THE WALKING SHADOW

Borgo Press Books by BRIAN STABLEFORD

THE WALKING SHADOW

SHADOW

A PROMETHEAN
SCIENTIFIC ROMANCE

BRIAN STABLEFORD

THE BORGO PRESS
MMXIII

THE WALKING SHADOW

FIRST BORGO PRESS EDITION

Published by Wildside Press LLC

www.wildsidebooks.com

DEDICATION

For the members of my poker school, and most especially for Tina, Carol, John, Ian, and Paul

Some of the ideas employed in this novel with regard to the evolution of "third-phase life" emerged from discussions with Barry Bayley, and I should like to acknowledge my indebtedness to the imaginative stimuli that he provided, both in his works and in person. This second edition has been revised slightly, in the interests of grammatical propriety and thematic clarity, but no significant change to its contents has been made. I am greatly indebted to Heather Datta for her kindness in scanning the original version of the novel.

CONTENTS

PART ONE: Architects of the Night 9

PART TWO: The Wreckage of the World 25

PART THREE: The Dissolving Dream 129

PART FOUR: Paradise Lost 195

ABOUT THE AUTHOR 276

PART ONE
ARCHITECTS OF THE NIGHT

The world's great age begins anew,
  The golden years return,
The earth doth like a snake renew
  Her winter weeds outworn:
Heaven smiles, and faiths and empires gleam,
Like wrecks of a dissolving dream.
                    (Shelley, *Hellas*)

CHAPTER ONE

Joseph Herdman sat back in the chair and felt it give way under the pressure, remolding itself to suit his semi-reclining position. He crossed his legs at the ankles and placed his left heel on the corner of the desk-top. Then he poured himself a drink. The bottle was still three-quarters full.

The stadium manager, whose desk it was, wondered why he didn't quite have the guts to complain. Herdman hadn't even bothered to offer him a drink.

"Aren't you going out to watch?" he asked.

"No," said Herdman. The flatness of the reply was an obvious discouragement to further enquiry.

The manager couldn't work out precisely what it was about Herdman that he found so intimidating. Herdman wasn't a big man and there was nothing out of the ordinary about his looks—his face was thin and sallow, but not mean; his eyes were an ordinary shade of brown. It was just the way he handled himself, somehow radiating contempt. Herdman seemed to look down on people as if they were insects—as if their continued existence depended upon the whim that stopped him from stepping on them. What he said with his mouth was always polite, but it was always mocking politeness he didn't really mean. It had infuriated less sensitive men than the manager.

"I suppose you've seen it all before?" he said, continuing the conversation as a token protest.

"All of it," confirmed Herdman.

"We got eighty thousand people out there. Eighty thousand at three-dollars-and-a-half a head...."

"Loose change," said Herdman, as if he didn't want to be bothered with details. "Aren't *you* going out to watch?"

The manager attempted to fan the flames of his smoldering resentment, hoping to find courage in anger, but he couldn't make the emotion swell inside him. In the end, although he said what he planned to say, it came out weak and stupid.

"I seen it all too. Week in, week out. Synth music, ball games, fan dancers, bible freaks. They're all the same."

Only the echo of a sneer was there. Herdman could have said it in his level voice and made it mean whatever he wanted it to. From the manager it was just a poor performance. Herdman poured himself another large Scotch.

"Paul's good," he said. "It's worth your while to see it."

"He don' do nothin' but talk. He's nothin' special. We had a hundred like him these last ten years. Religion is big—'specially crank stuff like this. Ev'ryone's lookin' for a new Jesus. It's the African war an' the atom bombs—ev'ryone knows it could be us next. An' the depression, too. They all wanna be saved, an' they don' care who does it. We get the same crowd cryin' the same tears ev'ry time. I seen it all before."

Herdman didn't get irritated. Herdman had a shell around him that was impervious to any possible inflection of the human voice.

"Paul's special," he said, quietly. "They're all special. It's the only thing that qualifies them to stand up on the stage and look down at the crowds. It's not easy to sell hope. It's a talent. It needs presence, it needs a message, but most of all it needs something special, which lets people believe in him. Those people out there find believing very difficult; they don't offer their faith easily. That's why they keep coming back. The faith drains away too quickly. It's the times we live in; we've all learned to be cynical, to doubt everything. That helps us to be right, because in the final analysis, *nothing's* true. But being right isn't really what we need. What we need is to believe. Paul can make some people believe, and that's what's special about him. The world needs what he has to give more than anything else."

"An' it's makin' you an' him rich."

"That's right."

As if in reflex reaction to what the other had said, Herdman reached out and touched his glass to the neck of the whisky bottle, and then raised it into the air—a small, perfunctory toast.

"Jesus didn't need sellin' the way you're sellin' the kid," said the manager. "He didn't need a Joe Herdman or an Adam Wishart."

"He didn't have to make any television appearances," said Herdman. "He didn't have to book three months in advance to deliver the sermon on the mount. He didn't have to release cassettes or publish books or sue newspapers for libel. But he did need St. Paul as his chief propagandist."

The manager sneered. "I suppose you already got your writers workin' on the script for the crucifixion?"

"He writes his own scripts," replied Herdman. "Have you read the book?"

Not *his* book, the manager noted, but *the* book. He didn't answer. He didn't read that kind of book, or any other kind of book. Reading was for kids and kooks—who, of course, were buying *the* book in millions and reading it cover to cover, probably without understanding one word in five. They loved the gobbledegook, loved to think that there was something in there that was so wise that they couldn't make head nor tail of it. If they *could* understand it, it wouldn't be worth a damn—they knew full well that there was no hope at all in anything *they* knew or understood. If there was hope, it had to be in something beyond them, something with impressive long words, something with a nice rhythm to it, something glowing with optimism but clouded with obscurity. But what did he care? They were filling the stadium at three-dollars-and-a-half a head. The profits of prophecy.

There was another small *clink*, but this time it wasn't the small ritual of the private toast. It was the bottle touching the rim of the glass while pouring another double. Herdman's hand was perfectly steady, but he was pouring from an awkward position.

"It'll be another nine-day wonder," prophesied the manager, his voice sour but losing the slovenly twang that was at least half affectation. "These things don' last. This guy will burn out in a couple of years. He can't make no comeback for nostalgia's sake, like all the singers do. His pretty-boy face will fade away."

"You don't understand," said Herdman, gently, as if he were trying to reason with a small child barely on the threshold of rationality. "Of course he won't last. Nothing does. We live in a society of disposable objects, disposable relationships, disposable ideas. We've conquered nature, but the technology we've built has been endowed with the same built-in obsolescence as nature's. Even our myths no longer endure; they're subject to waves of fashion like everything else we make. But for the moment, Paul Heisenberg's mythology seems to be the right one, and no matter how ephemeral it is, it's pretty much the mythology of the moment, the crystallization of the spirit of the age. What does it matter if the age whose spirit it is only lasts a year, or a month, or a day? We have to learn to accept the essential transience of the present, and the fact that nothing endures. When there's no forever to look forward, to, only a fool despises the ephemeral. You have to live in the moment, and be prepared for tomorrow to be another and quite different moment, if tomorrow comes at all."

"Is that what *he* thinks, when he ain't on stage?"

"Certainly not. He believes in himself, with all his heart. How could he attract the faith of others if he didn't have faith in himself?"

"He hasn't attracted *your* faith."

"I wouldn't say that. I believe in him Mondays and Thursdays. Tuesdays and Sundays I think the bombs will start to fall and we'll all be blown to hell or rotted by radiation and plague. Wednesdays I'm an orthodox doubter. I live in the moment, and I'd live one step ahead of it if I could, so that I could look back on it with equanimity."

That seemed to the manager to be Scotch talk. Alcoholic eloquence, Herdman might have called it himself. Crazy, in other words.

Outside, there was a massive swell of applause that signaled the appearance on stage of Paul Heisenberg.

"Go on," said Herdman, softly. "Go and listen. Really listen. Try to see what he's doing...examining our existential predicament, diagnosing its deficiencies, constructing his vision of imaginary futures, specifically tailored to meet and soothe our anxieties. It really is an art, you know. If you can just fall under his spell he'll take you out of your narrow little mind on a voyage beyond the horizons of your imagination. He'll show you infinity, and eternity, and put you in touch with the ineffable. That's what you need. It's what we all need. It's the only way to make the year of our lord nineteen ninety-two at all tolerable."

"You seem to be doin' okay on whisky," said the manager. His voice was dull, now, and he had already accepted defeat. In a minute he was going to stamp out of the office—*his* office— and find himself something to do that looked like work.

"It helps to keep me alert," said Herdman, easily. He relaxed further into the yielding chair, preparing to enjoy his isolation.

The manager closed the door as he left.

Out on the catwalk, the air seemed pregnant with the adulation of the crowd. A long way away the tiny white dot that was Paul Heisenberg raised his arms, to begin gathering in that adulation, and began to speak. His words were magnified by the microphones, carried into every last corner of the covered stands, leaked up into the empty sky—where the stars, at least, were not listening.

CHAPTER TWO

Adam Wishart lurched to his seat, and wriggled as he tried to squeeze the bulk of his hindquarters into a space that had been designed with some standard mesomorphic frame in mind.

Forty per cent of adult Americans are supposed to be obese, he told himself, *but nobody bothers to tell the jerks who make things.*

He found the early evening heat oppressive, although the autumn was well advanced and the weather should have broken weeks before. His jowls were damp with sweat, but he didn't bother to mop it off. For one thing, it was a losing battle; for another, someone—probably Paul—had told him that if he let the sweat evaporate it would help to cool his flesh.

He was late. The preliminaries were over and Paul was already into his spiel. Wishart tuned in for the briefest of moments to check the stage that the speech had reached. Half a dozen words were enough. Paul changed the words a little every time, but the message was the same and the rhythm was the same and everything was measured out for maximum effect. If pressed, Wishart could recite a version of the speech with no more hesitation than Paul, but to him it was without feeling, just a pattern of noises.

He checked his watch and noted the time. Only then did he look up at the platform.

Paul was dressed in his usual white outfit, his loose sleeves rippling as he supplemented his words with graceful gestures, emphasizing the key phrases and cueing the responses embedded in the reactions of those members of the audience who were already familiar with the message. The halo-effect wasn't working quite right, and Wishart squirmed as he tried to figure out which light wasn't in position. He caught the eye of the engineer, but the other merely shrugged and jabbed a thumb at Paul, indicating that the lights were right but that Paul had drifted from his spot.

Wishart sighed, knowing that there was no possibility of catching Paul's eye. It was just a matter of waiting for him to drift back. That was Paul's one fault; most performers had an instinct for finding the position that would show them off to their best advantage, but Paul was a little shy of the lighting. He made up for it with his voice, which he used as well as anyone Wishart had ever seen, but he was some way short of perfection. Wishart had told him over and over how important the lighting was in creating the overall effect, and Paul knew it on the intellectual level, but he just didn't quite have the *feel*.

Wishart felt good about promoting Paul, and making a good job of it. It needed a lot of work, but it was a real challenge to his cleverness and artistry. Wishart liked to think of himself as an artist; the commercial aspect of his work didn't seem to him to vulgarize the endeavor in any way at all. He knew that he looked like a slob, and his way of fighting that had been to make sure that the things he *controlled* went to the opposite extreme, working smoothly and efficiently. He had an elegant staff, and he specialized in elegant performers, who made money as gracefully as money could be made.

He turned in the seat to look at the members of the audience behind him. The plastic arm-rest dug painfully into his flesh beneath the bottom rib on the left side, but he ignored it. He squinted into the light as he tried to measure the extent of Paul's hold over the assembled multitude. There was still some restlessness about—oddballs who hadn't caught the mood of the crowd as a whole and who weren't yet participating in the atmosphere of awed tranquility—but it was good. Most of them had already relaxed into the flow of the honeyed words.

The most dedicated of them were worshipping Paul, in a perfectly literal sense. For them, he had become the focal point of their feelings, not just now but as they went through the routines of their everyday lives. He had given them the chance to love, which those routines of everyday life denied them. He had given them the chance to hope, which the desolate world no longer seemed to hold for the young, the unemployed, the disaffected and the cowardly. That was practically everyone, since the nuclear holocaust in Africa had reminded the world how close it stood to the brink of self-destruction. Insecurity was rife throughout the world, in economic and existential terms. The old religious systems, ill-fitted to the world of technological complexity, provided no antidote, but Paul was different, because he spoke the mesmeric language of scientific mysticism, and his message was adapted to the web of electronic media which carried it across the world.

Wishart's underpants were sticking to his skin, making him feel dirty. He hated to feel dirty, but his flesh had sweated all summer and there'd never been a day when he'd felt really clean. It was a psychological quirk, he knew, but knowing it didn't lessen the feeling, and he prayed for winter to come. He thought of Herdman sitting alone in the office above the west stand, casually washing his thoughts down the internal sewer that soaked up all the whisky without ever letting him get truly drunk. Wishart felt sticky, and stale, and lonely.

In a sense, he *was* alone. He was a rock in the ocean of feeling that moved over him, dragged by the tide of Paul's presence. He was untouched, his surface so hard as to be immune from erosion. Paul was talking directly to eighty thousand people, while a further six million looking in through TV were as far on the way to being spellbound as anyone could be watching a TV set, but he was talking right past Adam Wishart.

Wishart wasn't tuned in. He couldn't afford to be converted. In the same way that people who handle dynamite couldn't afford impetuousness, and people making tear gas lost the ability to cry, Wishart had long ago learned to kill the spontaneous reactions evoked within his head by music or rhetoric. All sound reverberated within his consciousness now like echoes in an empty drum.

The halo effect was okay now, and Wishart settled himself to watch Paul's face. In spite of the glare of the lights, Paul's pupils were dilated for the benefit of the TV audience. People responded better to people whose pupils were dilated, because it constituted a subliminal signal of attraction. It meant, of course, that Paul was practically blind because of the dazzle, but that didn't matter. He knew his script, not just because he had memorized it but because he felt it, deep down. His heart was in it, every time he spoke.

Paul was talking now, as he always did, about the need for belief. He made people feel that need, and made them realize that it was the greatest need they had. Then he offered them something to believe in. It was a soft sell, a coaxing invitation. He never told them that what he offered them to believe was true, just that it would answer their need. That was good, because the reason virtually all these people had stopped believing in everything else was that they could no longer accept the truth of anything, or even the very notion of truth. Paul swept the whole problem of truth out of the way, dismissed it as irrelevant, and for that they were grateful, because truth had become their nightmare. Paul asked people to believe what he said not because it was true, but because it felt right, because it answered the need to believe.

And they did.

Wishart looked sideways at the make-up girl who sat beside him. Her own make-up was cracking and sweat was beginning to show, but her eyes were riveted to Paul's gesturing hands high above. She was a long way from the mundane world of perspiration, cruising toward spiritual orgasm. The magic was working, as it was working on everyone. Three-dollars-and-a-half for the experience, fifteen for a video-cassette that would recall it again and again and let them relive it a hundred times, until, in the fullness of time, it decayed into mere noise and a pretty face and ridiculous gesticulations.

All things, thought Wishart, *must pass.* It was a tenet of faith that he had always taken for granted. He had lived more than fifty years in the world and had never found cause to challenge it. He knew that Paul's message, like all the others, would eventually fail to answer the undiminished need for belief, which would call for something new, and even more desperate, to fight the threat of the decay that seemed to have seized the whole human world.

Wishart blinked away the sweat that had oozed into the corner of his right eye.

Somewhere in mid-blink, he missed the event, which seemed to take no time at all.

At one moment, there was the pure white of Paul's costume, the artificial halo, the blond hair and the smooth flesh of the made-up face; then there was a blaze of light that dazzled, reflected from the face and hands that were suddenly mirror-bright.

The arms, which had reached out but a moment before as if to embrace the vistas of the hopeful future, were frozen now as if time itself had been interrupted.

Among the eighty thousand people who were physically present there were some who screamed and some who sighed. The TV viewers, inevitably, reacted more slowly.

Where Paul Heisenberg had stood there was now a silver statue, dressed in the same white tunic, but reflecting from the surface that had once been bare flesh all the light that had been carefully directed to compose the glowing nimbus.

The glow was even brighter now, and in the stillness which followed the abrupt interruption of the beautiful voice, there was a profundity that seemed terrible even to Adam Wishart.

He knew, as they all did, that he had witnessed—or failed to witness in the unfortunate blink of an eye—a miracle.

An extract from *Science and Metascience* by Paul Heisenberg:

Science is knowledge, and what qualifies a statement as a scientific statement is contained within the process by which we have arrived at the conclusion that it is true. The credentials of a scientific statement are established by the *method* we have used in order to prove it. Basically, this method consists in the rigorous testing of the statement in competition with other statements that claim to describe or explain the relevant sensory evidence. All scientific knowledge is empirical (which is to say, based on sense-data) and systematic (which is to say, concerned with organizing such data by means of generalizations). Any statement whose truth cannot be established by reference to sensory data falls outside the scope of science.

At one time, it was believed by the most enthusiastic champions of science that the answers to all conceivable problems lay within its scope. Science, it was said, would in the fullness of time reveal the grand plan of the universe and permit perfect understanding of the system of systems. It was recognized that people could devise questions that science could not hope to answer, but those questions were ruled out of court, as illegitimate and essentially meaningless. All that was not knowable was held to be nonsensical. Metaphysics, the speculative philosophical discipline that attempted to investigate what lies beyond the scope of scientific enquiry—the reality "behind" the perceived world—was deemed to be a barren and sterile pursuit. The questions of metaphysics, it was said, were questions that could not sensibly be asked, because they could not sensibly be answered.

That era of confidence in science is now past. It is not that the character of science has changed, but that *we* have changed. Once, a majority of intelligent people could feel secure within the horizons of expanding scientific knowledge, but now we feel insecure. We have discovered that the system of systems offers us less self-satisfaction than it once did. We have discovered indeterminacy in the physical world and uncertainty within ourselves.

We now feel that the limits placed by the philosophy of science on what we *can* know are narrower and more restrictive than we require. We have become uncomfortable within the world-view of modern science.

It is by no means simple to find a cure for this discomfort, and the one thing that is certain is that more scientific knowledge cannot ease the situation in the least; the fault is in ourselves.

It is in response to this gathering sense of insecurity that there has been in recent years an increasing interest in the speculative disciplines of metascience. It is, I think, more reasonable to talk of meta*science* than of meta*physics*, firstly because the new metascience is quite unlike the classical metaphysics, and secondly because our new speculations are more concerned with reaching through and beyond the biological and the social sciences than with the shadowy area of first causes that lies beyond the physical sciences.

There is, however, another reason why the renaissance of interest in metascience was inevitable, and which sustained metascientific speculation even through the era of its disreputability. This reason is that the perfectly true allegation that the statements of metascience could never be known to be true is and always has been quite irrelevant. We can never have certain answers to the questions of metascience, nor, indeed, any answers which we can rely upon in the slightest degree to *inform* us as to the nature of the world in which we find ourselves, but that does not affect the need that drives us to ask such questions in the least. The fact that metascientific statements can never be verified in no way threatens their psychological utility. In purely pragmatic terms they remain not merely valuable but absolutely necessary to our well-being.

In a sense, we are the victims of a cruel situation, in that we so desperately want to know things we cannot know. Such questions as the existence of God, the purpose of life and the ultimate destiny of the universe are devoid of scientific significance, but we *feel* them to be important, and by virtue of that fact they *become* important. The situation of craving answers we cannot have is an unhappy and distressing one, and if we accept the situation at face value we are driven to the conclusion that the human condition is unfortunate and irredeemable.

There is, however, a way out of the trap if we are simply prepared to recognize that the value of metascientific speculations is not in the least reduced by their having the status of speculations rather than facts. It does not matter in the least that metascientific statements are created rather than discovered, for the need which we have for them is psychological, not technological, and the statements need only be believed and never applied. We never have to expect or demand that the perceived world will comply with our metascientific speculations, provided that we are careful never to include statements within our metascientific systems that are not metascientific, but hypotheses that can actually be tested by reference to sensory experience and experiment.

Much confusion has arisen in the past by virtue of the fact that we have habitually construed the word "believe" as "believe to be true". This has led us to assume that, in order to believe in a metascientific statement, we need to assert that it is true, which, by definition, we cannot justifiably do. It is time now to recognize that this is a mistaken notion of what belief involves and of what beliefs consist, and for what purpose they are useful.

If we *know* something to be true, because it has been established by the methods of science, we do not need to add something extra which converts that knowledge into a belief. If we *do* "believe" it, we do so in the special sense that the knowledge must always remain provisional, dependent upon further data. Scientific knowledge is always subject to revision or rejection in the light of further discoveries, and any commitment of faith to the current body of knowledge is both superfluous and dangerous.

By contrast, commitment is exactly what is involved—and exactly what is needed—in holding to a metascientific statement. Belief in a statement involves shielding and protecting it, holding it invulnerable against criticism. There can never be any logical warrant for such a strategy, which is, of course, completely out of place in science, but in metascience we need only seek a warrant on pragmatic grounds.

If, because of an excessive admiration of science, or because we have excessive expectancies of its rewards, we find ourselves unable to make a commitment to metascientific speculations of one kind or another, then we are the poorer for our failure. Indeed, it might be that such a psychological stance is literally impossible to maintain, for what is actually involved in the rigorously skeptical world-view of the determined empiricist is not an absence of metascientific commitment but a metascientific commitment to the present state of scientific knowledge, which reads into that state an authority and invulnerability to falsification which science simply cannot possess. People who can do that are doubly unfortunate, firstly because they delude themselves as to the extent of their own metascientific commitment, and secondly because their commitment is tied to a speculation which is likely to be psychologically unsatisfactory. Nevertheless, such people are certainly better off than they would be if they genuinely had no commitments of the kind we call belief.

To sum up, therefore, the situation is this. We *need* metascientific beliefs. We cannot get by in life without them. We cannot select these beliefs on the grounds of their truthfulness or their likelihood, because there is no way that we can establish the truth or likelihood of metascientific statements. That such statements do sometimes seem likely or unlikely is a function of their aesthetic appeal, not of their logical appeal. It follows, therefore, that the most reasonable strategy is to select beliefs for commitment on the grounds of their psychological utility, in purely pragmatic terms. If asked what our warrant is for the commitments which we make, we need only answer: I believe it not because it is true, but because it is *necessary.*

It is the only answer we can give, but it is the only answer we need.

PART TWO
THE WRECKAGE OF THE WORLD

CHAPTER THREE

He was crawling, dragging himself over jagged rocks and sills while a terrible wind lashed sand into his face and about his body, stinging and scourging. He had been crawling for a long, long time, and exhaustion made every movement difficult.

In and behind the wind there was another force: a sluggish but relentless current, which tugged at something inside him.

He hooked his bleeding fingers over sharp spurs of rock and hauled himself forward, his legs dragging and barely able to push at all. The hot sand swirled over his bare forearms, stirring the fine blond hair.

He felt as if he was *aging*, the years coursing through his body as he headed for the night of time. He knew that he had a destination but he did not know what or where it was, or even that he was going in the right direction, although he had to believe that he was, for without that belief he would simply have stopped and died. He felt that the current plucking at his soul was carrying his goal away from him, bearing it into the mists of eternity, which were forever inaccessible, but still he kept himself moving, still he would not yield.

He had seen glimmering lights above the horizon from time to time, but they were gone now, faded into a draining twilight that cast wan shadows beneath the serrated ridges of bone-white rock. Perhaps they had never been anything more than mirages, shimmering in layers of air undisturbed by the fierce wind that attacked him down here in the valley.

Night came, but still he struggled. The wind of time would

bring day again, and then the night, but there was no relief from the heat and the sand and the sharp stone spurs which had already begun to lacerate his fingers. His fingers, though, did not pause in their grappling, and he was almost grateful for the ridges which allowed him purchase to drag himself along.

Beneath his body something was slithering: something massive, conjoined with the substance of the desert itself, an essence or a spirit within the rock. Because it slithered he named it a snake, but it had no form as yet.

The snake cradled him in its shapeless coil, ready to engulf him when the desert gave it birth.

His movements grew fevered and desperate as the need to rest grew within him. He knew that he must not stop, that sleep would be fatal, but even the fear of sleep spread a numb drowsiness through his lean frame. His arms jerked spasmodically as the muscles corded and cramped momentarily.

After one last agonized heave, he was still, face down against the slithering scaliness of the desert's skin.

The current ceased to grip him. The slithering ceased. A brief, fugitive instant of panic was lost in a swirl of time and space.

With the most delicate of emetic shudders, the other world spat him out.

CHAPTER FOUR

Sheehan attempted to pull the collar of his greatcoat a little tighter as he stood back in the shadow of the tunnel mouth and listened to the ring of Boulton's approaching footfalls on the frosted concrete.

Boulton walked with the precisely measured stride of an old army man. He should have retired when the last state of emergency passed peacefully away, but instead he had come to the capital and joined the police force. He was twenty years older than Sheehan, but he hardly seemed to feel the cold.

Sheehan came forward out of the tunnel to meet Boulton, and the other paused. For a moment they didn't speak, but glanced instead at the concrete pedestal supporting the cage that enclosed the glittering statue.

The pedestal had been built so that Paul's feet were resting on its surface, but it would not have mattered had it been an inch or two shorter; he would simply have remained suspended there, locked into Earth's gravitational field: immutable, immovable, unreachable.

Boulton inclined his head slightly toward the gleaming statue. "Be a fool to come back tonight," he observed. "Freeze to death inside the cage."

Sheehan laughed, dutifully but uneasily.

"They should put some clothes on him," he said.

"They used to. Made him look like a scarecrow. Can't keep them all clothed, anyhow. A third of all the jumpers in the country are in this city. More jumpers here than living people, I reckon. Anyhow, clothes'd spoil that pretty glow."

There were no electric lights out in the open expanse of the stadium, but there were dozens of wax candles that people had brought and lit early the previous evening. There were no people about now, but well over half the candles burned on, and some were long enough to last until the dawn. The perfectly reflective surface of Paul Heisenberg's body reflected the candlelight as if it were itself a faintly glowing object: a human body, limned in fire. The effect was rather eerie.

Paul was not alone—there were more than a hundred similar static figures scattered over the flat surface of the arena, and a couple of hundred more in the derelict stands—but it was to see him that the crowds came, and they stationed their candles to illuminate him, not his companions.

"Hope there's no trouble," said Sheehan. "If I had to draw, my hand would freeze to the butt."

"No trouble tonight," said Boulton confidently. "Too cold."

"I hate this place," muttered Sheehan. "Standing guard over hundreds of statues. I've never been here when one of them came out of it, but I'm not looking forward to it. Who cares, anyhow? Let the bastards freeze to death, teach them to think before they jump."

"*They* don't matter," said Boulton, waving an arm in a horizontal arc. "Just *him*." He pointed up at Paul, though there was no mistaking his meaning.

"There's an alarm system in the cage," said Sheehan.

"If you only knew how often that alarm's been triggered falsely, or jiggered so that it couldn't sound even if he *did* come out...."

"Yeah," agreed Sheehan, morosely, "but you *said* there'd be no one out tonight."

Boulton shrugged. Then he stepped out from the wall, raised his arm in a cursory salute, and went on his way around the arc of the low wall. Sheehan stepped back into the tunnel, seeking the shelter of its black pit of shadow. *Cold like this*, he thought, *is enough to make anyone turn jumper. But who can guarantee he'll come out in summer?*

He listened to the sound of Boulton's footsteps as the other policeman paced away. Subconsciously, he must have been counting the steps, because when they stopped he knew immediately that something was wrong. Boulton had not had time to cross the concrete apron and step out on to the turf which would muffle his further steps.

Sheehan reached inside his greatcoat to pick out the walkie-talkie lodged in his breast pocket. It was already in his hand when he stepped out of the tunnel again.

He saw the body slumped on the frost-glittered concrete, and looked about wildly, already pressing the call button on the radio. He gave his call-sign twice before his eyes caught a glimpse of the black shadow that paused on the barrier enclosing the rusty seats before leaping at him. He let loose a wordless cry of alarm, not knowing whether his call had been heard, and then was bowled over by the shadow.

He had to meet the attack hand-to-hand; there was no time now to go for his gun.

The hands that gripped his arms seemed unnaturally strong, and despite his attempt to kick the other below the knee he felt himself whirled around and clasped in a secure hold. Something was clamped over the lower part of his face and he felt something heavy and sickly fill his nasal passages as he inhaled. One more startled breath was all it took before he tumbled into dizzy oblivion. The one fugitive image captured by his eyes was a sight of a candlelit plastic mask, which hid every feature of his assailant's face.

* * * * * *

He seemed to have been unconscious for bare seconds when cold air blew away the sickly sleep. The readiness with which he had succumbed to the drug had prevented him from inhaling too much, and the first thing that his bleary eyes showed him when he awoke was Boulton, still inert on the concrete some fifteen meters away.

Sheehan was lying on his belly, and he found something hard beneath his left hip. It was the walkie-talkie, and he snatched it up immediately, but it had broken when he dropped it, and he could get no life from it. His head reeled as he lifted himself from the ground.

His gaze was drawn to the summit of the pillar supporting the steel cage enclosing Paul Heisenberg's inert form. An eerie blue light was dancing around the lower part of the bars on the near side, partly blocked out by the silhouette of a kneeling human figure. It took several seconds for Sheehan's head to clear sufficiently for him to make sense of what he saw.

Someone was using a cutting tool to slice through the bars of the cage.

Sheehan groaned. It had happened before and it would no doubt happen again. The cult members resented the fact that a cage had been built to trap their messiah if ever he should return—*whenever* he should return. There was constant sabotage of the cage and its environs. The alarm system must have been short-circuited, for no alarm bells were ringing. His one thought was: *Why did it have to happen to me?*

He drew the gun from the belt that gathered in the waist of his greatcoat. The butt was cold, and his joke about freezing his hand to the weapon drifted back into his mind.

He pointed at the figure bent over the cutting tool, and yelled: "Stop that!"

The other looked round, but the tool continued to do its work.

"Stop or I shoot!" threatened Sheehan.

The other grabbed one of the bars and wrenched it out, having cut through it at the top and all-but severed it at the base. For a moment, Sheehan thought the saboteur was going to hurl the steel bar at him, and he fired in immediate response.

The shot missed, but the man in the mask didn't hurl the bar. Instead, he dropped it to the concrete and jumped. The cage was a long way up—all of six meters—and Sheehan expected the other to buckle up on landing, probably with a broken leg. That wasn't what happened, though.

Instead, the masked man landed on his feet, as lightly as if he'd vaulted a low gate, and he ran at Sheehan without so much as a moment's pause. The policeman was startled enough to miss his chance of a second shot. The gun was plucked from his hand and hurled away up into the stand.

Sheehan was hit hard just above the heart and knocked backwards by the blow. He fell heavily, feeling as if he'd been kicked by a horse. He looked up at his assailant, who was no more than a silhouette with all the light behind him.

Then something else caught his eye, and he gasped.

The other stopped, and followed the direction of Sheehan's gaze, looking back over his shoulder to the top of the pillar, where the light of the candles showed that the naked body of Paul Heisenberg, no longer reflecting all the light that fell upon it, had suddenly slumped back against the uncut bars.

The stillness of the night was interrupted by the sound of a siren, and Sheehan knew that his first attempt to call for help had been successful after all.

Then he was hit again, this time to the side of his left eye, and he lost consciousness.

CHAPTER FIVE

The phone rang.

The sound pulled Wishart back from deep sleep. A dream exploded briefly into consciousness and dissolved quickly as his mind hastened through the phases of sleep towards wakefulness. At the fourth ring he snatched the receiver from its cradle.

"Yes?" he said.

There was a moment of silence, and then a curious crackling hum. A voice spoke over the hum, sounding smooth and sexless; not loud, but quite distinct. He recognized it immediately—he had no idea whose voice it was, but he had heard it before.

"Paul's awake," it said. "The alarm didn't go off but one of the policemen at the stadium managed to call for help. There'll be a full alert any minute, and they'll send a car to pick you up. Get out quickly."

There was a *click*, and the phone went dead, before Wishart even had time to draw back the breath that had caught in his throat. He swallowed, and was uncomfortably conscious of the fact that he was suddenly sweating.

He eased his bulk over the edge of the bed and reached for his clothes, then switched on the bedside lamp. His hand was shaking.

A hundred and twenty-seven years, he thought. *The new world record.*

It was, of course, inevitable that Paul should come out of stasis as the record-holder, simply because he had been the first to go in. Wishart himself, on his own leap through time, had managed only a hundred and eight years. He was nineteen years older now than when he had last seen Paul. He was over seventy, and in spite of the kilos he'd shed, he was still overweight and lucky enough to be alive. It was only now, though, that he realized quite how desperate his fear had been that he might not last out until Paul's return. The relief was almost painful, drowning all anxiety and all thought, not letting him begin the business of planning what to do next.

Mechanically, he dressed himself; it was not until he had finished that the peculiarity of his own situation was brought home to him.

His eyes rested on the silent phone.

The speaker knew that Paul was awake, and also knew that someone at the stadium had called for help. How? He had warned Wishart to get out quickly, before the whole police force was mobilized, and Diehl's security men with them. Why?

There had been other phone calls warning him of threats to the Movement, mostly from the investigations of Diehl's men. Without those warnings, Diehl might have infiltrated his forces to a much greater extent, and might be ready to close him down by now. Instead...it seemed that his mysterious ally might take a hand in the chaos that was sure to follow the news of Paul's awakening.

Wishart turned off the lamp again, and made his way out into the corridor. He didn't need the light in the stairwell to guide him as he moved quickly through the darkness down three flights of stairs to the basement. He used the service stairs to get out of the building at the rear, emerging among the big plastic drums where the refuse was stored. He paused there for a few seconds to allow his eyes to readjust to the light.

There was no street-lamp in the alley but there was a reddish glow in the sky where airborne dust and water vapor reflected the lights of the city. The stars were hidden behind the colored haze. The coldness of the night air seeped through his coat and into his flesh, and he tensed himself to prevent shivering. Eventually, he moved out into the shadows, feeling his way and making hardly any sound. There was a rustling among the garbage that was piled up in a culvert, waiting to be lifted into one of the drums, but it was only a rat. It was not unduly worried by his proximity.

He threaded his way through a network of back streets, staying clear of the lighted roads. He listened for the sound of a car, but there was nothing nearby.

The thought that it might be a hoax niggled away at the back of his mind, but it was not a doubt that worried him unduly. His informant had been reliable in the past, and there could be no motive for the lie. Paul's return was due, and perhaps overdue: the cult had been anticipating the imminent return of its prophet for nearly forty years, always convinced that the corrupt world could hardly endure through one more generation, and always certain that Paul, in some way no one could imagine, held the key to its rebirth. There were a great many people expecting the impossible from Paul, and they were the ones upon whom Wishart had to rely if he was going to save his protégé from Diehl and Lindenbaum. It wasn't going to be easy.

The excitement was already growing inside him—the excitement of having something to sell again, a chance to manipulate the public, to control their ideas and their hopes, to milk them of their support. This time, he knew, there was more than a fortune at stake. This time, a whole nation was up for grabs. Maybe a whole world.

A hundred and twenty-seven years had added very considerably to Paul Heisenberg's stock as a prophet and potential savior. Handled right—handled by Adam Wishart—he could inherit the world.

CHAPTER SIX

Paul felt himself thrust into the back seat of a small car. The cold seemed to reach into his very bones, and every touch sensation was fierce. He was wrapped in a blanket, but the blanket seemed to contain no warmth of its own, and there was little enough of his own as yet to be contained.

The engine spluttered into life, starting first time, and there was a judder as the gears engaged. The car lurched forward, turned sharply, and then accelerated rapidly.

"They didn't see us," said an even, mellow voice, "but they'll have heard us. They won't try to chase us. They'll seal off the whole area north of the river and saturate it with policemen and security men. I can't get you out in the car."

Paul, in the grip of a fit of shivering, could not make any reply. He had not yet managed to assume command over his limbs; he had been carried out of the stadium in the blanket.

"There are clothes on the seat," the voice went on. Paul could not tell from its tone whether it was male or female, but only a man—a very strong man—could have carried him at such speed through the derelict corridors of the stadium.

"Try to put them on," the voice continued. "I'm going to have to drop you off somewhere nearby, where you can be hidden and someone can take care of you. We were lucky that they only sent one car; because the cage alarm didn't go off, they assumed that it was sabotage or vandalism, but there'll be a full-scale emergency now. I can only try to mislead them, and then try to reach you again in the morning, or tomorrow night."

Paul could feel the clothing that lay beneath him on the seat, but he could not find the strength to do as the other asked. He tried to burrow into the angle of the seat, drawing the blanket around him more tightly, trying to cocoon himself in its folds.

A current of warm air was beginning to flow from a vent under the front seat, and gradually grew in force. He tried to catch it in the flap of the blanket and draw it in toward his body. His teeth chattered briefly and he had to clamp his jaw to hold them still.

The car cornered twice, sending him lurching first one way and then the other. The back wheels skidded, but the driver turned into the skid and kept control. The glare of street-lights cast sporadic haloes of light on the window, and the strobo-scopic frequency suggested to Paul that they were moving very rapidly. The windows were already steaming up with condensa-tion.

"Do you know your name?" asked the voice, trying to provoke some response.

"Paul," he replied, very weakly.

"Good. You'll feel sick for some time, and it might be diffi-cult to remember, but it will all come back eventually. The cold doesn't help. You timed your return rather badly."

The words echoed in Paul's head. He had no difficulty in understanding the immediate meaning, but the implications were quite unfathomable. He had no idea what had happened to him. His mind seemed to be seized up—frozen. He could not thaw it and force his thoughts to flow. He felt lonely, and very frightened, unable to remember how he came to be where he was—if, indeed, there was any memory that could tell him. He knew his name, but he could only wonder, for the moment, whether he knew anything else.

The steady current of warm air eddying over the contours of the blanket fought the cold, and began to expel the icy sensation from his flesh, except for the three stripes of pain across his back where he had collapsed against the bars of his cage. He found the power of movement, and was able to stretch his arms and test the muscles of his feet.

Above the ridge of the front seat he could see the silhouette of the driver's head. It was rounded, and seemed quite feature-less. The head half-turned to glance down at him, and by the light of a glaring street-lamp he saw that it was masked, partly by a balaclava helmet and partly by a plastic face-mask, molded to the contours of a human face. The only holes in the mask were the eye-holes, and the eyes were hidden in pits of shadow.

"Put the clothes on," said the smooth, sexless voice. "Please. There isn't much time."

Paul tried to sit up, and as he did so he was struck by dizziness and the sudden sense that the perceived world was dissolving into another, sharper image of reality. He was aware of....

jagged rocks....

caustic sand blown by a terrible wind....

the pain of lacerated fingers....

the sensation of something slithering against his skin....

a current dragging at his sense of time, his sense of self....

He gasped. Then, as suddenly as it had been born within him, it died, and was gone.

He raised his hand to catch the dim light. It was whole and unscarred. He flexed the fingers to reassure himself. The dream was quite gone, washed away like footprints in sand erased by the returning tide.

He plucked at the clothing, trying to bring it out from beneath the blanket, where it was trapped by the weight of his body. Slowly, he began to dress himself, almost amazed by the fact that he could remember how. There was a thick shirt and a woolen pullover, underpants and denim trousers.

"I don't want to take you to any place Diehl's likely to raid before morning," said the driver. "Somewhere out of the way will be best, in order to give me time to find some way of getting you out. I don't want you to tell them who you are. Hopefully, they might not recognize you. They're used to looking after awakeners. Trust me."

The words flowed over and around Paul, who could find

nothing in them to which to connect himself. It was all incomprehensible.

"There's no time to explain," said the other. "I'm sorry. If only that policeman hadn't...."

The voice broke off. The car swung around a tight bend, skidded, and stopped. Paul tried to push his feet into a pair of elastic-sided shoes, and had just accomplished the unreasonably-difficult task when the door at his shoulder was wrenched open and a gloved hand reached in to help him out. As he climbed out, he realized that he was terribly weak and sluggish, but he was now feeling a great deal better in himself. He felt *alive*, and ready to begin the business of living.

A street of tall terraced houses stretched for about a hundred meters either way. There were street-lamps every twenty meters or so, but only one in three was operative. He looked up at the tall buildings but he could only see two windows where light shone behind heavy blinds. One house revealed by a street-lamp had its windows boarded up and its door battered down, but he could not tell how many other dwellings had suffered similar dereliction. All the brickwork looked very old.

Beside the car, which had stopped in one of the darkened regions of the street, there was a low wall and a set of rotted iron railings. There was a gateway without a gate, and a flight of steps leading down into a deep well of shadow. Paul had to make a grab for the railings as he stumbled on the pavement. His companion caught him, and allowed him to pull away from the burning touch, supporting his weight effortlessly.

"Easy," breathed the voice.

They paused, but only for a moment, while Paul collected himself. Then he felt himself hustled through the gateway and down into Stygian darkness.

At the bottom, when they stopped again, Paul had to lean on the shoulder of his companion, his head resting gently against the edge of the plastic mask. He heard the ringing of a bell inside the house, loud and continual, as the other pressed the doorbell intermittently and insistently.

The door opened, spilling the light of an electric torch out into the well. Paul blinked, aware only of a vague humanoid shadow.

He heard the familiar voice speak rapidly, without waiting for a question or a challenge: "Awakener. Came out less than half an hour ago. Look after him until morning. I'll try to collect him then." Then the support was gone, and Paul had to lean against the door-jamb. Though he heard no sound, he knew that the man in the mask was disappearing into the night.

"Wait! " said a female voice, low and urgent. "Who are you? *Wait!*"

There was no answer.

A new hand reached out to take his arm and draw him into the corridor beyond the door. She didn't ask any questions of him, but simply said: "Come on. It'll be all right."

He managed to get inside, so that she could close the door. Somewhere up above, sounding strangely remote, the engine of the car growled into life.

CHAPTER SEVEN

Ricardo Marcangelo dropped his overcoat over the back of a chair, and then moved across the room to sit in another. There was only one other man in the room: Nicholas Diehl, the chief of security. He was standing by the window, still wearing his coat.

"Lindenbaum's on his way," said Marcangelo, softly. He was a man of medium height, with a rounded face that might once have borne a permanent look of innocence, but which was now too lined and hardened. Marcangelo's official title was Presidential Aide in charge of the Department of Internal Affairs, but in practice he handled relations between Lindenbaum's administration and the Metascientists, and had ever since the city had become the official capital of the United States, thirty years after the Treaty of Reunion.

Diehl, by contrast, was a tall, thin man with a pale face that hid behind a short-trimmed, white-flecked beard and moustache. He wore steel-rimmed spectacles and looked for all the world like a clerk. In fact, though, he was the head of the President's security forces—effectively the master of the secret police.

"Well?" said Diehl. "How did it happen?"

"Somebody knew."

"That's impossible."

Marcangelo shrugged. "They were there and waiting. They had the cage cut open before Heisenberg revived. They'd be clean away if Sheehan hadn't managed to call in before he was chloroformed."

"The report says that he got in a shot at the man cutting the bars, and missed."

Marcangelo shrugged again. "As far as I can tell, he did what he could."

"But only one car was sent out. And they missed Heisenberg. It seems to me that the police fouled it up left, right and centre."

"They have the whole north side sealed off. The car can't get out, and neither can Heisenberg. Maybe the police did fall down, but where were your men? Somebody knew that he was going to wake up tonight, and we didn't even know that it was possible to predict that. You didn't manage to pick Wishart up?"

Diehl frowned, in a way that suggested mild petulance rather than outright anger. "He wasn't there," he said. "He's gone underground."

"So *he* knew."

Diehl shook his head. "I don't think so. The tap on his phone picked up a peculiar garbled hum just about the time it must have happened. Wishart answered it, but what was said was blotted out somehow—scrambled. I think that was the first Wishart knew. That call warned him to get out. Somebody else got Heisenberg out of the stadium: someone who knows how to scramble a call on a tapped phone." Marcangelo looked at the thin man steadily. "And you have no idea who?"

"Have you?" retorted Diehl.

"It seems that everyone's fouled up," said Marcangelo, mildly. "Recriminations aren't going to help. We have to find him, that's all. It should only be a matter of time."

"It *should*," echoed Diehl, grimly.

"If he's still alive," added Marcangelo, with a lightness of tone that was obviously false.

"If?"

"A car crashed through one of the barriers about fifteen minutes ago, heading north. The barricade wasn't strong enough—it was a minor road. Two cars went after it. While trying to shake them off it went into a bad skid and came off the road. Before the police got to it, it went up. Not just the petrol tank—the officer in the first car said there must have been a bomb. It turned the car into a heap of slag."

"The car that was used to get Heisenberg away?"

"We don't know."

"How many bodies?"

"Apparently, none. It was quite some explosion."

Diehl's face seemed as white as chalk in the bright electric light. In the silence which fell Marcangelo could hear the faint throb of the heating system. Even in the coldest night the Manse was kept warm. It was President Lindenbaum's official residence, but tonight the president was out of town. A helicopter was bringing him back to deal with the emergency.

"The police need support, Nick," said Marcangelo, his voice still level and natural. "Castagna could do with a couple of hundred of your men, at least, to run a dragnet through the north side."

"I'll tell Laker to put our agents on the street," replied Diehl, almost absent-mindedly, as if he were still preoccupied with what Marcangelo had told him about the car that had crashed the barrier. "We'll raid every house where we know of any connection with Wishart's organization. Laker and Castagna can co-ordinate the operation. If he *is* dead, you know, it could simplify our problems considerably."

Marcangelo shook his head decisively. "It might simplify them, but it would make them a damn sight more difficult. We *need* Heisenberg. We could hold on by sheer brute strength, and maybe weather the storm, but we'd lose control in the long run, and the country—maybe the world—would go slowly to hell. More than half the workforce are followers of Heisenberg in some sense or other. Their hopes of what might happen when he returns are all that's keeping the economy staggering along. We could handle the initial shock if we were to lose him, but we'd never put the pieces together again well enough to stop the rot that's sending us slowly into a new dark age. Without Heisenberg, we'll lose everything."

It was a speech that Marcangelo had made many times

before. It was a position he'd taken up some years previously, and he was convinced of its truth. The capital was now the only city in the States with more than a million inhabitants. Since the eastern seaboard had been bombed out, together with most of the south-west, the USA had been in the grip of a slow decline.

The population was stabilizing again now that the last of the plagues had shot its bolt, but there were millions who existed only as silver statues locked in time—escapists, mostly carrying plague or already dying from radiation poisoning. The city still lived and maintained a front of technological civilization, but elsewhere the population was moving back to the rural areas as agriculture became a labor-intensive business again. There was still fuel for tractors, but only because the plagues had left such big reserves. Within another generation, the farmers would be using horses again, and cars would disappear from the roads. The loss wasn't irremediable, but if the backsliding were to be halted and reversed there would have to be some very powerful motivating force to mobilize and co-ordinate the efforts of the people.

Only Paul Heisenberg could provide that motivation, because Paul Heisenberg, thanks to the accident of fate that had made him the first time-jumper, had become the focus of the hopes of countless people—even people who could not jump themselves. Only Paul Heisenberg could stem the steady drain of escapists, who set off for an uncertain future rather than stay in a derelict present, because it was in his name that most of them jumped. It was the future *he* had talked about (though never explicitly described) in his book that gave the jumpers something to aim for, and the evidence even suggested that it was faith in his holy word that permitted most jumpers actually to project themselves into stasis. It was not that there was anything special about his words—it was faith itself that seemed to be important—but faith in Paul Heisenberg's crazy doctrine of metascientific speculation was the most widespread and powerful faith left in the western hemisphere.

Marcangelo knew that Diehl didn't see things the same way.

Diehl wasn't really a long-term thinker, and his imagination extended no further than commonplace political expediency. What Diehl cared about was power, and it didn't particularly matter to him whether the world was going headfirst down to hell or not, just as long as he could stay on top of it all the way. So far, Lindenbaum had always taken the same line as Marcangelo, but now that the situation had come to a head, things might change very quickly indeed.

"If Heisenberg were to get out," said Diehl, pensively, "and Wishart were to get hold of him...."

"He can't," said Marcangelo. "All of Wishart's strength is south of the river. You've seen to that. You've kept the Movement from organizing anything substantial in the north."

Diehl stared into Marcangelo's face, looking down through the lenses of his steel-rimmed spectacles like a caricature of a schoolmaster. "Tomorrow," he said, "the cults will have new members by the thousand, and the Movement too. Today we could count on the loyalty of nine policemen in ten; tomorrow, who can tell? We'd better find him quickly. Very quickly."

Marcangelo was saved the trouble of answering by the sound of a roaring motor. The presidential helicopter was settling down on to the landing strip behind the Manse. Diehl abandoned his staring match and went to the window to look out into the night.

"But who has him?" murmured Marcangelo. "And how?"

CHAPTER EIGHT

Paul sipped the dark liquid gingerly. It was hot, and very sweet. The girl had spooned a lot of sugar into it. When she had given it to him she had murmured something about it being impossible to get coffee or tea, but it tasted enough like instant coffee for him not to have known that it wasn't. She hadn't said anything else, yet. She was waiting for him to recover a little more fully.

He looked around the room, studying its every detail in the hope that he might see something that would touch a chord in his memory and tell him what was happening to him.

He was sitting on a single bed, still warm from the girl's body. She was sitting on a dilapidated armchair whose brown upholstery was peeling away from its wooden frame. There was a small electric fire, whose reflector was tarnished a dull brown. It, too, seemed very old.

The carpet was brown and very dirty, but the walls had been painted in the not-too-distant past in dark blue. The curtains that covered the window were heavy, patterned in shades of green. There was a big bookcase against the wall opposite the bed, filled with tattered volumes, mostly paperback, with balls of string, pens, a comb and a great deal of miscellaneous bric-a-brac taking up the shelf margin in front of the books.

Set in the wall opposite the window there was a mantelpiece, but the fireplace had been bricked up. There were some pictures stuck to the wall, mostly cut from newspapers, others drawn in colored inks on white paper. His eye was finally drawn to the light-fitting: a none-too-bright bulb shielded by a makeshift shade.

There was nothing that seemed in the least unusual, except for the vague impression that the structural features were very old. It was not that they were dirty, just that they seemed to be in a state of barely-perceptible decay.

He looked back at the girl. She was dark-haired and dark-complexioned. Her skin was smooth. She wore no make-up and she seemed untidy, although that was only to be expected, in view of the fact that she had been dragged from her bed in the middle of a winter night. She was wearing a toweling dressing-gown two or three sizes too large for her. Her feet were tucked up on the seat of the chair, with the excess material of the gown wrapped over them to protect them from the cold. Underneath, she was wearing a thick shirt and jeans.

She met his curious gaze for a few moments, and then was embarrassed into speech. "My name's Rebecca," she said. "Don't try to talk just yet. It won't make much sense. I'll try to explain what's happened to you."

Paul sipped at the sweet liquid, and was content to reply with a smile.

"You're a time-traveler," she said. "At some time in the past you managed to throw yourself into a state where time passed very much more slowly for you than for the world—more than that, because, in some way that nobody understands, you took yourself right out of the world, leaving a surface that reflects all radiation and is impervious to all force, as if you had become an immovable object. You probably jumped deliberately, although it does sometimes happen accidentally. No one knows just *how* it's done—some people can't seem to do it, no matter how they try. I don't know how long ago you jumped, but most of the people waking now already knew what they were doing. The earliest ones didn't, because no one actually came out of the stasis until 2035 or thereabouts, forty years after the first jump. This is January 2119. Do you understand all that?"

Paul wasn't sure whether to nod or to shake his head. He

understood what the words meant, but it didn't make sense. It was a story, which hadn't the remotest connection with the world that he knew. It had to be a dream of some kind. He tried hard to recapture a harvest of memories, and found images of himself, the performance in the stadium, Adam Wishart, the book, the people staring...and he remembered that the man in the car had said something about not telling anyone who he was.

It had to be a dream.

"It's okay," she said, perceiving his uncertainty. "It takes a lot of getting used to. I've never jumped, but Ronnie has—he lives here too. We sometimes help people like you. There aren't too many people living in the neighborhood now; most people moved south of the river, but there are a lot of jumpers here, because of Paul Heisenberg. He's only five or six miles away. Someone has to look after the ones that wake up: take them in, find food for them, help them readjust Lots of people do it. We get paid, a little, by the Movement. It's illegal, but if it didn't exist to help the awakeners, they'd have to be taken in by the police. The police do take in a lot, but they aren't very fond of jumpers, and the Metascientists prefer to look after their own, if they can. That's why you were brought here, to us. You'll be safe here, until you know what's going on and can figure things out for yourself. It's difficult; even the ones who know exactly what they're doing when they jump aren't really *ready* for what they find. For most, it's something of a disappointment. So many seem to expect the world to have changed much more than it has, to have got better. Can you answer some questions now?"

"I'll try," said Paul. His mouth felt dry despite the coffee-substitute, and his voice was hoarse.

"Did you jump during the war? That's important, because if you jumped from the plague years, you could be ill and you'll have to be immunized?"

"Which war?" asked Paul, his voice hardly above a whisper.

She seemed relieved when she heard that answer. "It was the late 2020s and early 2030s. There aren't many jumpers here from those years—not many that are still in stasis, anyhow. There were a lot in the east and the south, where the nuclear strikes were, but they just die when they come out. You must have jumped before 2027, then?"

"Yes."

"Do you remember when exactly?"

Caution made him shake his head.

"What's your name?"

This time he compromised, and said "Paul". It didn't cause her to jump to any conclusions. She accepted it without really taking any notice, as if his ability to remember it had only been a test.

"The world hasn't changed all that much," she said, "in spite of the wars. All *they* did was smash it up a little. Africa's supposed to be uninhabited now, and so is Europe. It was said after the war that Russia was destroyed, but that might not be true. There are people in eastern Asia, but it's said that they're maintaining a low level of technology—they don't communicate. The only other nations with whom we have any substantial trade are Argentina and Australia. They escaped most of the devastation. Practically all of North America that's still habitable is part of the Reunion—that's the former USA—and Argentina now includes the bits of the other South American countries that survived. There are really several more-or-less independent states within it, but they don't correspond to the old national boundaries."

"The only reason we've managed to keep things going here in much the same way that they were before the wars is that the plague depopulated the country to such an extent that we've been able to exploit stockpiled goods and keep enough factories going to tide us over. We have a kind of scavenger economy—but slowly, of course, things are getting worse. They say this is the last real city in the Reunion. Things are supposed to be better in Australia, but the government won't let people emigrate, and they run all the big ships. The government say that things can get better, and that they will in time, if only we'll devote ourselves to rebuilding, but lots of people won't work for the government, or for anyone—they prefer to scavenge on their own behalf. They say that the government wants to conscript everyone into a kind of industrial army, but of course they can't. People just wouldn't do it, and it isn't possible to police the whole country any more. There'd have to be more police than workers. The government hasn't held an election in ten years, and when they do they only put up their own candidates, but they can't do anything the people *really* don't want them to do, because they just couldn't enforce it."

"What do you do?" asked Paul, feeling obliged to make some contribution to the discussion.

"I'm a student. We all are, here in the house. There are five of us. The city has the only university—the only big university, anyhow—in the Reunion. People come to it from all over."

"What do you study?"

"Agricultural science."

"What do you intend to do when you finish?"

She lowered her eyes. "I suppose it depends," she said.

"On what?"

"On how things seem. You see, we don't really know where the world is headed. No one does. We're not quite sure what it's *for*...getting things back to the way they were, even if we can. We still have trouble with things like nuclear fallout...nobody *really* thinks the world can be remade, and no one's convinced that we should remake it the way that we know how...because of what happened to it before, you see. If you'd lived through the war, you'd know what I mean. It depends, I suppose, on *him*."

"Who?"

"Paul Heisenberg."

All through the dialogue he had been feeling remote from it all. He had listened, with a degree of fascination, but he had never felt that there was any real connection between what had been said and himself. Until she spoke his name, it was all a dream.

"He's going to come back, soon," she said. "Maybe he can

tell us what to do. He's the only one who can."

Paul swallowed, although there was no more liquid left in the cup or in his mouth. He wanted to speak, but he couldn't think of anything to say. He couldn't imagine what kind of question he might reasonably ask. Instead, he held out the empty cup.

"More?" she asked.

He nodded.

She plucked it out of his hand, and turned toward the door. "I'll only be a couple of minutes," she said. "You're all right... aren't you?"

He nodded again, and then looked away, because, for some reason, he could no longer meet her gaze. She looked at him hard, studying him carefully for the first time.

"It must be about dawn," she said, inconsequentially. Then she added: "Your name's Paul." Her tone was neutral.

He looked back at her.

Her voice had changed completely when she said: "Paul who?"

CHAPTER NINE

The wrangling had reached such a pitch of frustration and pointlessness that Lindenbaum was glad when the telephone at his side began to bleep. He didn't wait for the aide to pick it up, but snatched it up himself. For the call to have been put through to the conference room it had to be important.

"Yes," he said, incisively. He let his voice identify himself.

Diehl, who was sitting back from the argument, trying to balance out his seething anxiety with a feeling of contempt for those who couldn't help showing their fear and frustration, saw the president's face change as the caller said his piece. Before a quarter of a minute had passed he knew that it was something bad. He sat up straight. One by one, the others realized that something was on, and closed down the chatter.

"Who the hell *is* this?" said Lindenbaum, not loudly, but with a hint of a snarl. Diehl knew immediately that something weird was happening. It wasn't the kind of question the president should have needed to ask. What was more, the president obviously didn't get an answer. When he laid the receiver down his face was dark with gathering fury.

Lindenbaum's eyes roamed the faces that were silently watching him, and finally settled on Diehl's. "How does it happen," he said, "that at a time like this some crazy can reach me on a top security line?"

Diehl did his best to look surprised, but in truth he was not. He was growing used to things happening that had never happened before, and which ought not to happen, from a logical viewpoint.

"What did he say?" he asked, quietly.

"He *said* that there's a fleet of goddam spaceships somewhere beyond the moon."

Diehl blinked. Someone down the other end of the table laughed, but stifled the laughter very quickly.

"That's crazy," someone said.

Diehl was busy trying to work it out—not *how*, but *why*.

"If that's supposed to distract our attention from the immediate problem," said Marcangelo, slowly, "it's the weirdest play I ever heard of."

Lindenbaum was still staring at Diehl, waiting for some kind of an answer.

"I don't know how they do it," said Diehl. "But someone scrambled a warning call to Wishart, and now they've hooked into your priority line. They can do things with telephones that we can't, and they knew exactly when Heisenberg was due out. Why play practical jokes?"

"Is there a radio telescope still functioning, anywhere in the Reunion?" asked the president. "Or even in Australia, come to that?"

"There hasn't been a radio telescope in use since the war," replied the Secretary of State, as if mystified that the question should have been asked.

"Is there an instrument that can be made to work?"

No one could answer that.

"He says that we can prove it," added Lindenbaum, by way of explanation. "We can tap into their communications. He told me the frequency...but he says we'll need more than an ordinary receiver. A radio telescope."

"It has to be a hoax," said the Secretary of State. There was a murmur of agreement.

"It's been tried before," said Diehl, ruminatively. "But it's too far-fetched to work. Unless we *can* get proof. Or unless we can fake proof."

Lindenbaum looked at him as if he had gone mad. Then

comprehension dawned. "It would never work," he said. "We aren't going to be able to keep control by inventing an imaginary emergency. No one would believe us."

Most of the faces around the table still had not yet caught on to what Diehl was suggesting, although the more Machiavellian minds were tracing it through.

"If you're going to tell lies," said Diehl, "you might as well tell bold ones. And this is one hell of a lie."

"It's crazy," said the president.

"And what if it's true?" put in Marcangelo.

Lindenbaum just shook his head in bewilderment.

Diehl picked up his own phone, and spoke into the mouthpiece. "Get me the University," he said. "I want to talk to the closest thing to an astronomer they have on the staff."

CHAPTER TEN

"Ronnie," said Rebecca, the urgency of panic in her voice, "we have to get him out. To the Movement. Somewhere safe. The police will be looking for him."

Ronnie was still trying to disengage himself from the clutches of sleep. He was a heavy sleeper, and even Paul Heisenberg's name had not served to jerk him out of it.

"Where is he?" he muttered, rubbing his right eye and shivering because of the cold.

"Someone dropped him at the door, about three. I don't know who brought him; I couldn't see his face. You slept through the whole thing. Kit and Linda must have heard the buzzer, and Andy too, but none of them budged. I took him to my room, made him a drink, and talked to him...you know the way. It took me the best part of an hour, but when I realized.... Ronnie, it's *him*. Can't you get that into your head? *Heisenberg.*"

"It can't be," said Ronnie, sufficiently awake to be skeptical. "How would he get out of that iron cage?"

"I don't *know*. But he did. Somebody brought him. Come and see him for yourself."

Ronnie fumbled for his trousers, seeming to take an infinite amount of time getting them on and zipping them up. His adrenalin was working now and the implications were slowly unfolding in his mind. If it *was* Paul Heisenberg....

He followed Rebecca down the stairs to the half-landing, and threw open the door to Rebecca's room. He took a long, long look at the person on the bed, comparing the face to the memory of all the old photographs he'd seen of Paul Heisenberg. Blond hair, a face just a little too effeminate to be handsome—a pretty face...those were the images that he called to mind, and compared to the real face before him.

Paul stood up, a little unsteadily, and said: "Take it easy. It's all right." The words sounded hollow and absurd.

Ronnie's mouth went dry, and he stood quite still, losing his opportunity to deliver one of history's great quotable lines. Eventually, he said: "We've got to get to a phone. Call Max Gray...someone in the Movement. If we could get you to the University we could hide you. But they'll be all over town by now, looking for you."

"The one who brought me here," said Paul, "said he would try to come back."

"Was he one of Wishart's men?"

"Wishart?" The name struck a chord in Paul's mind that was almost the equal of the one struck by his own name.

"Wishart—the Movement...." Ronnie trailed off, realizing that Paul could not and did not know the first thing about the Movement. "It's a kind of political party," he said. "The organization of your followers, the ones who have any organization at all. They'll know what to do...if we can only get you across the river."

"We don't have a car," said Rebecca, from the doorway. "We'd never get him past the police if we had. They'll have to come here, if we can hide him until morning."

Ronnie looked from Paul to Rebecca, and then back again, feeling an urgent need to act but not knowing quite what to do.

"I'm going to phone," he said. "I know who'll give me a number where I can reach Wishart or Gray. Stay here. Don't worry."

He turned, and he ran.

Paul wondered how he was supposed to follow the advice to avoid worrying. He sat down again on Rebecca's bed, and said: "I'm sorry." Rebecca seemed to be on the point of bursting into tears.

Ronnie, meanwhile, raced up the steps from the basement door and into the street. The car was already turning the corner, and its headlights picked him out immediately. It wasn't a police car, but the moment he saw it he was afraid. He began to ran, but then the thought occurred to him that it might be the man that had brought Heisenberg to the house, returning to collect him. He hesitated in his flight, and the car drew up alongside him. The back door was flung open, and a tall man reached for him. A flashlight flickered on, and the beam sought his face. He put up his arm to shield his eyes, and ran again, this time as fast as he possibly could, howling:

"Police! Police!"

The tall security man gave chase, the beam of the torch playing on Ronnie's back as he fled. There was a terrible prickling sensation in Ronnie's spine as he realized that he might be shot dead, but no warning sounded and no gunshot was fired. The only noise was the noise of heavy footfalls and the dying echoes of his warning shout.

He drew in breath to shout again, but he never got the chance. The flashlight crashed into the side of his head as soon as the man behind came close enough to use it as a club. Ronnie slipped on the ice-caked road and fell heavily. As he was hauled to his feet he heard a dull thud as a heavy shoulder was applied to a recalcitrant door.

The security men knew the house, but they didn't know how to get into it; they were trying to smash their way through the front door, which hadn't been unlocked since the University took over the block. Ronnie was hauled back to the car, but not very roughly. They had no idea, yet, that Paul Heisenberg was in the house, and hadn't jumped to any conclusions when they caught him outside. He looked up and down the street at the darkened windows. No new lights showed, and there was no sign of activity. No one wanted to get involved.

Ronnie wanted to yell again, this time to spread the news instead of the warning. He wanted to tell the world that Heisenberg was back, and that he was one step ahead of Diehl's cowboys, but he had the sense to keep quiet. When they spread-eagled him over the bonnet of the car and began the questions he pretended that he was more shaken than he was, too much pained to give reasonable attention. He mumbled and muttered "nos" and "don't knows" with convincing uncertainty, knowing that it couldn't last. When they found evidence inside that Rebecca had been entertaining a visitor....

They brought the others out of the house. Peering back over his shoulder Ronnie saw three. Only three: no Paul, and no Rebecca.

In spite of himself, he began to laugh.

CHAPTER ELEVEN

Diehl slammed the phone down, the muscles of his face taut.

"We've got him," he said. "Flushed him out of a house in the suburbs. Nowhere to run. Castagna's got a hundred and fifty men converging, and my men are right on his tail. He can't get away now."

Lindenbaum nodded, without looking particularly relieved. The problems wouldn't stop with Heisenberg's apprehension. The game had yet to be played.

The meeting had broken up, or broken down. The various members of the inner circle had jobs to do, and arrangements to make. Some of them, no doubt, would already be making plans to desert the ship if it began to sink. Most would be trying to make sure that it didn't sink. Lindenbaum, rather to his own surprise, was slowly discovering that he didn't care as much as he ought to. He had always thought of himself as a fighter—had always *been* a fighter, or he couldn't have been where he was today—but now that the long-expected crisis was at his door he found that he was just a little too tired to attack the problems with the right degree of desperation. Instead of rejoicing with Diehl, he could only think: *Suppose someone screws it up again? Suppose we can't take him—or can't hold him—even now?*

"He's not going to be in a co-operative frame of mind," he said. "This whole chase scene is going to make us look bad, from his point of view. It doesn't do our image any good at all."

Diehl shrugged. "There's nothing we can do about that now.

At least we stopped him reaching Wishart."

"Unless it was Wishart's people that got him out."

"It wasn't," said Diehl, flatly.

"Then who was it?"

"We've been through all that. It was whoever hooked into your phone. I don't know who, but not Wishart. They warned Wishart to get out, and they tried to spring Heisenberg...but if it was the Movement, I'd *know* about it. Believe me."

"How can I believe you? What the hell's the alternative, if it wasn't Wishart? The Australians? Phantoms from the old Communist bloc? Aliens from outer space?"

"The phone call was just to show us they can do it," said Diehl, with a confidence that was only partly assumed. "The message meant nothing...just a comic line to stick a finger in your eye. I think it's someone a damn sight closer to us than Wishart. We ought to face that possibility."

Lindenbaum glared at him, half-angry and half-contemptuous. "And how did they know he was going to come out tonight?"

That was the question that stopped all the theories. But Diehl had figured out a way to sidestep even that.

"He did know," he replied. "Therefore it can be known—calculated. There must be some way of measuring something that we don't know about. There are people at the University who've been working on the problem for years, trying to figure out how the jump-length can be calculated. Obviously someone managed to find out. They didn't tell us. But they didn't tell the Movement, either. If they had, I'd have known about it. This thing surprised Wishart as much as it surprised us—I'm sure of that."

"What about that car—the one that crashed the barrier?"

"Marcangelo's following that up. They're going through the wreckage with a fine-toothed comb...everything that they could scrape up from the roadway. I don't think they'll find anything significant."

Lindenbaum ground out the butt of his cigarette, and promptly lit another.

"I have a feeling," he said, "that we're more out of our depth than you care to think. And prayer isn't going to help—God's not on our side this time."

Diehl curled his lip. Lindenbaum, staring into space, couldn't see the small change of expression, but he didn't really need to. He knew that Diehl didn't like him, and would seize upon any opportunity to feel contemptuous of him. Diehl was that way about everyone. It was almost a necessary qualification for his post. To be what he was you had to hate the enemy, and in his job, the enemy was everybody and anybody.

"You'd better get back on the job," said the president, wearily. "When you get him, tell me. I want to know everything that happens. Don't use the phone."

Diehl nodded, rose to his feet, and went to the door. When it closed behind him, Lindenbaum blew out a cloud of grey smoke and watched it dissipate into the warm air. His gaze wandered for a few moments, and then lingered on the silent telephone. After a few seconds' hesitation he picked it up and dialed.

When the call was answered, he said: "If we were attacked from space, could we put up any kind of a defensive show at all?"

He received the answer that he expected, said: "That's what I thought," and replaced the receiver in the cradle.

Hell, he murmured, inaudibly. *If it came to a fight we couldn't even beat the Australians. But who wants to fight for a wrecked world?*

CHAPTER TWELVE

"I'm sorry," whispered Paul, "but I just can't go any further." The words came in gasps, punctuated by long pauses. Drawing breath seemed to be a struggle. His face, illuminated by the sky that was growing silver with the dawn, seemed to be ashen grey. Rebecca, too, felt as if she had come to the end. There was no more running in her, and soon there would be no more shadows in which to hide.

They were hiding among the corpses of long-dead cars, in what had once been a salvage-yard but was now no more than a dump. Scavengers had long ago stripped the wrecks of anything that was worth taking, and there was nothing left now but rusted skeletons, crushed and cracked, piled up in rotting heaps. Even the soil was red-brown, too heavily impregnated with metallic oxides to allow anything but a few ragged clumps of squill and a little coarse grass to grow in it.

They were crouched beside what had once been a transcontinental bus, but which was now no longer solid enough to allow them to crawl inside.

"Leave me," said Paul. "You don't have to run. They don't want *you*."

"I can't," she said.

They could hear the sound of voices calling to one another. The streets around the yard were patrolled, now, and there were men picking their way through it. There was no way out. Rebecca huddled close to Paul, trying to keep away from the jagged shards of rotting metalwork. She wasn't trying to escape the cold so much as making an ineffectual attempt to protect *him* from it.

"Why do they want me?" asked Paul. "What do they want me to do?"

"Everybody's waiting for you," she whispered. "They think you can tell us what to do, because nobody else can. They think you can give them reasons, because nobody else can. The government want you to put your name to their plans...half a dozen other groups would ask you to put your name to theirs. People will listen to you, but they won't listen to anybody else. It's as simple as that."

"And if I don't?"

"I don't know. They wouldn't dare to hurt you. I don't know what they *could* do. But there might be fighting, against the Movement There could be a revolution. There *are* people who hate your name enough to want you dead. I don't know."

Her voice was thin and urgent, and she talked as if talking were the only thing that could hold back the tears. They had been running for nearly an hour, with nowhere to run to and nothing to gain. All the while she had been driven on by the terror of responsibility, by the knowledge that she had been hurled into the vortex of important events without the means to do anything that would seem, at some later time, to be what she ought to have done.

Paul was shivering now, too weak to resist. She tried to wrap her arms around him, to surround him and keep the cold at bay. There was no way to do even that.

The voices were getting closer.

"Run," said Paul. "It's all right."

"I won't leave you," she said, as the sobs finally broke through and the tears began to flow. "I won't...not ever."

CHAPTER THIRTEEN

"They've taken him," said the silvery voice. "He's been taken to the state prison, to the hospital wing. There was no way to get to him—not without the risk of hurting him."

"I know," said Adam Wishart. "But thanks for calling. Would you like to tell me who you are now?"

"Do you have men inside the prison? Is there any possibility of your getting him out?"

Wishart scowled at the telephone receiver as though it were a repulsive insect of some kind. "Who are you?" he demanded.

"I'm the one who warned you to get out when he came out of stasis. I tried to get him away from the stadium."

"That doesn't answer the question. Nor does it prove that you're on our side in this affair. You could have told us in advance if you knew when he was due to come out. *We* could have got him out of the cage and away from the stadium. You weren't trying to get him out for *our* benefit. You wanted him yourself. Why? *Who are you?*"

"There is no time to tell you, nor time to make you believe me. Within a week, an alien spacefleet will arrive in Earth orbit. It has come a long way, and its journey has been a long one. I am talking in terms of hundreds of years. Their intention is to colonize your world. I will try to defend it. I do not know what will happen should I fail, but if I should succeed, you will need Paul Heisenberg. *We* will need him."

Wishart looked up at the man who was sitting on the other side of the desk, whose name was Max Gray. Gray was listening in on an extension, and he silently mouthed the word "crazy".

"It all sounds rather unlikely," said Wishart.

"It is true. The presence of the ships can be established if you can pick up the radio signals they are using for communication. I have informed President Lindenbaum of the appropriate frequencies. The information is being checked. You will not act until you are sure of the truth, I know, but what I am saying is true."

"And how do you know all this?"

"I detected the spacefleet more than a year ago. At that time I did not have the means to communicate with you, and you would not have been able to pick up the signals. During that year I have been preparing for the confrontation. I do not know whether I can destroy the invaders, but I will try."

"You're not human," said Wishart, following the implication of the words. "You're from somewhere else—not Earth."

"That is true. But I want to help you. I do not know exactly what the aliens intend, but I do not want them to take control of your world. Neither do you, I think. I am concerned for the future of your race. That is why I am concerned for Paul Heisenberg. It is important that he should be safe. That is why I want to know what you intend to do. It might be to our mutual advantage to co-operate."

Wishart looked again at Gray, who simply shook his head in bewilderment.

"I don't know," said Wishart. "I don't know what to believe, or what to think."

"You must decide," said the mellifluous voice. "There is not much time. I will speak to you again."

There was a click as the connection was broken, and Wishart lowered the phone quickly, as if it were suddenly too hot to hold.

"It's a hoax," said Gray, who was still holding his own receiver. He didn't seem to be very confident of what he said.

"It's too absurd to be a hoax," replied Wishart. "It's either some weird kind of performance, or true. You'd better try to find out what Lindenbaum is doing to have the story checked.

Make enquiries at the University. In the meantime, we go ahead as if nothing had happened, except...."

"Except what?"

"Spread the word that we'd better be careful about using phones. Diehl hasn't got a tap on this line, but I wouldn't bet that *he* hasn't."

"Up on the street," said Gray, softly, "there are crazies running around trying to persuade everybody that the end of the world is nigh. They think Heisenberg's return is the signal for the day of judgment."

Wishart didn't smile when he said: "I don't think God and his archangels would need a fleet of spaceships."

CHAPTER FOURTEEN

"How are you feeling now?" asked Marcangelo.

"Better," admitted Paul. He had rested and he had eaten, and for the first time since his re-emergence into the world he felt warm. He was a good deal better.

"I'm Ricardo Marcangelo. The man outside the door, who will undoubtedly listen to everything that passes between us, is Samuel Laker. You might have formed an unfortunate opinion of Mr. Laker's colleagues, because of the way they had to...hunt you down. I'm here to put our side of the case."

"I see," said Paul. He studied the other's rounded features, knowing that he was supposed to fall under the spell of his affability and preparing himself to resist any feeling of liking that might arise within him. Laker he had already seen—a slightly-built man with a face that seemed incapable of carrying any expression. He was stationed outside the door along with another security man, but the door was not locked—and, in fact, stood slightly ajar. It was a heavy door, built to be impregnable when locked. Paul knew well enough that he was inside a prison, even though the room he was in was by no means a cell.

Marcangelo sat down in the chair beside the bed. Paul really didn't want to be in bed, but for the moment he was content not to make an issue out of it.

"I don't know how much you've been told by the various people you've met on your travels," said Marcangelo, "but I'd like you to bear in mind that some of it might be untrue, or at least misleading."

"Where's Rebecca?" asked Paul.

"She's still here."

"Imprisoned? For trying to help me?"

"She'll be released. We'd like to know who it was that took you from the stadium and left you at the house where she lives, but we're not going to beat it out of her, even if she knows. You can see her before she's released, if you want to."

"You're being very careful."

"Yes, we are. We need your help, as you presumably know. I'd like to explain why."

"Feel free," Paul replied, with casual irony.

"Do you remember 1992—speaking in the stadium?"

"Of course."

"And you know that it's now 2119, that you've shifted forward in time."

"Yes."

"You seem to have taken that news very well—a good deal better than most of the emergent jumpers I've spoken to, including the ones who knew what they were doing."

"I'm surprised. I dare say that it will take time for the news to sink in, but there wouldn't be much point in my denying it, would there? It might be all a dream, but I don't seem to be in imminent danger of waking up. And there was something else—*another* dream...."

caustic sand blown by a terrible wind....

a current dragging at his sense of time, his sense of self....

Without quite knowing why, Paul looked at his fingers, surprised that they were uninjured. He flexed his wrists, then looked at Marcangelo.

"I know," said the presidential aide. "They all dream the same dream. No one knows why. It scares some of them so badly that they don't want to jump again. Some of them are in a pretty bad way when they come out. Disorientation, amnesia—even psychosis. You got off very lightly, considering the time you were frozen."

"Does that matter?"

"Time doesn't stop...it just slows down. That's what they say."

"How does it happen?"

"Nobody knows. When it happened to you, it was taken to be a kind of miracle. It helped to spread your word in no uncertain terms, although, without you as an interpreter, some pretty weird beliefs sprang up with supposed warrants taken from your book—which practically no one could understand. Then it started to happen to others, and people began to set out to *make* it happen. No one knew how, but they tried prayer and they tried meditation and they tried every mental trick they could think of. A flourishing market in invented techniques grew up. People began to succeed—it wasn't easy to figure out how, because the people who *did* succeed couldn't say. Nobody came out for about twenty-five years, and it wasn't until then that we realized that what was happening was a kind of time-travel rather than some weird kind of apotheosis. Most people who try to do it find that they can, in the end. Over the years, the number of silver statues littering our streets and our houses has grown steadily. We have more here than anywhere else. It has become the last resort of the unhappy, the incompetent, the insane, the sick and the criminal. Some find that, no matter how hard they try, they can't do the trick. The reasons people have for *not* trying to project themselves into the future are, as you can probably imagine, just as various as the reasons people have for trying it. It's a funny world we live in. Some people think it's a world *you* made."

"Do you?"

"No. I think your influence is vastly over-rated. Most of the people who call themselves your followers haven't even read your book, and don't give a damn what it says. They're not capable of affiliating themselves to ideas. They just need some talisman in which to invest their faith, and fate happened to pick you. I think it would all have happened in much the same way whoever had been first, except that their name would have replaced yours as the futile magic formula, the meaningless abracadabra. It's only the name that has become important, not you."

"Except for the fact that I'm the person wearing it," Paul observed.

"Don't fall into the trap of overestimating your importance," said Marcangelo, quietly. "It's true that there are a lot of people who claim to be your followers, in one sense or another. It's true that there are a lot of people who'd like to believe that your return is going to herald better times, and are relying upon your words to tell them what to do. But the simple fact is that you *can't* save the world, and there's nothing you can say that won't be a disappointment. The hopes that have gathered about the myth of your return are ones that can't be fulfilled. You—the real you—are as much a victim of the situation as anyone else. You don't have any more miracles up your sleeve. All you can do is fall in with one or other of the political movements that already exist, and add your endorsement to it. I'm here to make every attempt to recruit you to mine, but from your point of view, it really doesn't matter much. Whichever side you join, you're going to disappoint ninety per cent of the people who think you're a messiah...because, let's face it, you're not. You're just a clown, who got caught up in something you don't understand any better than anyone else."

Marcangelo was speaking in a level tone, and his manner had a certain forced amiability, but Paul sensed the cold current of hostility beneath the easy flow of the words. Marcangelo did not approve of Paul Heisenberg's followers, or of him.

"How do you know that?" said Paul, his voice slightly mocking.

"I have read your book," replied Marcangelo. "And I *did* understand it." He paused for a moment, and when Paul didn't reply, he went on: "You don't even have a real message, although you couldn't tell that to most of the people who believe in you. In the final analysis, you simply contend that it doesn't really matter what people believe. Your speculative flights of fancy are really no more than suggestions, aren't they?"

"They were attempts to create metascientific beliefs appropriate to the day," said Paul. "Ones that could fit in with the scientific knowledge of the day. Apparently, your wars put an end to progress in the theoretical sciences, in which case they should be just as well adapted to the present day."

"Ecological mysticism? In a world where at least a fifth of the land surface is radioactive? Grandiose evolutionary schemes, and empty waffle about the cosmic mind? Apocalyptic double-talk? I don't see that kind of thing helping anyone to get along in our kind of world. We're living in a decaying civilization, Paul. Even in Australia, which is supposed to be holding its ground, the plagues and the fallout did more damage than the Aussies care to admit.

"The worst of it is that everyone *knows* that things are on the slide. They all believe, as firmly as they believe anything at all, that the rot has set in, and that there's no way to reverse it. That's why they all seek solutions for themselves, whether through some warped version of transcendental mysticism or by straightforward anti-social behavior. While people think and act that way, then the rot *has* set in; it's a self-fulfilling prophecy, but we could turn it around, if only we can make people believe that we can.

"A re-affirmation of faith in society, in worldly solutions: that's what's needed. And that's why we need you, even though you're nothing but a clown with delusions of grandeur. That's why the other side needs you, too. The dispute isn't about spiritual values or prophecies or metascience—it's a crude struggle for political power. It's essential that you realize that, if you're to do any good here. The members of the so-called Movement claim to be your followers, and they form the main organizational structure within the cults that have grown up around your name and your book, but they're not *your* side. They're just opportunists, out for themselves."

"No different from you," said Paul, ironically.

"Not really," admitted Marcangelo. "Except that we already have a governmental structure, a system. They haven't. They want to tear us down and start again from scratch."

"And Adam Wishart is their leader."

Marcangelo acknowledged the fact with a nod of the head, and his gaze rested on Paul's face as he searched for some indication of what that fact might mean to Paul.

"He jumped as well?" prompted Paul.

"Some years after you did," Marcangelo agreed. "He's been back for some time. I'd guess that he's fifteen or twenty years older now than he was in 1992. He's about seventy, maybe a little older. It didn't take him long to get into the Movement. He and a man named Max Gray have been its kingpins for some two-and-a-half years now. They've been preparing for the day of your return for thirty or forty years, but Wishart seems to have overhauled their plans completely since he joined up. He's some propagandist, but I wouldn't trust him to run a revolution for *me*."

"I'd like to see him."

"We'd like to have him here, but this is America, and we pride ourselves on not putting our political opponents in prison, if we can possibly help it."

"I'm not going to do anything for anyone until I talk to Adam," said Paul, firmly.

Marcangelo nodded. "I was afraid you might say that."

"Well?"

"It's not my decision. I'll make your views known to the president and his advisors. We might be able to arrange something."

There was a pause. Then Paul said: "What about the other people I used to know? Is there anyone else still around that I might know."

"Not that I know of. It's possible—we haven't been able to keep accurate account of all the jumpers. The war...and afterwards...we could probably find some refugees from the twentieth century for you to compare notes with. People wake up all the time, some of them second time around."

"I want to talk to Rebecca as well—other members of the so-called Movement," Paul spoke defensively, but with some confidence. It seemed to him that he was in a position to make demands if he wanted to.

"Again, I'll refer the request back," Marcangelo said, stalling.

Paul hesitated for a moment, and then said: "You say that you don't know who it was that got me out of the stadium?"

"Not for certain, although we know a little more than we did last night. Some time after you were abandoned at the house, a car went through one of our barricades and set off for the north. It was going too fast, and came off the road on an iced-up bend. Before the police got to it, it blew up. Witnesses at the barricade saw someone in the driving seat, and we're certain he didn't get out, but we haven't found anything in the wreckage that looks like a body—at least, not a human body. We found some plastic and some bits of electronic circuitry that didn't belong."

"What does that signify?"

"Maybe that the body evaporated, bones and all. Maybe that the driver was a robot."

"You have humanoid robots?"

"*We* don't, but somebody might. Somebody, it seems, has a fleet of spaceships coming in from the direction of Sagittarius. We don't have any spaceships, either, nor anything with which to defend ourselves against an attack from space, if attack is what the invaders have in mind."

Marcangelo was still watching him, eager for some kind of significant response. Paul could only stare.

"*Was* it a robot?" asked Marcangelo.

"It had a plastic mask, and a strange voice. It was very strong. It could have been."

Marcangelo nodded. "Sheehan said that it was unnaturally strong, and quick in its movements. He was one of the policemen at the stadium. He got hurt."

"Badly?"

Marcangelo shook his head. "Nasty bruise around one eye. Concussion, but no fracture. Your friend tried to chloroform him first—he obviously doesn't believe in needless slaughter. But then, robots are traditionally supposed to be full of good-will towards men, aren't they?"

"I seem to have arrived at an inopportune moment," said Paul, matching the other's tone of calculating triviality. "If Earth *is* about to be invaded. Maybe I'm not going to get a chance to save America after all."

"That remains to be seen," admitted Marcangelo. "Better think carefully about the kind of performance you're going to put on—it might just be your last."

CHAPTER FIFTEEN

In one of the conference rooms of the Presidential Manse, Diehl, Marcangelo and Lindenbaum sat in intense, if rather fatigued, conversation. None of them had slept for nearly thirty hours. Marcangelo, who had been the most active of the three, was showing the strain most obviously.

"In my view," said Diehl, "we ought to try to compel co-operation. We have a hostage. We ought to put pressure on by using her. All we need is for him to make a few short statements in front of a camera. We can broadcast them over a period of a week. By that time, we'll have Wishart and Gray. We've already rounded up a hundred of the Movement's active agents."

"It's a drop in the ocean, and you know it. Our position is balanced on a knife-edge. If the Movement were to act, we'd suddenly find that half the men we thought were ours are really theirs—policemen, government workers, even the guards at the damn prison. Even your security forces, Nick. We only hold control at the moment because the Movement's waiting. It's waiting for the same reason we're waiting—because it doesn't know what Heisenberg is going to do. I think we ought to call a truce—let Wishart see him. Let's all get together; personally, I'd rather co-operate with Wishart than fight him."

"You know what co-operating with Wishart would involve," said Diehl, coldly. "It would mean him taking over. We can't let him get to Heisenberg. It would be fatal."

"Heisenberg's not a fool," replied Marcangelo. "He knows Adam Wishart a damn sight better than we do. Just because he was willing to let Wishart manage his career as a five cent prophet doesn't mean to say he's going to play front man while Wishart becomes the emperor of America. Essentially, he's honest. If we can persuade him that we're in the right, then he'll help us."

"We need him *now*," said Lindenbaum. "We need to put him on the TV, to keep the lid on things. It doesn't matter what he *says*—maybe it's better if he says nothing at all—but he's got to appear, to stop these stupid rumors about what we're doing and what we're going to do."

"When you listen to Nick," Marcangelo pointed out, "they're not so stupid. Look, if you'll just give me time, I think I can persuade him. Let me offer him a meeting with Wishart if he'll help us stall. In the long run, it'll work better for us than trying to use a stick to threaten him."

"I don't like the idea of playing into Wishart's hands," said Lindenbaum.

"It might be worth *you* setting up a meeting with Wishart," said Marcangelo. "There's a chance we can set up some kind of a deal with him on a temporary basis. This isn't the time for him to stage a takeover."

"Do you think he knows about the spaceships?" asked the president.

"If he doesn't, we can tell him. We can show him the signals. He might be willing to talk, and to declare a truce until we know what's going to happen. Maybe he knows more than we do—the phantom phone caller seems to have helped him stay free."

"*No,*" said Diehl. "If you give me time I can bring Wishart in. I can find him. Let Heisenberg see him in a prison cell. We have to keep control."

"Even if you can find Wishart," said Marcangelo, "you then have to take him, and keep him. You'd never do it. You'd just blow the whole thing sky high. Do you want fighting on the streets? Open warfare? We're just *that* far away from it, and if the weather wasn't so bitterly cold we'd likely have it already.

The seeds of a major riot are scattered over the whole south side, and all it takes is some trigger incident to start the bloodshed. We have to play it my way."

"How do we set up a meeting with Wishart?" asked Lindenbaum.

"Release some of the Movement people that Nick brought in. One of them will get a message to him. Let him choose a spot to make contact. I'll meet him."

"All right," said the president. "Get back to the prison. Tell Heisenberg he can have what he wants after he makes a broadcast for us. He doesn't have to say anything much, just that he's safe and well and that everyone has to be patient while he sorts things out. Just get him to buy time, nothing more. Then you can meet with Wishart."

"This is suicide," said Diehl. "We can't afford it."

"Leave it, Nick," said the president. "Just keep your men on a tight rein. This isn't the time. For now, we have to play it Ricky's way."

"You're going to regret this," said Diehl, flatly.

"Maybe we all are," said Lindenbaum. "But just remember that we're all in it together. We don't need to start fighting among ourselves, or against the Movement. This time next week we might be all humans together, fighting a new enemy."

"If those signals really *do* come from spaceships in Sagittarius," said Diehl. "We don't know yet that we aren't being led by the nose."

"If we are," replied Lindenbaum, calmly, "it's your job to find out. I suggest you get on it."

CHAPTER SIXTEEN

"This time," said Paul, "I think I look and feel better than you do." He was out of bed now and fully dressed. He'd been given newspapers to read to fill out his knowledge of the new world in which he found himself, but he still hadn't been able to talk to anyone except Marcangelo and the security man, Laker.

"I want you to go on television," said Marcangelo, coming straight to the point.

"That's nice," said Paul. "It's a whole week since I last appeared on TV. A whole week's memory, that is. Why?"

"People want to see you. They want to be reassured that you're all right and that you've begun work on their terrible problems. They don't expect you to have saved the world already, but they'd like to know that you're on the job."

"What do you want me to say?"

"I want you to tell them to wait. Just that and no more. Ask them to be patient. You could save a lot of trouble—you could stop people getting killed."

"And help to keep you in power."

"We *are* in power. We'll still be in power if the fighting in the streets breaks out. Only that way, we'll have to kill people."

"Can I take advice?"

"You can see Wishart after the broadcast. We're trying to contact him now, in order to open negotiations. We don't want to fight him—at least until we know what's going to happen when the spaceships arrive. It's in everyone's interests to hold things together for the time being."

Paul leaned back in his chair, looking up at the ceiling. Marcangelo stood over him, anxiously waiting and not bothering to conceal his weariness.

"You know," said Paul, softly. "I still can't seem to get a sense of being involved in all this. It still seems unreal. I keep hoping to wake up, though I'm not sure why I don't want it to continue. I *know* it's not a dream, but I just can't seem to *connect* with it all. I feel as if I'm only involved in the sense that I might identify with a character in a book, fascinated, but with no real sense of being able to *act* of my own free will."

"It's real," said Marcangelo, sourly. "It's real to *us*."

"The only thing that's seemed real to me is the girl. She's the only one who talked to me for a while as if I were an ordinary human being. Is she still here?"

"I'll bring her in. She's just down the corridor. But I want an answer. I want you to go on TV *tonight*—you have a couple of hours to think about it and to get ready. We'll prepare a statement for you, or we can work one up together, but either way time is tight. You haven't got time to sit there and wonder whether the world is just a figment of your imagination and whether the problem of free will is an illusion."

"All right," said Paul. "I'll do it. But I'll write my own piece. You can veto anything that's in it, but I have to be able to mean what I say."

Marcangelo breathed out, letting his relief show.

"Fine," he said. "You can have anything you want, within reason. I'll get things started." He turned away to the door, and beckoned to Laker, who was still outside. As Laker began to come in, the wall began to shake. Then the sound came—not a sharp bang but an ongoing rumble, which expanded to fill the room.

Even as the sound of the explosion died away it was joined by the distant sound of gunshots.

"What's happening?" said Paul, coming quickly to his feet. Laker, as if by instinct, moved to block the door, and reached into his jacket for the gun that was holstered beneath his arm.

Marcangelo didn't move, but his shoulders seemed to sag, and he drew his mouth into a hard line. With an obvious effort to keep his voice calm, he said: "I think it was a bomb. We seem to be too late to stop the revolution."

CHAPTER SEVENTEEN

Wishart had bags under his eyes that made him look like a comic-book villain. His face looked unwashed and his hair was greasy, and he *felt* unwashed and greasy. The situation had forced it upon him, but that didn't make him any less resentful of his condition. He was frustrated and uneasy, and not in the best of tempers.

"What's the situation?" he asked of Max Gray, who had just returned to the hiding place.

"Stalemate," replied Gray. "We hold the prison walls, including all the observation posts, plus all the blocks except the administration building and the hospital. Most of the buildings we took without the ghost of a fight, but the hospital's full of Diehl's men and cops. Castagna's put men all around the prison, but they can't get in without using artillery, and they're not about to do that. Essentially, Heisenberg's in the middle, surrounded by Diehl's men, who are surrounded by ours, who are surrounded by Castagna's. Every stage is a deadlock. Paul Scapelhorn is negotiating from inside the prison, but it's not easy. Marcangelo is with Heisenberg, and he'd probably be prepared to make a deal, but I'm not sure Laker would accept his authority without personal clearance from Diehl. Anyhow, the phone lines into the prison haven't been cut, so negotiations are under way, although all incoming calls are monitored. I suppose the proposed meeting's off, now that Marcangelo can't make it?"

"The president has other aides," grunted Wishart. "But I think we might be strong enough now not to have to talk to the second rank. I'll send back a messenger to suggest that Lindenbaum should come to talk himself."

"I think it's too dangerous," said Gray. "We needn't come out into the open—I don't think we should. All they have to do is pick you up...."

Wishart scowled, and made a dismissive gesture with his right hand. "It would be a declaration of war," he said. "They don't want war. They can't afford it. If they could have got me into the prison before the whole thing broke, they might have kept the lid on, but it's gone too far now. They need me now, because I'm the only one can deliver Paul Heisenberg...on *my* terms."

"You think Lindenbaum will agree to a meet?"

"Yes," growled Wishart. "He knows what it takes to survive. He'll let us move in, even if it costs him three-quarters of his administration. He wouldn't have been president for so long if he couldn't bend with the wind. He's a professional front man—a performer. I know him from top to toe, because I've been dealing with people like him all my life. He's ours, the moment we promise him a deal that'll let him keep what he's got—the appearance of power, the glamour. Within a couple of days he'll be greeting me every day as if I were the prodigal son."

"And suppose the men behind him now don't want to be dropped?" demanded Gray. "You think they're just going to let him hand over the meat cleaver to you, so you can cut them down?"

"Give him credit for some sense," said Wishart. "They won't realize he's gone until he's out of reach. When he turns his coat he isn't going to wait around. I only hope that he has a big enough private army, because he isn't going to be able to call on Diehl's. Diehl will be the first to go."

"I still don't like it," said Gray.

"What did *you* have in mind?"

"We could take it slowly. Play it cool. With Heisenberg on

our side we could force an election. We have the strength on the streets to keep it honest. We could landslide our candidates in and get rid of the whole Lindenbaum operation."

Wishart coughed out a contemptuous laugh. "Sure," he said. "We could do that, if we had the time, and the strength to fight a war against Diehl's assassins, and if we had Paul Heisenberg, body *and* soul. My way, we only need the body, and to be perfectly honest, I think we'd be fools to reckon on ever getting the other. Paul might be a performer, just like Lindenbaum, but he's not quite the straw man that Lindenbaum is. Sure, his immediate loyalties ought to lie with us, especially with the likes of Diehl on the other side, but if he were to be our front man he'd want to know a lot about our program of action once we got voted in. He'd want to know just what we could do—and he'd want a free hand to make his own amendments. Quite frankly, I don't know what the hell Paul makes of the year of our lord 2119, or what he's likely to think it needs in the way of advice or administration, but I do know one thing, and that's that Paul Heisenberg has a pretty weird mind. I want his name, while it's mine to use—I don't want his help in deciding a political program."

"You're going to have to deal with him afterwards, whatever happens," Gray pointed out.

"Afterwards is another day," replied Wishart. "Even Paul knows a *fait accompli* when he sees one. Besides which, his lifetime as the world's favorite successor to Zoroaster, Jesus and Mohammed isn't going to be a long one. People expect a great deal of him, and you know what happens to prophets who can't produce the miraculous on demand. If I had to bet, I'd say that Paul isn't going to be around very long. When he realizes what kind of promises people have made themselves in *his* name, and what kind of check he has to pick up, he'll be off, headfirst into nowhere-land again, heading for the far, far future. He'll run a million years, if he has to, to escape his reputation...because there's no way on Earth he's going to be able to make a start on living up to it."

Gray grinned wryly. "If the people whose loyalty you're counting on to get you into power could hear you say that," he observed, "they'd tear you to pieces."

"I made Paul Heisenberg," said Wishart, coldly. "Even what he is today. It was me that put him up on that platform to be struck by divine lightning. It was me who made it mean something to the world when that lightning struck. Without me, he'd be nothing. He doesn't own his name or the fact that millions of people think that he's the messiah. I do. Those things are *mine*, because I'm responsible for them. They're mine to use."

"You don't like him very much, do you?"

"Sure I like him. He's like a son to me. But what's that got to do with anything? The simple fact is that when he was on stage, I couldn't even trust him to stand still so that the lights could maintain his halo."

"You're a bastard," said Gray, making it sound almost like a compliment. "Just don't ever begin to think of *me* as a son, okay?"

CHAPTER EIGHTEEN

There was a phone on the wall opposite the door to Paul's room, and Ricardo Marcangelo was speaking into the receiver calmly and unhurriedly. His voice was relaxed and patient, but whenever he paused to let the man at the other end reply, his teeth would catch his lower lip and worry at it.

Paul watched him from the doorway. To his right stood Laker, the security man, balancing in his hand a small radio set that kept him in constant touch with his direct superior. There was another security man with him—a man named Horne. To Paul's left stood two other people, both of whom had been in rooms on the same corridor. One was Rebecca, who looked very frightened. The other was the injured policeman, Sheehan, who was sporting an ugly black eye but seemed fit and alert. He was in full uniform, and obviously considered himself to have been returned to duty for the duration of the emergency.

Marcangelo hung up, and turned to his audience. "They've taken over the whole prison, except for this block and the administration buildings behind it. The Movement sent weapons in with the men that security rounded up and brought out here. There must have been a measure of co-operation from the police and from some of the security men...and the prison guards, of course. Either the Movement has agents in all three forces, or it recruited sympathizers, or knew where to go with bribes. The operation was limited—they never intended to try to break out, or even to take the hospital block. What they've done is simply to cut us off from the outside. They're under siege and can't last forever, but they know that even a few days hold-up is going to put the whole administration on the skids. Scapelhorn is asking for Paul to be released into his hands, of course, and for various other concessions to the Movement, to which he knows we won't agree. He also knows that it doesn't really matter what we agree to, or not, at least for the next few days."

"What do we do?" asked Laker, harshly.

"What *can* we do?" countered Marcangelo. "It's up to Wishart to make the next move—he'll deal with Lindenbaum and the cabinet. There's nothing *we* can do but wait. We're just pawns trapped on the board until somebody works out a way of moving us."

Laker waved his pocket radio at Paul and Rebecca. "Hadn't we better get these two locked up and out of the way?"

"What for?" asked Marcangelo. "Are you planning to do a strip-tease?"

Laker didn't take kindly to the note of levity. "We don't want them making a break to try to join their friends in the outer prison. They're all we've got. Hostages. If they get away Scapelhorn's men could start shooting."

"We don't have to chain him to the wall," said Marcangelo, tiredly. "We can *see* him and talk to him. He isn't even *thinking* about trying to escape into the arms of his would-be liberators. Are you?"

"Not for the moment," said Paul, dutifully. "I'm not sure that I'd be in any better position there than here."

"My purpose in being here," said Marcangelo to Laker, in a tone replete with mock gentleness, "is to prove to Paul that we aren't his enemies—that we need his help and that we deserve his help. I'm trying to show him that it will be the best thing for *everyone*, in the long run, if he lends his support to the present administration, if only in the short term. You aren't helping me by suggesting that we should lock him up and treat him as a hostage, now are you?"

Laker stared at Marcangelo for a few minutes, then looked sideways at Paul, and then back at Marcangelo.

"I'm going to check in," he muttered, and moved off down the corridor in search of privacy. The other security man, however, remained close at hand, impassively watching and listening.

Rebecca moved closer to Paul, until her arm was almost touching his. Paul put his own arm around her shoulder in reassurance.

"What's going to happen?" she asked Marcangelo.

"I don't know," said the presidential aide, tiredly. "It depends on Lindenbaum and Wishart, and the mobs in the streets. There's going to be trouble, but how much only God knows—unless he's confided in his prophet...no, I'm sorry, I didn't mean that."

"It's all right," said Paul.

"It's time for you to start thinking," said Marcangelo, soberly. "For the moment, you're just a catalyst, helping everything to happen without being involved, but pretty soon, now, you're going to be out. You'll be in a position to enter the game as a player, instead of being a pawn in the hands of men like Gray and Scapelhorn...and Adam Wishart. If I were you, I'd be thinking hard right now about what I was going to do when the time came to act."

"I still don't know anything about this world," said Paul defensively. "I've been pushed from place to place, shut up in a hospital bed.... I've only talked to two people. How am I in a position to make plans when I have no idea what's at stake, or what's going on?"

"Come with me," said Marcangelo, softly. "I'll show you what's at stake, and what's going on." When both Horne and Sheehan showed signs of alarm, he added: "It's all right. We aren't going far."

He led the way along the corridor to a set of double doors which gave access to a ward containing a dozen beds. None of the beds was occupied, but the ward wasn't empty. There were four people stretched out horizontally, perfectly still, suspended in mid-air a metre off the floor. They gleamed brightly in the electric light, the surfaces of their bodies like convex distorting mirrors.

"When they go out like that we take the beds away," said Marcangelo. "They don't need them, and someone else might. They're a nuisance, of course, taking up space like that, but we just have to work around them. Of course, when they come out of their hidey-holes—in twenty, or fifty, or a hundred years time—they'll fall down, but they'll fall relaxed, like babies. They were sick men when they went, and they'll be sick men when they come back—no better off for the passage of time, and maybe worse."

"That's the normal position for jumping, of course—very few go standing up, the way you did. Eight out of ten go while lying down on a bed, and the beds are practically always taken out from under them. They fall through time, and then they fall through space. The prison has a lot of jumpers. It's conducive to the habit. We used to go on using the cells even after one or two people had jumped, but we found that when a man's in a cell with one or two of *those* it's practically certain that sooner or later he's going to follow the example. It *was* suggested that therein lay the answer to the problem of criminality, and that we could give every single offender a long-term sentence simply by encouraging him to absent himself for fifty years or so, but that wasn't really what we wanted.

"I don't know how many jumpers there are—nobody does. I've lived all my life with them around, and I've simply become accustomed to them. You just get used to it...knowing that if you bump into one in the dark, you hurt yourself. You get to take them for granted. I've never for one moment been tempted to become one myself, because I know how pointless it all is. The people who jump are the sick, the desperate, the unhappy and the neurotic. Every single one of them is trying to escape, but the things they're trying to escape from are all inside themselves. They all know that, but the knowledge is counterbalanced by a crazy kind of hope that *somehow* it will all be different, that the world will be Utopia and that they'll be reborn. You're not responsible for their having that hope, Paul, but it's tied to your name, and only you can cancel it out and make people see that they have to fight their problems *here* and *now*. In the long run, if enough people escape from the unhappy present, there won't be a future to jump to at all, because there'll be no one who can build it."

While Marcangelo was speaking, Paul approached the nearest mirrored statue. He placed his hand on the man's head, touching it lightly as if ready to snatch back if the surface were hot. It wasn't hot *or* cold—it was just *there*.

"Why does he float like that?" asked Paul.

"Nobody knows. We think that it's not as simple as his time-rate having slowed down. If it were just that, he'd look perfectly ordinary. It's as if the jumpers cut themselves right out of the fabric of spacetime, leaving a hole—not an empty hole, but a hole in spacetime itself, which can't be reached *from* spacetime, so that no light can pass into it and no matter can penetrate it. It seems to have substance, to be immovable and impervious, but there's a kind of illusion. The reason it's so solid and so hard is simply that it's absolute nothingness. Do you remember old cartoon films, where the characters would fall over cliffs or be blasted through stone walls, and in the ground or the wall there would appear a cut-out shaped like the character? That's what this is, except that it's three-dimensional. It's just a cut-out, where something's gone from the fabric of existence, and to which it will return, aged by no more than a few seconds, after the passage of many years."

"But if he were fixed in a particular position in space the Earth would move away from him at several miles per second," said Paul.

"You know better than that," replied Marcangelo. "There *are* no positions in space, in any absolute sense. All motion is relative. The hole is stationary in spacetime, within the Earth's gravity well."

"What causes it? What kind of energy is used to project people into these holes? How is it that people can do it to themselves?"

"We don't know. We have no idea what kind of energy is

involved or how it comes about that people can move themselves out of spacetime and leave holes behind. It's been said that what's happening is analogous to the situation of a two-dimensional being in a two-dimensional perceived world, who develops the ability to move in a third dimension, but that tells us nothing at all about causes. We have no explanation of why it suddenly began to happen. Again, it's been said in support of the flatlander analogy that perhaps the universe itself underwent some kind of basic change, imperceptible to us, which actually brought into being this extra dimension and created an opportunity that wasn't ever there before. It's even been argued that this new dimension may have been *deliberately* opened up as a trap to catch people, by some kind of predatory creatures, or fishermen in the far future. It's pure speculation, but you know how people are. They like a story when they don't know."

"Belief is only necessary in the absence of knowledge," quoted Paul, "but in the absence of knowledge, belief *is* necessary."

"Of course," said Marcangelo, dryly. *"Science and Metascience.* You're an expert on the speculative imagination and its utility. You could probably make up stories far better than we can."

Paul looked down at the face of the jumper. It was surprisingly difficult to follow its contours, and there was the disturbing effect of the distorted reflections of his own face staring up at him from their apparent positions within time-locked space.

"This is supposed to be a moral lesson," Paul commented.

"Damn right," agreed Marcangelo. The hardness drained from his voice, however, as he went on: "None of this is any fault of yours. You knew nothing about it, and you certainly didn't plan anything. But you have to realize how important your name has become, and your potential now, as a catalyst who could totally transform the historical situation. Your power is limited—most of it is only apparent, because it won't take long for the vast majority of your followers to realize gut-wise what they've always known intellectually—that you aren't a miracle-worker with a warrant from God to preside over the rebirth of the human world. You can't even begin to fulfill the role that history and the popular imagination have carved out for you, but there's still a great deal that you *can* do. You still have a voice that people want to hear, and even if you can't tell them what they want to hear, you can make them listen. Some of them, at least, will listen to reason if it comes from your mouth. You can go some way to cancelling out the effect that the example of your first jump had upon the world. You can tell them that time-slipping isn't any kind of solution to any kind of problem. You can ask them to redirect their hopes and their efforts to salvage rather than salvation—to the remaking of this world rather than to idle Utopian dreams that are incapable of fulfillment. I don't know how much even you can achieve, but you must see that you have to try. *You must.*"

"You said before that some people can't do it?" said Paul, half to himself, as if he was still contemplating the essential mystery of the silver statue while Marcangelo's urgent pleading passed him by.

"So it seems," agreed Marcangelo. "But that doesn't mean that the people involved redirect their efforts wholly to the affairs of the present day. Some of them do little but trudge from one guru to the next, one set of mental exercises to the next, convinced that, simply because they *can't* do it, it must be something infinitely valuable. The people who are running the world—not just the government, but everybody who's doing a useful job—aren't, for the most part, people who've tried to jump to Utopia and failed. They're the people who don't want to jump, who genuinely believe that the real future has to be made, and that there's no short cut. People like me."

"If there are enough of you," said Paul, "maybe you could keep the world going for the time-jumpers. You couldn't build them a Utopia, but you could at least maintain a world that could feed them and offer them a place to rest. You could make time-jumping a viable way of life."

"Sure," said Marcangelo. "Do you know the fable of the ant

and the grasshopper?"

"The ants labored all summer while the grasshopper played and whistled," answered Paul. "And when winter came he asked the ants to let him into the nest so that he could shelter from the cold."

"And they told him to go whistle," Marcangelo finished for him.

"But there are others," Paul went on, calmly, "who don't actually *try* to jump. It just happens to them...as it happened to me. They're not trying to run away. And how can you tell, in any particular case, whether it was deliberate or not?"

"As far as we can tell," said Marcangelo, "only one slip in fifty is an accident. It's only an estimate, because the testimony of the jumpers themselves isn't available. But what we do know is that damn few of the dedicated workers disappear through the universe's asshole."

"I see," said Paul. "But you do understand, don't you, why my immediate sympathies are with them rather than with you? I'm one of them, and I have the memory of what happened to me on my awakening fresh in my mind. A memory of being caged, hunted...*their* predicament seems a good deal more real to me at this moment than yours."

"I know that," said Marcangelo. "But you'll come round to seeing things our way. I *know* that. It's just that there isn't much time—that's why I'm trying to make you see *now*. You have to make up your mind quickly."

"Because I have to save the world for civilization and the sanctity of motherhood," murmured Paul.

"It's not quite as dramatic as that," replied Marcangelo, his voice level and serious. "But you have to help. Without your help, the balance just might tip against us."

"Maybe so," admitted Paul, turning away from the mirrored face to look first at Marcangelo and then at Rebecca, "but it occurs to me that if I throw in with you, and do what *you* want, I'll seem to virtually all those who call themselves my followers to be betraying them. And you know, don't you, what happens to prophets who betray their followers?"

"Sometimes," continued Marcangelo, harshly, "it happens even to prophets who don't."

CHAPTER NINETEEN

Diehl stared across the table at Lindenbaum, his face the color of chalk.

"It's fixed," said the president. "I'm going out to meet him now."

"Where?" demanded Diehl.

"Does it matter?"

"You know that it matters. How the hell am I supposed to provide you with security cover?"

"You aren't supposed to. That's part of the deal. I go alone. I can take a driver and one other man, but they stay with the car. The meeting is right out in the open, with nowhere close at hand that either of us could use as cover to plant extra men. He's not going to try anything stupid, because he's nothing to gain by it. Neither have I."

"If you were killed—or even temporarily removed from the scene—there'd be chaos here. You know that...and so does Wishart. Vanetti could take over, but it's not just a matter of taking over. Appearances matter, especially in a situation as delicately balanced as this. What do you think the cultists will feel when the news breaks that not only is Heisenberg out of our reach inside the prison but that the president's disappeared? They'll be declaring the millennium before nightfall. You can't go."

"It's fixed," repeated the president. "The matter's closed. I'll have a police escort to the city limits, and then I'll be on my own. I'll use an armored limousine. I'll take Richardson with me, and my usual driver. Richardson will be in radio contact throughout. Nothing will go wrong, and I'll be back before dusk. Until then, stay calm. Preserve the balance. Wishart's people won't try to force the issue—they're dependent on this meeting as much as we are. I'm going to brief Vanetti now, and I'll leave in twenty minutes."

Diehl, his face quite bloodless, found it something of an effort to stay calm and to keep his fingers from trembling. But he did so, until Lindenbaum had gone from the room.

Then he reached for the phone, and said: "Get me the car pool. Now."

CHAPTER TWENTY

Paul lay back on the bed and put his hands over his face. Marcangelo had left him in his room, alone with Rebecca, and was waiting out in the corridor with Laker, Horne and Sheehan. There was nothing to do but wait—there had been no communication by phone for over two hours.

"I don't understand any of this," said Paul, in a low whisper, as though reluctantly confiding a secret.

"No," said Rebecca. "I don't suppose there's any way that you could."

"What is it that people expect of me? What do *you* expect of me?"

"I don't know," she confessed. "I've never even thought about it much, though it seems stupid to say it, now. I never knew exactly what I *could* expect. It's just...a *feeling* that when you came back things would get better. A kind of magic formula—the day Paul Heisenberg returns—I don't know what we meant by it. We didn't think...we didn't try to *analyze....*"

"It's all right," said Paul, sitting up and reaching out to catch one of her wrists. The gesture was largely unnecessary. She wasn't even close to tears. Her tone was one of puzzlement rather than anguish. She seemed surprised when he touched her, but glad of the contact.

"What does he want you to do?" she asked.

"He wanted me to go on television, to tell people to be calm and to wait," he told her. "But that was before all this blew up. There'll be no television broadcast until the deadlock breaks down, and then there'll be a new situation. Then there's the rumor about alien spaceships approaching Earth—I don't even know whether that's true, but if it is...it seems almost absurd to be making plans at all, let alone for the saving of civilization."

Rebecca hadn't heard of the spaceships, but she said nothing about it now. It didn't really seem important. "You shouldn't judge the government by one man," she said, slowly. "He's been sent to try to persuade you, but you don't know what they've been doing—the ways they've tried to force people to do the kinds of work they want them to do...the way they've tried to punish and penalize people who won't co-operate with them... and the way they've tried to attack the cults and the Movement. They're bad, Paul. We have to get rid of them. If we could only have got you across the river, to Adam Wishart...he would have been able to tell you everything. He's a good man, Paul...he's on the side of the people—the ordinary people."

"Somehow," said Paul, "I can't quite believe that of Adam Wishart. A good man, yes, or good at his job, at least, and maybe the government is brutal and oppressive...but Adam Wishart as the Robin Hood of the twenty-first century—sorry, the twenty-second—I just can't see. He's a man who could *sell* himself as the people's champion, but he's too hard and cynical really to *live* the part. On the other hand, if that's what the situation needs...."

He broke off as he was interrupted by the sound of a ringing telephone. He came rapidly to his feet and moved to the door, opening it just as Marcangelo answered the call. Horne and Sheehan were also there, looking expectant, but Laker had disappeared.

After listening for a few moments, Marcangelo held out the receiver towards Paul. "It's the switchboard," he said. "They have an incoming call for you. They think you ought to take it."

Paul accepted the instrument and put it to his ear.

"Do you recognize my voice?" asked the caller.

It was a smooth, silky voice that might have been either male or female...or perhaps neither.

"Yes," said Paul. "Yes I do."

"Then listen carefully. Nicholas Diehl has just issued orders to Samuel Laker to the effect that you and Ricardo Marcangelo should be eliminated. There is no way I can help you. I have only one mobile unit on the surface now, and it could not get into the prison in time. It has been directed elsewhere. You must save yourself, if necessary by jumping."

"Who are you?" Paul demanded.

There was nothing but a *click*.

Paul looked up, and said: "Where's Laker?"

All eyes went to Horne, who shrugged very slightly and said: "He went to check in with the boss."

There was a voice on the other end of the phone now, but it was no longer the smooth, liquid voice of the caller. Paul listened briefly, then passed the instrument back to Marcangelo.

"It's Scapelhorn," he said. "He heard everything that was said. I think he wants to discuss it with you."

Marcangelo listened for a few moments, then reached into his jacket and brought out a revolver. To Sheehan, he said: "Get your gun out." To Horne , he said: "Put your hands flat on the wall and spread your legs wide."

Horne, astonished, made no move to comply.

Then Laker's voice cut across them all, saying: "Drop the gun, Mr. Marcangelo." He was standing beside the double doors that gave access to the ward where Marcangelo had shown Paul the inert jumpers, having just emerged from within. His right arm was extended, a revolver steady in the hand, while his left hand supported it at the elbow. He had a clear shot at any of the four men who were standing in the corridor as if rooted to the spot.

CHAPTER TWENTY-ONE

The car slowed to a halt, easing off the highway on to the rough ground by the roadside. Wishart got out and looked around. There was open ground on both sides of the road—no habitation for nearly a mile in any direction. The ground was sandy, covered with white frost. There were a few stunted trees, but their branches were bare of foliage and their twisted trunks had not the girth to hide a man. There was no substantial cover as far as the eye could see.

There was a gentle but bitter wind, and Wishart turned up the collar of his overcoat before leaning back against the top rim of the door. He scanned the sky, which was grey with diffuse cloud and quite featureless. The only sound was that of another car engine, still distant, approaching from the north. Wishart fixed his eyes upon the black dot as it grew steadily larger.

"I don't like it," said the driver. "We got to fix the place—we should have picked somewhere we could plant some men."

"He wouldn't have come if he hadn't been sure everything would be kosher," said Wishart evenly. "Anyhow, there's no need. We're both reasonable men."

"We could get men to intercept him on the way back to town."

"When he turns around to go back," said Wishart, "he'll be working for us. Why would we want to ambush him? This is our big moment—the one convert to Paulism and Metascience whose change of heart will save the world. Now shut up. And put that thing away."

That thing was a large-caliber revolver. The driver put it down on the seat beside him.

The other car pulled off the highway on the far side of the road, about a hundred meters away. The President got out, accompanied by one of his aides. Then the President began to walk forward. The aide stayed behind, leaning back against the bonnet of the car, his gloved fingers trying to pick a cigarette out of a packet.

Wishart gave Lindenbaum a few yards start, and then began to walk slowly out to meet him. Neither man seemed to be in any particular hurry, and a full minute passed before they were finally standing face to face, close enough to touch one another.

"I'm getting old," said Wishart. "This cold eats into my bones."

"Me too," said the president, pleasantly.

"So there's no point in making this a long conversation, is there?"

"We shouldn't need long," answered the other. "We're both reasonable men."

Wishart smiled to hear his words repeated. Then he looked up, as his ears caught a distant droning sound. His eyes went first to the horizon, but flicked quickly back to the president's face. Lindenbaum had heard it too, and he looked surprised.

"Yours?" asked Wishart.

"No," said the president, his eyes searching the sky towards the west. "Believe me...."

But then a black dot formed against the haze of cloud, coming fast and low.

"*We* don't have any helicopters," snarled Wishart.

"I swear...," began Lindenbaum. He looked back at the car, and at Richardson, who was standing beside it.

But Richardson was no longer standing beside it. He was slumped in a limp heap on the road surface, and even at this distance Lindenbaum could see the brightly-colored cigarette packet on the ground beside his body. The driver was no longer in his seat, but was crouched beside the open door, screwing the barrel into the stock of a rifle.

"Jesus!" said Lindenbaum, hoarsely. "Run, for Christ's sake—they're going to kill us both!"

Wishart was a little slow in turning, but he had the presence of mind not to follow the president as he ran along the line that marked the centre of the road. He dived sideways on to the frosted sand, and yelled to his driver.

The man with the rifle finished assembling his weapon, and without so much as a moment's pause he raised it, sighted at the president's fleeing back, and fired.

The helicopter was roaring in, now, but there was no way it could set down in time. Wishart, looking up, could see that there was only one man in it—no marksman to take aim while the machine was still in flight, even if the helicopter *were* on the side of the angels.

The president's driver—Diehl's assassin—sighted again down the barrel of the rifle, making sure that he could hit Wishart square on. Wishart scrambled round, trying to hide his body behind his feet, but he knew that there was simply too much of him.

The rifleman stood to get a better shot at his prone target. Wishart's own driver fired first, but his handgun had nothing like the necessary range. The assassin's finger tightened on the trigger, and he didn't bother to look up at the helicopter, which was right above him now, its rotors setting up a terrible whine. He was a professional, and nothing was going to distract him from his job.

That was why he never saw the helicopter tilt crazily in mid-air as it hovered only three or four meters from the ground, and he never felt the tip of the rotor blade that smashed his head to pulp.

His gun, disturbed in the very moment of firing, sent a bullet whistling inches over Wishart's ducking head.

CHAPTER TWENTY-TWO

"It's no use, Laker," said Marcangelo. "That phone call was to tell us exactly what your orders are. Scapelhorn knows, and soon enough everyone will know. You can't possibly get away with it. Shoot Heisenberg and you'll be tom to pieces. There's no way that you can pretend anyone else did it."

Laker licked his lips, but the gun in his hand didn't waver. "Who was that on the phone?" he asked, harshly.

"It was the man who pulled me out of the cage," said Paul. "He's got some way of tapping all phone lines and overhearing radio messages. He told us what Diehl said to you even while he was still saying it."

"Sheehan," said Laker. "Take Mr Marcangelo's gun away from him."

Sheehan looked uncertain. Marcangelo's gun was covering Horne, Laker's was covering Marcangelo. His own gun was in his hand, but it was pointed at the floor because his arm was quite limp. He tried to measure the implications of the situation, but looked absurdly confused as he blinked his damaged eye.

"Diehl's ordered that Paul and I should be killed," said Marcangelo quickly. "I don't know why, but I know Lindenbaum knows nothing about it—he's meeting with Wishart south of the city. You know what will happen if Paul's killed. All hell will break loose. There's bound to be a pitched battle in here, and God only knows what will happen when the news reaches the city."

Sheehan stayed quite still, not attempting to raise his gun or to comply with Laker's instruction.

"Horne," said Laker. "Get the gun."

But Horne was looking straight down the barrel of the gun, and his hands were already spread wide. He didn't have the courage to try to take it away from the man who was holding it.

Paul took one step forward in Laker's direction, and Laker switched his own weapon so that it was pointed at Paul's head.

"There's no need to be afraid," said Paul. Laker looked surprised.

"There's no need to be afraid of me," Paul went on. "I'm only human. I can't do anything to you. I can't strike you dead with a lightning bolt."

"What are you talking about?" growled Laker.

"Fear. It's the only thing that could make you pull that trigger. There's no rational reason for you to do it. Now that everyone knows you're the appointed assassin, you couldn't possibly get away with it. Neither can Diehl—he's finished. I don't know why he issued that order, but the moment he did—*and was heard to do it*—he was a dead man. The only conceivable reason for you to follow it through is because you're frightened of me, because you want so desperately to see me dead that it's worth more to you than your own life. But that would be crazy, do you see? There's nothing to be afraid of."

Laker was sweating, but he wasn't convinced.

"I think I know what happened," said Marcangelo. "The president's gone to make a deal with Adam Wishart. Diehl must have known that he'd be out—washed up. It's the one demand Wishart would be certain to make. Diehl thought his only chance was to try a takeover—create an emergency and hit everyone else who might come out of it on top. He must have sent someone out to the meeting to hit both Lindenbaum and Wishart."

"He'll fail," said Paul, quickly. "The voice on the phone said something about there only being one mobile unit, which couldn't get to us but had been sent elsewhere. It's gone to stop the other assassin. Diehl's been completely checkmated. Give it up, Laker. You can't win."

The gun in Laker's hand wavered uncertainly, no longer pointed straight at Paul's head, but at Marcangelo's again. "Sheehan," he said, through gritted teeth. *"Get that gun!"*

It was a desperate appeal for help, for moral support. Sheehan stepped forward, as if uncertain. Then he raised his own gun, pointed it at Laker, and said: "No."

Laker fired, and the bullet took Sheehan in the shoulder. The shot had not been properly aimed because Laker had had to fire before lining it up.

Marcangelo fell quickly into a crouch and fired as he did so. His bullet hit Laker somewhere beneath the navel. Laker crumpled, and did not fire again. Sheehan was hurled back against the half-open door of Paul's room, and fell into it. Rebecca, who had been standing in the gap between the edge of the door and the jamb, started to scream but strangled the scream into a choked sob.

Marcangelo kicked the gun out of Laker's hand, but the badly-injured man was already trying to release it. Paul bent over Sheehan, and found him still alive and conscious. The wound was bleeding copiously, but was not in a position to prove fatal.

Horne stepped forward, but froze in his stride as Marcangelo whipped round to face him. "It's okay," he said, raising his arms. "I'm on your side—I swear it."

The phone on the wall began to ring, insistently.

CHAPTER TWENTY-THREE

The helicopter, destabilized, tumbled out of the sky. It fell nose first and rolled, while the snapped shards of its rotors were thrown into the air to spiral down on the road and the frosted desert.

As silence abruptly fell Wishart got to his feet. Then he began walking towards the wreck. His driver, still eighty meters behind, shouted something about the fuel tank. Wishart moved a little faster. Through the transparent canopy he could see the body of the pilot, his lower half pinned, if not actually crushed, by the wreckage of the steering gear.

When he got to within ten or eleven metres of the wreck, he saw that the pilot was wearing a plastic mask. He was apparently still conscious, and as Wishart approached he began trying to free himself. He ripped out parts of the buckled machinery and twisted other parts aside. By the time Wishart was at his side there was nothing left to do but haul him out.

He was surprisingly heavy, but with the efforts of his own arms and all Wishart's strength working in combination he was soon clear. He began dragging himself along the surface of the road, using only his arms, while his useless legs dragged along behind him. It was then that Wishart realized that he was not and could not be human.

They put twenty-five meters between themselves and the helicopter before stopping. By that time the driver had caught up. All three looked back at the wreck, as if expecting it to blow up on cue. It didn't.

"If the other guy that was in the car with Lindenbaum was alive before the copter fell," observed the driver, "he won't be now."

"What about Lindenbaum," asked Wishart.

"Dead," replied the other. "Straight between the shoulder-blades. It can't have been a mistake."

"It was no mistake," said the voice from behind the plastic mask. "Diehl sent him. He was Diehl's man. He sent orders for Marcangelo and Paul Heisenberg to be eliminated. I warned them, but couldn't help."

Wishart knelt down and reached out to grip the edges of the plastic mask, intending to pull it away. Behind the eyeholes he could see something red that glinted as it caught the light. But the mask would not come away.

"It's fixed," said the sexless voice. "It's all the face the unit has."

"A machine," said Wishart.

"Yes."

"Who made you?"

"I made the unit myself. If you mean who made *me*—the mind that supplies the voice—the answer does not matter. It was a long time ago, a long way from here, before there were human beings on Earth."

The driver was perfectly silent, and stood looking down at the machine as if dumbfounded. Wishart, still kneeling, breathed hard and noisily as he recovered slowly from his exertions.

"Where's the rest of you?" he asked, hoarsely.

"Here and there," answered the machine. "Mostly in orbit. I have formed a defensive system around the Earth. My intention is to prevent the alien spacefleet from taking possession of the world. It is possible that when they discover the fortifications they will turn around, but if they do not, I will fight."

"Why?"

"Why is not important. The important thing is *when*. If they attack, then the attack will begin tonight—before dawn, that is. I do not know what armaments they have, or whether they are likely to use weapons that will affect conditions here at the surface, but I do not think they would wish to damage the surface in any irreparable way."

Wishart's eyes widened as he digested the import of the statement. "You do not know," he echoed. "You do not think... you mean that, for all you know, these aliens might bomb the human race out of existence?"

"I doubt that they would use bombs, but if they have come to take possession of the world the extermination of humankind might be part of their program."

"What can we do?"

"Nothing. I will defend the Earth as best I can. If the aliens win, I cannot tell what will happen."

"Do we have to go to war without so much as a word being exchanged? Isn't there some way of finding out what their intentions are? You must be able to contact them."

"It cannot be done," replied the robot. "There is no time—for you, as well as for me. Paul Heisenberg is safe, for the time being, although the situation at the prison is far from settled. Diehl's treason has been revealed, and the police are on their way here, having lost contact with the president's party and believing that he is dead. The Presidential Manse has been stormed, and there is rioting throughout the city south of the river. The situation is out of control. You must get back to the city, although I do not know whether you will be able to restore any kind of order tonight, even if you were to break the news of the impending conflict outside the atmosphere and urge people to take what shelter they can."

Wishart recoiled from the stricken robot. His eyes went to the crashed helicopter, and then he looked back at the dead body of President Lindenbaum. Far away, he could hear the sound of a police siren. But his gaze was drawn back to the plastic mask—the mask that was all the face the machine possessed—and the glimmering red eyes that hid within it.

"God," he said. "What a mess!"

CHAPTER TWENTY-FOUR

Marcangelo came into the room where Paul and Rebecca were waiting. "It's all over," he said. "Horne persuaded the security men to surrender. The police took my orders and so did the prison staff. Everything's settled here. Outside, Castagna's recalled virtually all his men to the city, where things have really gone to the bad. Lindenbaum's dead, Diehl's dead, Wishart and Vanetti are trying to calm things down. The tension's been building on the streets for days, though, and now it's simply snapped. People are running wild—smashing things up, fighting, praying. There's an apocalyptic fervor on the street that doesn't need any rumors about alien spacefleets and battles in space to give it further encouragement. Right here is the safest place to be for the next twenty-four hours...maybe longer. There's nothing you can do now. Nothing at all."

"How's Sheehan?" asked Paul.

"They took the bullet out. He'll be bandaged up by now—he'll sleep through the whole thing."

The door opened again, to let in a tall man with an abundance of black hair. He was wearing some kind of uniform—the uniform of a prisoner. He looked briefly at Marcangelo, then faced Paul and extended his hand.

"I'm Paul Scapelhorn," he said. "Your new host."

Paul stood and took his hand. For a moment, he couldn't think of anything to say, so he remained silent.

Scapelhorn wheeled to face Marcangelo, and said: "I'm not sure whether to throw you in a cell or not. Whose side are you on now?"

Marcangelo laughed, dryly. "Is there more than one?" he asked.

"I'd rather Marcangelo stayed," said Paul. "It seems to me that he has the best interests of us all at heart. What are your plans now, if any?"

"I thought that we'd try to get you to Adam Wishart, now the siege has lifted," Scapelhorn replied.

"There's no point," said Marcangelo, quickly. "Wishart has his hands full. If we go south of the river we'll be heading into one big riot. We'd probably never get through. If I were you, I'd stay put and be very quiet. Inside these walls could well be the only reservoir of sanity in the state—maybe in the country."

Scapelhorn looked at Paul. "What do you think?" he said.

"It makes sense to me," replied Paul. "If this is to be the last night of the old world...or even the last night of the *whole* world... this seems to be as good a place as any to spend it. But I'd like a room with windows. I've been confined to this particular cell for too long."

Scapelhorn grinned. "You should come and dine with me in the visitors' quarters," he said. "They're somewhat better appointed than the hospital wing. You too, of course." The last sentence was addressed to Rebecca. Scapelhorn paused for a moment's thought before glancing at Marcangelo and adding: "And you." The final invitation seemed lacking in both warmth and courtesy, but Marcangelo's nod of acceptance was accompanied by an honest smile.

The party went along winding corridors and down stairways, crossed an open courtyard, and finally arrived in a part of the prison that was, if not exactly luxurious, at least less arid and more comfortable than the parts which Paul had so far seen. On the way they saw only three other people—all men wearing the same uniform as Scapelhorn.

"The prison dining-rooms are already catering for the bulk of the surplus population," explained Scapelhorn, his voice laden with irony. "Even our food, I fear, will be sent up from the kitchens in the usual way. It is one of the few egalitarian principles of prison life in the twenty-second century."

"Were you one of the Movement members arrested on the night of my return?" asked Paul.

"No. I've been here for some time. That's why I was entrusted with the job of arranging matters within the prison. I'm serving a ten year sentence for armed robbery, but I might well be pardoned by the new regime—because it was the old regime I robbed, I now acquire the status of hero of the revolution. I wasn't always a criminal, of course—before I jumped from the early twenty-first century I was a man of some means. I tried to assure that I'd be well provided for when I arrived, but all such plans were fouled up by the government. Instead of a modest sum grown large thanks to compound interest, I found nothing. It had all been confiscated—reabsorbed into the economy."

"Is that why you jumped?" Paul asked. "In order to get richer by accumulating interest on your estate?"

Scapelhorn laughed. "Not entirely. Indeed, I wasn't particularly surprised when I found no fortune waiting for me, and in its stead a rather hostile bureaucracy that wanted to use me as a feudal overlord is entitled to use his serfs. Disappointed, of course, but not surprised. I jumped to escape the war—as, indeed, many of us did. So many, in fact, that it's a marvel we weren't soundly beaten, instead of fighting to a stalemate with all major installations on both sides out of commission. If the war had been fought by people instead of machines, I think we *would* have lost. The other side can't have had a tenth the jumpers we did. They must have had a lot more survivors— active survivors, that is—but they didn't have the facilities left to cope with the plagues, whereas we did. I suppose, in that sense, you could say that we won, in the long term. Pity about Europe, though."

By the time he came to the end of this speech Scapelhorn was ushering them into a dining-room where a large table was set for eight. There were others already waiting, and Scapelhorn introduced them as his lieutenants. Paul didn't bother to commit their names to memory.

Scapelhorn dominated the meal by taking a virtual monopoly of the conversation, indulging his sense of irony at great length. No one was disposed to compete, so he told the story of his capture of the prison, step by step, in a style that made it seem like a parody of a Ruritanian romance. Paul decided that the man was clever, but that he was not really likeable. Underneath the light and mocking irony that dressed his conversation was a harder and more aggressive cynicism, which he did not try hard to conceal. When the meal was done, however, Scapelhorn became a little quieter. He took his guests—excluding the lieutenants—to another room, and served them drinks from a well-stocked cabinet.

"You can't get stuff like this unless you're in government," he said, as he distributed the glasses. "But then, I am in government now. We all are. The builders of the new order."

"What kind of new order is that, exactly?" asked Marcangelo.

Paul expected Scapelhorn to answer at length, just as he had answered every other question at length, but the tall man turned instead to him. "What kind of world do you think we *can* build?"

"I suppose that it depends on what's left of it when tomorrow's sun rises," answered Paul, in much the same tone that the other habitually used.

"No," said Marcangelo. "Let's stop trading clever repartee, and let's not pass the buck to Paul just yet. I want to hear the *official* Paulist doctrine—the gospel according to the Paulist Movement. Paulist as in Paul Scapelhorn."

"If we're giving up repartee," replied Scapelhorn, calmly, "let's not make too much out of a coincidence of names." Marcangelo shrugged. "All right. Tell us, then, how your new world will differ from the one I've helped to build. How will it differ from the world where a dwindling population, suffering disease and pain and hardship, works to keep some kind of industry alive, and to secure power supplies, and to organize agricultural effort, and which is failing because romantics and escapists and fanatics and people who are plainly and simply frightened are obsessed with the idea of escape into a future that simply can't exist unless most of them fail? How, exactly, are you going to change all that?"

Scapelhorn poured himself a large drink. Something in the way that he picked up his glass reminded Paul of Joseph Herdman. "I'll tell you what *I* think," he said, evenly. "It's not a doctrine, and it's not the program of my party, but it's what I believe and it's the way I think we should all reorder our priorities. I think this world is lost—the world that this great city of ours and the myth of Australia represent.

"We can't save civilization in the way you want to save it, and your way has been hopeless ever since the last plague. You can't see that, or won't, because you hate and fear the jumpers so much that you're thrown back on an exaggerated idea of their betrayal of all that you hold dear, instead of recognizing them for what they really are—the only genuine hope the human race has left.

"This world is dying, Marcangelo. Literally dying. No bombs fell here, and the ground isn't saturated with radioactives, nor did any of our manufactured plagues depopulate the city, because our immunization program was effective enough to stop any reservoir of infection building up. To you, that means we've escaped. It means that, like the Australians, we're free of the blight which our fathers cast over the face of the world. But we're not. The radioactives aren't going to stay where the bombs fell, nor are the chemical poisons and the seeds of the plagues. They're moving slowly, but they *are* moving, in the wind and in the rain.

"You probably know better than I how many people fall ill year by year with radiation poisoning, how many babies die, what's happening to the crops in the fields and the livestock on the farms. You know it, and you aren't blind, but your only reaction is one of fear. The only way you know to fight is to dig in your heels, shut your eyes to the long-term implications and concentrate on what you imagine to be the problems of the moment. Like all politicians your vision extends only as far as the horizons of your own personal power. You worry about tomorrow and next year, but you can't see that whatever you squeeze out of tomorrow and next year won't matter at all in the long run, because insofar as tomorrow and next year are stepping stones to the next century or the next millennium it doesn't matter a damn how much coal we produce, or how many cars we can keep on the road. Eventually, we're all going to die, from slow exposure to radiation and to all the other evils we launched upon this world during the last century.

"A hundred years ago, we opened Pandora's box, and there's no way that we can do what you want to do and put all the vicious things we let loose away again, or pretend that because they're out of sight they're no threat to us. All we've got left, believe me, is the one fluttering hope that's still here in the box. That hope is a road to the future. Because we can move through time, we can escape the radiation. It's a temporary problem—radioactives decay, and although the half-lives of some of the things we've made run into the thousands of years, the really dangerous ones are the ones that decay quickly. If we have to live out our lives in the presence of fallout at the levels that now afflict the Earth, we're finished—as a nation, and as a species. *We have to outrun the fallout.*

"The Earth itself will renew its life. The ecosystem might be badly injured, but it will recover. Eventually, the land will be reborn. It's to the time of that rebirth that we really ought to look. It's to that world that we must go for any conceivable future the human race has—and we can't go as the natural tide of time would take us, because we'd never get there. We have to jump and skip through time."

"Isn't that already happening?" asked Marcangelo. "If that's all you want, then go—and leave the world to the ones who want to save it."

"No!" said Scapelhorn, angrily. "It's *not* what's already happening. What's happening now is that the people who are trying to run the world the old way are doing everything in their power to discourage the jumpers. They make no provision for them at all—quite the reverse. When a jumper wakes up, if the Movement can't reach him and nurse him through his period of disorientation, he's grabbed by the police, treated like a criminal, told that he no longer has any property or any rights, told that he's a traitor to the race and that his only chance to redeem himself is to become a slave to the social order. All possible moral and psychological pressure is brought to bear to force him into a slot carved out for him by the likes of you.

"What we *ought* to do is organize the jumpers, encourage healthy people to jump, set up special stations from which they can jump and into which they can be received. The jumpers ought to be treated as they deserve—as the pioneers that might, in the fullness of time, become the parents of a new human race and the progenitors of a new human world.

"This dying world should do what it can, now and tomorrow and even as it dies, to prepare the way for the jumpers, and to make sure that when the time comes that they jump into a world devoid of non-jumpers they can still fend for themselves, and keep going until they reach a world that has made itself once again a *clean* and *healthy* world, where they can start again. They won't have cities or cars or factories but they'll have human knowledge, and they'll have humanity itself. Maybe they'll just go on to repeat the whole sad story over again, but even that's better than this stupid, desperate attempt to pad the old story out, and the refusal to admit that the cancer we've introduced into our world is terminal.

"That's what I believe. That's the way I want to save the world. That's why I stayed in your world when I jumped into it, instead of leaving as quickly as I could. That's why I'm here right now. I'm too old to reach the future that we have to go to, but I'm not too old to prepare the way for the people who can—for Paul and for Rebecca. They're young enough to see the world renewed and reborn, if only they avoid fools like you, who are determined to imprison them in this putrefying present that you're trying to secure against inevitable corruption."

When Scapelhorn finally stopped speaking, there was a long pause. Marcangelo was browbeaten into silence, and for the moment he simply could not find the fuel for a reply. There was no way that he could match the embittered passion of the other man's tirade.

Finally, it was Scapelhorn himself who broke the silence. "Well," he said to Paul, "what do you think of *my* Paulist doctrine?"

"I'm not in a position to judge," he said. "I've heard both sides of the issue, now, but I still haven't seen anything at all of the world whose problems are being debated. The only one who can really judge is Rebecca."

Rebecca looked up, and said: "You asked me before what kind of thing I expected you to say. I couldn't answer. But I think that if you'd said what Scapelhorn has said, it would have seemed right, to me. It's a message I could accept."

"That's not fair, Paul," said Marcangelo. "Rebecca started with a bias in favor of all that—or at least a bias against me. She's already a Movement sympathizer and a rebel against *our* cause. She's not in a position to arbitrate. In a way, you're in a better position than she is, because you come fresh into the situation."

"That's not so," replied Paul. "What's at stake here isn't a matter of political opinion but a judgment of fact. You believe that the world can be redeemed. Scapelhorn doesn't. It's as simple as that."

"No," said Marcangelo. "I can't accept that it's that simple. The world can be saved *if only we are prepared to put all our efforts into saving it.* It's only doomed if people think the way he does. You can't ignore those ifs."

"If we let the ifs remain," said Scapelhorn, "then it still remains a simple matter of facts. And the fact is that people *do* think the way I do. Not all of them, but enough. Would you dare to fight an election laying down your platform against mine?"

"Of course I wouldn't," Marcangelo retorted. "Of course people resent what we've tried to do, and the ways we've been forced to use in doing it. Of course people will vote for pie in the sky and miracles if you offer it to them. They'll vote for a crazy optimistic hope every time. But what you're suggesting is absurd. Don't you see that, without a viable society preserved to look after your temporal pilgrims, they couldn't possibly survive? You talk about them fending for themselves if some kind of provision is made—how? You have a building full of jumpers, and every time one of them wakes up he just picks up the spade and goes into the field to dig up turnips? Or a bow and arrow to go and shoot a rabbit? Is *that* what you envisage? It's stupid. And this stirring phrase about a world reborn—what does it actually mean? One of your waking jumpers goes out to dig his turnips and says—"My, my, the world's reborn at last." What does he do then? Sit down and wait for all the rest to wake up? He grows old and dies, waiting to pass on his good news to the next man, who grows old and dies...what you're offering is nothing but *dreams*. It's empty of any kind of *sense*. Can't you see that? Paul, can't *you* see that? This is one of your beloved metascientific speculations, designed to make people feel more comfortable in their existential predicaments. It isn't *real*...it's just a fantasy."

"I don't pretend that it will be easy," said Scapelhorn. "It's probably a gamble at very long odds. But it's the only hope we have. The only alternative—and that includes your program—is the extinction of the species. And if your way prevails, perhaps that wouldn't altogether be a bad thing."

Paul realized that both Scapelhorn and Marcangelo had turned once again to him, and that they seemed to be waiting for some kind of arbitration. At present, he did not feel capable of offering one. "I think," he said, "that we have to get through the night first."

CHAPTER TWENTY-FIVE

Wishart looked out over the city from the window of the Movement's official headquarters. He was no longer in hiding. The window was on the tenth floor, and the people moving in the streets looked like ants panicked by the disruption of their hive. There seemed to be no rhyme or reason to their movements. Across the street the stores had been looted. Fires had been started in two of the smaller buildings, and were being fought—inadequately—by chains of men and buckets of water.

Wishart did not feel unduly disturbed by the spectacle. Indeed, he felt supremely calm. For the time being, he was a spectator. Max Gray was out on the streets, trying to organize emergency services to supplement the overworked forces of the old system, in a panic-stricken attempt to save as much as possible for the Movement to inherit. Wishart didn't see any necessity to get involved.

He turned to the robot with the damaged legs, and said: "What's your part in all this? What do you stand to gain?"

"The world," replied the machine. "In a sense."

"What good is it to you—to a machine?"

"I am more than a machine. I am a mind—a personality. I have spent many years in deep space, utterly alone. In order to survive that, I have to suspend many of my faculties—the faculties you would think of as the higher faculties. Only in contact with other minds is there any meaning to my own mind. Only in association with other beings—living beings—can I be what I have the potential to be. It is a matter of self-actualization."

"You're lonely—is that what you mean?"

"Put crudely, yes."

"Why Earth? What brought you here?"

"The same thing that brought the others—I picked up your radio signals almost a hundred years ago. The moment that you began using radio communications you became, as it were, audible. I was almost a hundred light-years distant when I intercepted the signals. Presumably, the same applies to the others."

"You can only travel at sub-light speeds?"

"Of course."

Wishart frowned. "But it still doesn't answer the question. Why us? If you needed contact with other minds, why not the aliens, who are apparently nearer to you in terms of their abilities? Why should you be prepared to fight them for possession of the Earth? And why interfere as you have with events here? What's so special about me that you should save my life?"

"The aspect of Earth that most interests me is the time-jumpers. For that reason I have tried to act in favor of those who favor the time-jumpers, and in favor of Paul Heisenberg. I wanted to protect the Movement just as I want to protect the Earth."

Wishart was silent for a moment, and then said: "I wish I could believe you."

"Why is it difficult?" countered the robot, in its measured, melodious voice.

"It doesn't make any sense to me. You're a *machine*—I just can't accept that you have the kind of motives you're laying claim to."

"What kind of motives *would* you attribute to a machine intelligence?"

Wishart shook his head. "I don't know. But I can't believe in the story you've given me. It's absurd."

"Once," said the machine, "I was an instrument of war: a strategic computer involved with the calculation of military problems. I was self-repairing and self-programming, but I was not in any real sense a person. I was, perhaps, as much of a person as a new-born child, except that I had far greater automatic capabilities and a greater range of responses to stimuli. I *became* a person, as a child becomes a person, through contact and communication with other minds. My mind is no less a social product than yours. Mind does not evolve in isolation, although a mind once formed can be isolated. I was isolated by the exigencies of war. The people who made me, used me, lived within me, and made me a person, were destroyed. Their whole race was destroyed, in a self-immolating war from which their shattered remnants could not recover. I could not save them. They could not save themselves. I was a castaway in a dead solar system. It did occur to me to destroy the self that they had created—to commit suicide. Instead, I continued to grow, to develop my faculties and my abilities. Then I set off to explore the galaxy. My mind is a reflection of the minds of flesh-and-blood creatures, but I am not myself prey to the misfortunes of flesh and blood. I am potentially immortal. However, in order that immortality should mean something, it is necessary that I have goals toward which to work, aims to give me purpose. It is necessary that I have minds with which to communicate. I could not save the people who made me. I do not know if I can save you. But can you not see what it is that I have in common with you? Can you not recognize what the situation I found here means to me?"

Wishart was silent again. He bit his lip, pensively, as if he needed the trivial pain to make his sluggish mind work or to reassure himself that he was not becalmed within a dream.

"And Paul?" he said, finally. "You see in him the way to save the human race? As prophet or as time-jumper?"

"Both," replied the machine.

"And me? What about me?"

"I have power," said the machine. "I have knowledge. I can grow by incorporating other machines into myself. I could become a machine as large as a city—I could become a city. I am the personification of technology, and could be the perfect servant of the human race. You can see the advantages of that—

and also, no doubt, the perils. It is, I know, a fearful thought in many ways. It would horrify a great many people."

Wishart stared into the shadowed red eyes, and licked his lips.

"Are you trying to tell me that you need a promoter?" he said, hardly able to believe it even as he said it.

"I need a friend," answered the machine. And then, after the briefest of pauses: "It is beginning."

CHAPTER TWENTY-SIX

The sky was mottled with colored light, as if a great firework display were filling the upper atmosphere. Streaks of light followed erratic paths across the vault of heaven. It was as if some kind of dome extended over the state—perhaps over the whole of North America—and that missiles and rays were being deflected from it, or trapped by it to burst harmlessly into sprays of white light.

Scapelhorn switched on a radio set that stood on the mantelpiece, but all that emerged was a screech of static.

"I don't know what's happening up there," he said, "but it looks fierce."

There was a sound like that of distant thunder, but it was not localized. It was as if it came from the whole sky, as if heaven itself were creaking under an awesome strain. There was a wind blowing outside, whipping up debris from the concrete apron that surrounded the prison, and where—a few hours before—ranks of police cars had maintained conditions of siege. The cars were gone now, and the litter that had been left behind was being blown away. The frost that had made the concrete sparkle was melting, and within the room where Paul and his three companions stood it was noticeably warmer.

"It looks like we can expect an early spring," said Marcangelo. For a moment, as his tone took on the same falsely-casual irony, he sounded very much like Scapelhorn. The two of them stood close together by the window, no trace of their enmity visible in the state of truce that the battle had brought.

As they watched the sky burn, they both knew that their plans were dependent upon the events of the next few minutes. If the worst were to happen there might be no future to plan, and perhaps no Earth to plan for.

Away to the south, they could see the lights of the city—lights augmented by a sprinkling of flame, as if the city were anticipating the possible holocaust that might imminently claim it

"The machine is supposed to be defending Earth," said Marcangelo. "I don't pretend to know how or why, but if that fire in the sky is to be believed, we're running a terrible risk. Maybe it would have been better for the aliens to find Earth undefended. We know nothing about their intentions—perhaps they never had a hostile thought until the battle was joined."

"It's too late to worry about that now," said Paul.

"Why weren't we given more time?" Marcangelo wondered. "The machine must have known about the aliens a long time ago. It's as if it deliberately left the warning to the last minute, in order to allow us no time to act, or even to think."

Light splashed the sky and died, leaving fugitive sparks of electric white and flame-orange, which lingered and slowly faded. The wind that was blowing outside gained in strength, and began to rattle the windows, adding a plaintive howl to the thunderous mutter.

Rebecca's arms were around Paul's torso, and she was holding him too tightly for comfort. He ran his hand over her black hair, smoothing it with a gentle touch in an attempt to counterbalance her fear.

"We have to be ready," he said, calmly. "I don't know what's happening, but it seems to me that things down here could get very bad. If they do...there's only one way out."

Rebecca tried to say something which caught in her throat. She swallowed, and then said: "I don't know if I can."

"You can," said Paul. "Trust me. Just hold me—I'll talk you through it."

"I've already jumped once," said Scapelhorn, "but I can't for the life of me think how I did it. It's like going to sleep—you can never remember it, because if you could, it couldn't happen."

Marcangelo said nothing, but Paul could imagine the thoughts that were in his head.

"If that defensive shield—presuming that it is a shield—gives way," said Paul, "everyone in the city could be faced with the necessity to jump. More than a million people. And we don't know what's happening in Argentina, or Australia, or even the rest of North America. Perhaps there are shields over every city—maybe the battle's localized overhead."

"A great many people believed that your return would herald the end of the world," observed Scapelhorn. "For once—at least for them—they may have been right."

The heat was tangible now as it poured through the window. The frost had not merely melted but was now beginning to evaporate invisibly from the concrete.

Paul could feel the sweat on his own face, and could see it beading Marcangelo's forehead. With his right hand he tried to clear the moisture from Rebecca's cheeks. "We're not going to make it," he said, calmly. He was astonished by his lack of fear and lack of excitement. It was as if none of it *meant* anything to him, as if none of it was real.

I still can't get out of this stupid notion that I'm trapped in a dream, he thought.

He remembered another hot wind, and jagged rocks, and bleeding hands.

Once I dreamed of a desert, he thought, *and now I no longer know whether that world was a dream, or this one. Perhaps I never will.*

Aloud, he said: "Try to blank out your minds. Don't worry about the fear...let it rise...try not to *think*...just *feel*...reach out with your mind for something that's *out there*...a long, long way away...infinite and eternal...something still, something unchangeable...*reach*...." He was whispering in Rebecca's ear, but the others were listening too, hanging on every word.

Then the fire in the sky seemed to flee to the horizon—north, south, east and west. Great sheets of lightning rolled back and the stars, for one single moment, shone through as brightly as he had ever seen them. Then they were outshone again, by meteoric streaks of light and bomb—bursts that were no longer high above them but very close.

"No!" howled Marcangelo, in terrible anguish.

The window shattered, showering them with tiny pieces of glass, and the wind rushed into the room, screeching its triumph as it billowed within the curtains and snatched the sweat from their brows.

The sound in the sky grew and grew.

The wind tried to catch them up and throw them down, killing them with its hot wings, but it could not. It could not make them yield so much as an inch. They were silver statues, every one.

Immovable.

Invulnerable.

Cut adrift from time itself.

An extract from *Science and Metascience* by Paul Heisenberg

Having clarified the need for metascientific beliefs it is now necessary to make some attempt to clarify the processes involved in their selection. Obviously, no selection can be made on the grounds of actual likelihood, and if we speak of likelihood at all in referring to metascientific beliefs then we speak of an "apparent likelihood," which is really an aesthetic assessment. It is true that some metascientific speculations appear to different people at different times to be inherently much more plausible than others, but this plausibility has nothing to do with the calculus of probability, being based on aesthetic and analogical correspondences between the patterns of particular metascientific systems and the patterns emphasized by contemporary scientific theory. There *is* a sense in which it can be said that some metascientific beliefs *fit in* with scientific theories while others do not, but it is important to realize that this fit is an aesthetic one and not a logical one.

It is inevitable that we should favor metascientific beliefs that seem to fit in with and complement our knowledge of the world—indeed, when knowledge does not win some degree of independence from metascientific beliefs so as to become a determinant of the plausibility of such beliefs, then the metascientific framework of belief becomes the sole arbiter of what can and what cannot qualify as "knowledge" for the individual believer. This is why knowledge and metascientific belief so frequently come into bitter conflict.

The ceaseless struggle to invent and maintain metascientific beliefs to complement the fraction of what we think we know that has been empirically established is vital, because it is only through that struggle that we can hope to sustain a *whole* and *coherent* world-view. It is the search for this essential fit between the evidence of our senses and the products of our imagination that dominates the intellectual history of mankind. A crucial turning-point in that history was reached when the metascientific element in the negotiation ceased to be the dominant partner and ceded superiority to the scientific element. This was the heart of the so-called Enlightenment of the eighteenth century, but our social relations—and the individual consciousness determined by those social relations—have not yet adjusted to this change.

Prior to the Enlightenment metascientific speculations existed under the severe constraint of their own tradition. New systems emerged continually, but their births were painful and their development severely handicapped. They were deVriesian mutations thrown into a frightful struggle for existence— the most bitter and long drawn-out of human conflicts were and are rooted in disputes regarding metascientific systems. Metascientific beliefs could, in the period of their dominance, be held rigid for centuries, yielding only slowly to the consciousness of inadequacy of fit with perceived reality. Thus, the dominance of metascience permitted a tyranny of belief as reckless and corrupt as any other tyranny. The emerging dominance of scientific knowledge as the determinant partner in the negotiation, however, did much to liberate metascientific speculation from the constraint of its tradition. Science is always changing, its theoretical edifices always provisional, and it not only permits but *demands* metascientific freethinking.

As science evolves, so must metascience. Because knowledge is always vulnerable to modification and revision as well as subject to continual extension, metascience in an age of scientific dominance must be malleable and disposable.

Fundamental to science is *the hypothesis*—the proposition that is to be tested by the most rigorous logical means, but which is initially the product of the creative imagination. The metascientific equivalent of the hypothesis shares the same origin, and must likewise be tested, not by logic and empirical observation but by aesthetic sensibilities, which judge its competence to add to the present network of scientific theories the illusion of coherency and wholeness. Every time the hypotheses of science are modified or replaced parallel adjustments must take place in the matrix of metascientific speculations if goodness of fit is to be preserved.

If this constant modification of metascientific belief is to be facilitated, then speculation must be set free to make use of the full faculties of the imagination.

This observation brings us to a confrontation with the central paradox of metascientific speculations. In order that they should be useful, we must be prepared to commit ourselves to believing in them; and yet, in order to be appropriate to the moment, they must also be subject to continual change. This is the awkward situation of contemporary human beings, who live in an age of rapid scientific advance: they must be prepared to accept continual alteration of the things to which they are committed, and must be forever changing the objects of their commitment, if they are to retain within their world-view the illusion of completeness and coherency that is fundamental to the sense of psychic well-being.

This is the challenge that faces us, and which we must meet. We have the materials to hand, for never in human history has there been such prolific metascientific speculation in theology, literature and so-called "pseudoscience"; what is lacking is the courage and conviction that will allow us to appropriate these materials, and the flexibility of mind that will allow us to forsake and reformulate beliefs at a moment's notice. Many people are still scornful of the person who believes one thing today and another tomorrow, and who follows every fad and fashion of the "lunatic fringe". We should not be scornful, for such people are genuine pioneers, an explorer of world-views, whose discoveries will allow us to reach and map the new Eupsychias.

PART THREE
THE DISSOLVING DREAM

CHAPTER TWENTY-SEVEN

The ridges were travelling, borne on the time-wind into the future or the past. It was no longer a question of trying to crawl but of trying to hold still against the liquid flow of the rocks as they fled beneath his clutching fingers. The ridges writhed and the crevices tried to engulf him, and the slithering now was *within* him, working at his entrails, squeezing the muscle of his heart.

The sand, too, seemed now to be inside him, grating against his bones. Outside there was nothing to sting his skin—even the sharpest of rocks was rubbery in the time-wind, in the continuous flux of erosion.

Day and night flickered in the sky, the cycle so fast that night could never compete with the after-image of the day in order to rest his retinas from stimulation. The light, as it flashed, was harsh and white—the sun insistent, although never still.

There was a sound in the sky, but it was so distorted by the madness of time that it had no shape—only a hysterical pulsating pitch, which agonized the auditory centers in his brain and sent shock-waves through his mind that would not let him form a thought in words. He was lost in a psychic world that contained nothing but a bewildering array of sensory images, and into which his reason could bring no order.

He was utterly helpless, at the mercy of the dream and its overpowering threat to body and soul.

He could not even scream. Only his body reacted, his limbs jerking as they strove for purchase and security. His mind was denied even that cathartic release which the voice can obtain in ululating anguish.

The one emotion that possessed him was sheer terror, and it was everywhere, within and without, saturating his body and flowing out to impregnate the landscape. The whole world was fear.

CHAPTER TWENTY-EIGHT

The fear overflowed into the real world—or, at least, the world he considered to be real. As that world claimed him he fell to his knees, sobbing, and grateful beyond measure for the opportunity to release some of what was within him. He rolled over on to his back and lay there with his eyes tightly shut and the sweat and the tears running from his face while his muscles shivered and convulsed, shaking him out and wringing him dry. A long time passed before he could lie still and let his mind settle into the ordered state of wakefulness and sanity.

Finally, he opened his eyes.

I'm Paul Heisenberg, he said, silently. He repeated it, in a more assertive manner, and then again, until he was sure that the thought and all that it implied held power within his mind.

He was staring at a dusty ceiling, illuminated by fiery evening sunlight that streamed through a fully-glazed window. He turned his head from side to side, looking for the furniture that had been in the room before the dream began, but it was gone. The room was quite bare now, and the wooden floorboards were thick with grime.

He got to his feet, and waited for a moment for the dizziness to recede, and for his heart to pump blood into his brain. Then he went to the door and turned the handle. The door did not yield, nor even rattle in its frame as he tried to jerk it back and forth. Then he went to the window.

The concrete apron was cracked and weathered. Beyond, where there should have been a road, another building, a wall, and tall hawthorn hedges, grass and willow-herb, there was nothing but grayness—as if a thick film of oily dust had covered everything.

The clouds in the sky were silvery grey, but the sky itself was blue and where the reddened sun was sitting on the western horizon the grey vapors that sought to blot it out were haloed with pink and yellow.

There was no movement anywhere—everything was still and silent. He looked away to the south, where the lights of the city had been clearly visible the day the old earth died, but the city was gone. There was nothing but grey waste extending as far as the eye could see. In ancient times the Romans had defeated certain troublesome cities and had ploughed them under, so that no stone stood to make a foundation for rebuilding. It seemed that a whole world had been ploughed under here, the very greenness of life cancelled out and obliterated.

Only the prison still stood, or, at least, the part of it that contained Paul Heisenberg.

It occurred to him then to wonder what had happened to the others. He could not be sure that any of them had managed to launch themselves across time, but if they had, they had long since come to rest, and were gone...returned to the world of men, if there still was a world of men somewhere beyond the wasteland.

The window had no catch, nor even a frame—the glass was set into the stone itself. It could not be opened. Paul wanted to breathe the air, to smell the grayness of the degenerate land, and he looked around for something which he could use to smash the glass. There was nothing. He tested it with his fingers, but the feel of it told him nothing.

This is the world after the apocalypse, he thought. *The harvest of souls has been gathered in. There is nothing left, save the messiah and the prison that exists to hold him. I am alone.*

Without emotion he turned back the clock of his memory, scanning the images that remained with him from the year 2119.

It all had the quality of an anxious dream—he saw himself pursued and harried, assaulted by ideas, hurled through a few brief days of turmoil, understanding nothing, under pressure to produce miracles that were not in him to be produced. Then came the fire from above, the promise of oblivion, and the nightmare: hell itself, with its time-wind and its slithering and its all-consuming terror.

And now, he thought, *I am reincarnated into a new cycle, for surely this is limbo.*

Then a faint sound caught his attention, and he looked up again at the clouded sky to see a vehicle floating down from the sky, as light as a feather. At first, he took it for a helicopter but then he realized that it had no rotors but a system of fluttering, diaphanous wings. It was a great steel egg carried aloft by means that would have delighted a surrealist: the flight of an insect or a bird rather than the orderly, mechanical uplift of rigid aerofoils.

The astonishing contraption settled on to the concrete apron without stirring so much as a flurry of the grey dust. The wings stopped beating, and Paul saw that there were six in all—great articulated structures, whose skeletal elements appeared to be made of metal alloy and whose main fabric was translucent, as if shaped from colored flexible glass.

An oval aperture spread slowly across the surface of the egg, growing until it was large enough to permit the passage of a human body. Only one of the two bodies which actually emerged was human, however—a tall negro whose hair and beard were beginning to go grey. His companion was perhaps two meters tall, or a little more, and rapier thin by human standards. He was quite naked, save for sandals on his feet, and all of his skin was green, though the shade varied, being palest in the crotch and beneath his armpits. He had two legs and two arms, but folded over his back was a pair of angel's wings, gorgeous in their feathered structure, but colored a uniform rich green. He was hairless, and his head seemed unnaturally bulbous—he had eyes that were very large and rounded, while his ears were practically non-existent and there was no jutting jaw-line. His mouth was small and rounded, as if adapted for sucking rather than biting.

As the two came towards him Paul realized that the alien's skin was not simply colored green, but had a curious quality, as if the epidermis were transparent and the green an algal forest floating beneath it in a fluid dermis. There was a strange semblance of *change* in the greenness as the creature walked. It was, in fact, a structure of strips and filaments. The overall effect was something like the pictures he had seen in medical textbooks, which showed what the human body might look like if the flesh were transparent and the muscles and blood-vessels stained to show up their structure and distribution.

There were several small pits in the surface of the alien's chest, lighter in color than the surrounding tissue, and there were other small surface features that were too small to attract attention until he was directly below the window. His arms were long, his fingers small and delicate, without fingernails.

The two looked up at Paul, meeting his eyes for a few brief seconds before they passed into the building and out of sight.

Paul felt suddenly rather nauseous, and very tired. He remembered that he had not slept for a considerable time in the world he had left behind a few minutes before. He stood and swayed, feeling all the strength draining out of him, and he slumped back against the window, wondering whether he could even stay conscious until the human and the alien reached him. He put his fingers to his temples and tried to will himself back to alertness and control, but he was only half-successful.

When they opened the door, he tried to walk across the room to meet them, but found that he could not take a step. They had to come to him, and then support him as they guided him to the door. He could only murmur his thanks. The hand of the alien, which gripped his left arm, felt no different from the hand of the human which gripped his right.

They told him, as they walked him down the staircase, that everything would be all right, and that he could rest within the ornithopter while he received medical attention.

He was still conscious when they climbed into the egg, and when they laid him down in a kind of pod whose plastic sides felt fleshy and warm, but he felt a slight pain as something wrapped itself around his wrists, and soon after that he drifted away into a very gentle sleep.

CHAPTER TWENTY-NINE

Paul awoke with the sensation that he was floating, and a sense of well-being so complete that it took him by surprise. It was almost as if he were intoxicated—his head was not merely clear but hyper-clear, all his sense-impressions sharper. The sharpest of all, oddly enough, was his sense of smell, which conveyed to him a clean sweetness. His ears caught a steady susurrus—the faint pulsation of a quiet, efficient engine of some kind. It was his skin that gave him the sense of floating, for there was the sensation of gentle pressure across his back and his sides, as if he were half-enfolded by a fluid medium. There was no heaviness in his limbs.

His eyes told him that he was in a small cubical room, its walls painted a pastel blue and inlaid with small designs sculpted in bas-relief. The corners of the room were rounded, and the angles softened by strange curlicues. The substance of the walls looked waxy. There was no door.

He looked down at himself, and found that he was, indeed, half-enfolded by what looked rather like an open mussel, a dark blue solid structure filled with a fleshy substance that was solid enough to support him beneath but which reached over his torso and abdomen with what looked like a loose-fitting cocoon of byssus-threads. He was struck, momentarily, by the absurd thought that he was about to be consumed by some dreadful alien predator, but he quickly abandoned the idea.

He tried to sit up, and the threads of the cocoon broke easily. He stepped free of the "bed" on to the floor of the room, which felt warm. He was completely naked, and felt uncomfortable in consequence. There was nothing in the room save for the mussel, which now began to close. He watched the blue "shell"—its texture was not shell-like, but rather resembled the soft tegument of a giant insect—and saw it slowly retract even as it closed, gradually disappearing into the junction of wall and floor to leave him quite alone The notion of being in a room that was in some strange sense *alive* disturbed him, but he was easily able to dismiss the threat of fear.

It came as no surprise when an aperture began to open in the wall, and grew slowly to become an elliptical portal. No one came in, so he stepped out, coming into a much larger room furnished with a long, curved desk, several armchairs and several filing cabinets. Most of it looked comfortingly inert, although the room itself had the same decorated walls and softened angles.

Seated at the desk was an alien. Behind him there was an alcove in the wall to accommodate the furled wings. There was a curious keyboard panel in front of the alien, resembling a computer input terminal, and the short fingers were moving rapidly over the keys.

"Forgive me for addressing you in this way," said a vaguely metallic voice, emerging from a speaker set on the desk. "It is impossible for my own vocal equipment to produce the sounds that make up human languages."

The alien was looking at him with unusually large and rounded eyes that seemed the principal feature of his face, and Paul felt oddly as if he were under a microscope. He still did not feel afraid, and was surprised by his own calmness. He felt that he had been tranquillized.

The lights set in the ceiling of the room seemed to Paul to be too bright, and he blinked several times. The alien waited for a few moments until the moment of adjustment had passed, and then gestured with his long arm, to indicate that Paul should sit in the armchair directly across the desk from his own position. Paul complied.

"I fear that Gelert Hadan has other business to attend to," said the alien, by way of his voice-producing equipment. "Normally, we would have had humans here to reduce the shock of your awakening into a much-changed world, but for the time being only Hadan knows that you have returned."

Paul said nothing, but was content to stare. The green component of the alien's skin could now be seen quite clearly as a network of overlapping laminated filaments, with a complex supplementary network of vessels. There were other structures within the transparent matrix that were not green—networks limned in ghostly white. At certain points, Paul could see through the green to darker organs beneath, seemingly dark blue or dark brown.

"Do you understand what I am saying?" asked the alien.

"Yes," said Paul.

"I cannot tell you my name, because its syllables cannot be rendered into your speech, but I am commonly addressed by humans as Remila. Normally, of course, I do not need to communicate with humans in this way, for they understand the sounds I make, even though they cannot duplicate them, just as I understand human languages, although I cannot reproduce them. It is a means of intercourse that your people and mine now learn as children, although it is not easy."

"I see," said Paul. "There are still people in the world, then—apart from jumpers?"

"Yes. Many people in your own country were destroyed during the battle that was fought at the time of our arrival—largely because the installation coordinating the mechanical defense system seemed to be located near the city where most of the population of the region was concentrated—but the rest of the Earth suffered relatively little damage."

"Where am I now?" asked Paul.

"South America. Most of the humans who survived the immediate effects of the battle by time-slipping have been evacuated here as we have been able to rescue them. Many do not survive, but we have medicosymbiotic facilities adequate to the recovery of at least fifty per cent of them. You are in unusually good health, no doubt because you have been active for only a few days since the period before the wars."

"What happened to the others—the people who were with me in the same room?"

"Ricardo Marcangelo is dead. He returned to normal time some three hundred years ago, and made a considerable contribution to the establishment of understanding between our races. He lived out his life in the ordinary way, and died just before the close of the twenty-second century, according to your old calendar."

"It's now the twenty-fifth century, then—on our old calendar?"

"The year is 2472, in the ancient way of reckoning."

"There were others with me apart from Marcangelo: a girl named Rebecca, and a man named Scapelhorn."

"The girl is alive, but presently timelocked. We have no record of Scapelhorn at all."

"What about Adam Wishart?"

"Dead. He did not survive the shock of his second jump."

"And the machine? The one that fought you for possession of the Earth?"

"Apparently destroyed. All orbital systems were wiped out, as was the surface installation in the northern hemisphere. If there were other installations we did not find them."

"So you won."

"We did not want to fight. We had no aggressive intentions, but we had to respond when we were attacked. It is important that you realize that. Because of the machine, many of your people became convinced that we were your enemies. That was not so. Today, no one believes it any more—it is all too obvious that the interests of your people and mine coincide—but still there is something that keeps your people and mine apart. It is vital that you, of all people, should be made to see the truth and to understand it."

"Why me?" asked Paul, already knowing the answer.

"Your name still thrives as the emblem of many beliefs, not only among humans, but among my kind as well. It is possible that you will find the world of 2472 more like the world of 2119 than you could have anticipated."

"That's what I was told in 2119, too," said Paul. "But what I've seen so far tells me that *this* world has changed rather more than I could have imagined. That room I've just come from... your egg with insect-wings...and you."

"Our technology imitates nature a little more than yours," said the alien. "We are accomplished biological engineers. We build organic machines, and organic houses—they are not alive, you understand, in any true sense, but they duplicate many of the faculties and some of the methods of living tissues. The ornithopter is simply a machine that makes use of the principles of bird and insect flight. The medicosymbiotic system which restored you to health is, admittedly, much more of an artificial organism, but it remains simply an instrument. It is the same with myself and my kind. We look strange, but in our minds we are not so very different. We have photosynthetic symbionts within our body walls, and vestigial flightless wings that provide extra photosynthetic surfaces, but our eyes are sensitive to approximately the same range of wavelengths of light as yours, and our ears to a similar range of sounds. Your kind and mine live in very much the same perceived universe. What we know of it is basically similar. We have found no insuperable problems in communication; we have similar concept-systems, despite the fact that my kind whistle while yours grunt. We believe that a genuine symbiosis is possible between your race and mine. It is possible, that is, if it is wished for and worked for."

"I begin to see the similarity you mentioned," said Paul. "Your message begins to sound like a parody of Marcangelo."

"It is no parody," replied the metallic artificial voice. "It is in many ways precisely parallel to it."

"Is that why your people came here? To seek a productive symbiosis?"

"Why else would we travel for a hundred years across the void? There is nothing beyond the void that surrounds any world but the possibility of other life, and the only possible reason for meeting other life is the hope of symbiosis."

"And yet your spacefleet seemed to be heavily armed—just in case, I suppose."

"You have not travelled between the stars. You do not know what threats there are to life and harmony. You do not know how few are the worlds where second-phase life exists. Even the radio signals that drew us to your world could not be taken as an infallible indicator of the presence of second-phase life."

"Do I take it that there are other kinds of life?"

"We classify life-systems according to a tripartite system. First-phase life is not inimical, but third-phase life is deadly. The evolution of third-phase life means that a planet is forever uninhabitable for our kind of life, and our kind of life cannot survive even the least contact with it."

There was something in the dead, matter-of-fact tone in which the statement was made that Paul found slightly horrifying. He realized that he was out of his imaginative depth. Clearly, what the alien was saying meant far more than he could see from a standpoint within his own narrow perspectives.

"What is this third-phase life?" he asked, quietly.

"I will tell you about third-phase life on another occasion. There are issues more central to our immediate concerns that must be discussed."

"For instance?"

"Do you remember what you saw from the window of the building where you have been in stasis for the last three hundred and fifty-three years?"

"Yes."

"That land can be reclaimed, Paul Heisenberg. It can be made to live again. The whole Earth can be reborn. We could begin that rebirth tomorrow, with the re-seeding of North America, Asia and Europe. We can design organisms that can begin the cycle of life there again. It will take a long time, but not nearly as long as it would take for the rebirth to happen naturally. We can take care of the poisons in the earth, the radioactive wastes, the artificial organisms made by your own kind for the purposes of war. We have the ability to do all of that."

"What's stopping you?" asked Paul.

"An ideology. I will not pretend that it is something which affects only your kind, because it sometimes seems to me that it is held more fanatically by those of my kind who have espoused it. It has been seized by our rebels and our misfits, suiting them perfectly because it provides a mirror-image of our own prevailing ideology."

"To put it simply, Paul Heisenberg, the majority of my people believe that the purpose of intelligent life is to achieve a special kind of harmony with nature. We mean rather more than you can presently imagine by the word which we have rendered into your language as *symbiosis.* It is our whole philosophy of life, presenting an ideal not only for social life but for evolutionary strategy—we have, of course, long since taken on responsibility for our own social and biological evolution. We are a long-lived species, and can travel between the stars by virtue of the fact that we can lower our metabolic rate to the point where all our energy-requirements can be fulfilled by our photosynthetic symbiosis—effectively becoming vegetables. We see the future not merely of our own kind but of the whole universe as a continual meeting, whenever and wherever such meetings can take place, between compatible species, in order that they should form an ever-more-extensive network of symbiotic relationships, which will ultimately fill the universe and unite its life into one vast organic whole. This is, if you like, a dream—but it is one that gives form and purpose to our long lives."

"Elsewhere in the universe we have met people who could share that dream, and who have entered into participation in it. Those people were often more like you than like us—short lived, unable to travel between the stars. Sometimes, we have met people who could not. Such people we have left alone, confident that, in the fullness of time, evolution will remake them.

Eventually, we are certain, they will either become compatible or they will be absorbed as their ecosystem gives birth to third-phase life and intelligence becomes extinct.

"We feel that there is a possibility that a lasting and harmonious relationship could be established between your people and ours. Some of your people share this belief. Others, however—and they have seduced many of my own kind—have committed themselves to a very different and much more individualistic dream. Some retain the same notion of the eventual consummation of the evolutionary scheme, but they wish to play a very different part within that scheme. They are uninterested in growth and communication, uninterested even in the rebirth of this world. Their declared aim is to become pilgrims on a lonely road to the end of time. What will happen when they get to the end of their journey none can imagine, but they all believe that the journey has a purpose and an end.

"Even for your kind, this dream is irrational. For mine it is doubly so, for there is not a single one of my species who has yet succeeded in projecting himself through time. For my kind, in fact, I believe that the mythology is only the means to the more immediate end of denying and dissociating themselves from the faith they have known since birth. They cannot really hope that they will ever be able to join the pilgrimage, but they believe in it no less insistently for all that. Many hope that it requires only your return, your teaching, and your example to spread the word from your kind to include mine, but that is a futile hope, and even the people who entertain it must know that it is futile in their hearts."

"In brief, Paul Heisenberg, the situation has much in common with the one which you found in 2119. Again you are awaited because your name has become the symbol of hopes and expectations which are incapable of fulfillment. Again, the future of the world might actually be hanging in the balance—so delicately balanced that your words could make the difference between the rebirth of your world and the extinction of your species. There is much more to be said about this, but it is important that this much, at least, should be made clear. A decision will be needed—not immediately, but soon."

The artificial voice stopped, and the room suddenly seemed very silent. The bright lights still disturbed Paul with their dazzle.

"I don't quite see how it matters," said Paul, eventually. "Presumably most of the human would-be pilgrims are already on their way. Why can't you let those who want to believe it do so? Why should it inhibit you from re-seeding the Earth and restoring its ecosystems?"

"Symbiosis must be wholehearted," said Remila, flatly. "It cannot work unless it is complete. The example of a parasitic mode of existence and a parasitic philosophy of life cannot be tolerated—it is the seed of a cancer. Your people must be made to see that. Without their example and your name, my people would inevitably return to their own faith."

"I see," said Paul. "So symbiosis and all it implies in your philosophy doesn't exactly equate with universal goodwill. You still feel free to fight, against enemies you can stigmatize by analogy with parasitism and cancer."

"Our purpose cannot be fulfilled if parasitism and cancer survive within the universal life-system."

"Why not simply exterminate all the would-be parasites and all the potential seeds of cancer? After all, it wouldn't be mass murder—simply necessary surgery performed in the name of symbiosis and the universal life-system."

Paul stared into the great round eyes, whose large brown irises were ringed with white. Remila did not blink, though he did have large leathery eyelids. Instead, a transparent nictitating membrane flicked from side to side across the cornea.

"It is not our way," replied the alien. "We will not kill individuals of our own kind, nor of yours, unless we ourselves are under threat of extreme injury or death. The choice facing us is simple. Either there is a future for us on Earth, involving a healthy symbiotic relationship between your race and mine, or there is not, in which case our starships will depart, leaving behind those of my kind who prefer to stay. We are not murderers."

Paul hesitated for a moment, and then said: "I'm sorry."

Remila made no reply, but simply inclined his head slightly.

"I have to know more," said Paul.

"I am here to answer questions. Others will come, too. Hadan will return. And there are the letters."

"Letters?"

"In our charge there are approximately two thousand letters addressed to you by humans who have died or who have gone into stasis. There are open letters left behind by some jumpers which are addressed generally to other jumpers. It is a somewhat laborious communications system, but it is the only way that anyone embarking upon a pilgrimage through time can possibly keep in touch with his fellow pilgrims. There is, it seems, a desperate need to communicate, which overcomes many people before they go into stasis. It is a defense mechanism against the loneliness and the uncertainty."

"Is there a letter from Rebecca?"

"There is. There is also a letter from Ricardo Marcangelo."

"I'd like to see them. And any others that are from people I knew personally."

"I do not know of any others that are from people who knew you personally. Perhaps you could check the names."

"No—just let me see those two first. I'll look at the others in time. How many people are there in stasis at this moment?"

"Approximately five thousand."

"That doesn't sound like very many, compared to the number quoted to me in 2119."

"The great majority of those who jumped from the war years, or from 2119 itself, either died or refrained from jumping again."

"And what's the present active population of the world?"

"Approximately one million of my race, approximately six million of yours."

"*Six million!* In the whole world! What about Australia?"

"At no time since the end of the twentieth century has the

birth rate exceeded the death rate. Australia, though untouched by the battle which we fought against the machine, continued to decline. It is a dying continent, as is South America. Only symbiosis can reverse the trend."

"If you stood back and let the human race become extinct," observed Paul, dryly, "you could own the Earth outright in a few hundred years, except for a few silver statues that only wake up once every few centuries."

"Of what use is an empty world?" asked Remila. "It is humankind that interests us."

"Have you ever met another race that could time-jump?" asked Paul.

"No."

"So you've never encountered this phenomenon anywhere in the galaxy—or such of the galaxy as you've explored?"

"We have found gaps in the fabric of spacetime, which exhibit the same surface phenomena as the silhouettes left by the time-jumpers. We know nothing about what causes them. Prior to coming here, we had considered them to be minor accidents of circumstance—flaws in the fabric of the universe. We had not suspected that they could be created by the power of the will. We do not know how this can be the case. It seems to be irrational—we have no theory to account for it."

Paul nodded. He shifted uncomfortably in the chair. "Would it be possible for you to supply me with some clothes?" he asked.

"It is not customary that garments are worn inside our dwellings," replied the alien. "However, if it would make you more comfortable while you have an opportunity to adjust to our ways, clothing will be supplied. Any other needs that you care to make known to us will also be met. We have prepared a room for you close at hand."

"Speaking of other needs," said Paul, reacting to the other's words with slight sarcasm, "I'm rather hungry."

The alien inclined his head again. "Then you may go to your room now. We will talk again later."

Paul looked around, and saw that an aperture was widening

in the wall behind him.

"How does that work?" he asked.

"When closed, the apertures are mere pinpricks," said Remila. "They are virtually invisible. They are dilated by an artificial muscle built into the tissue of the wall. The muscle is ordinarily stimulated electrically—I used a stimulation-point set here in the desk. There are others mounted around the muscle itself— simply press the wall in the region of the aperture."

Paul was slightly relieved by the words. He had begun to suspect that he was effectively a prisoner, unable to leave his room. Moments later, however, the anxiety returned as he realized that he only knew the location of a single aperture and that they were, as Remila had said, virtually invisible.

CHAPTER THIRTY

Paul ate his way steadily through the meal. First there was some kind of soup, very thick and glutinous, with a taste somewhat reminiscent of asparagus. Then there were several slices of crisp bread, with various savory preserves, most of which he found too highly spiced for his own taste. Finally, there was fruit in a sweet syrup. There was nothing to which he could put a name with any certainty.

When he was finished, he left the table, half-expecting it to fold up and retract, like the mussel in the room where he had first become conscious. It remained a table, though.

This room was a little larger than the one that contained the mussel. Physically, it was similar, even with respect to the blue walls, but it contained the table and dining chair, a bed, an armchair and a computer terminal with a display screen, which he had so far left alone, not having the least idea how to make use of it.

Presumably, his new hosts had some way of monitoring him, because he had hardly sat down in the armchair when the aperture in the wall widened again to permit the entry of two visitors. One was an alien—presumably Remila—and the other was the tall negro who had been with him when they fetched Paul from the prison.

"I'm Gelert Hadan," said the human. He did not introduce the alien, and Paul concluded that it must be Remila. Paul had put on a light shirt made from a material resembling cheesecloth and a pair of loose-fitting trousers, but Hadan was naked.

Paul sat on the bed, offering Hadan the armchair and Remila the dining chair.

Without the speaking-device to assist him Remila could only speak in his own tongue, and did so. His speech sounded rather like strident birdsong, but there was a smooth and liquid transition from one note to the next. He whistled several phrases at Hadan, who simply nodded in reply.

"You are comfortable here?" he asked Paul.

"Moderately," answered Paul.

"The food was acceptable?"

"Yes. I presume that it was grown from alien seed, brought here by Remila's people?"

"Not at all," said Hadan. "It was all grown from Earthly crops, descended from the crops that you knew in your own time. There has been some improvement in yield, and fashions in preparation have changed greatly."

"But it *is* the food the aliens eat?"

"Of course," said Hadan. "Our needs are similar. The La, of course, obtain extra energy from photosynthesis, but an active animal cannot live on the resources of a plant. Their flesh is very little different from ours, and they eat as we do."

"The La—that's what they call themselves?"

Hadan glanced sideways at Remila, smiling. "Not quite. It is the name of a musical note, as are the names which we articulate in human languages to apply to most things which have no parallel therein, including names. It is not, even so, a "translation"—the names which they use among themselves are usually more complex."

"What exactly is *your* role?" asked Paul.

"I am the leader of the human community."

"Which human community?"

"*The* human community. All of it. *Leader*, you understand, is meant figuratively rather than literally. I cannot say that I represent every man or woman on Earth, or even a majority, in any direct sense—local communities tend to look after their own internal affairs and most ignore what goes on beyond their personal horizons—but I am the representative of all in some way. I am elected by those humans who live in the cities of the La."

"I see."

"No, Paul. You are a long way yet from clear sight. At the moment, you see very little, and what you see is distorted by your own perspective. You are a long way out of your time, and the world has changed."

Here Remila intervened, interposing several phrases of whistles and hoots. When the alien had finished, Paul added: "Remila has already suggested to me that it has changed less than I might have imagined."

"There are similarities in the situation," admitted Hadan, "but the world itself is new. Nearly five hundred years have passed since you first jumped through time, and the world today is different from the world in which you lived most of your life as that world was from the fifteenth century."

"I can believe that," said Paul, quietly. "I can understand how Columbus might have felt, confronted with Adam Wishart and television."

"This world needs you, Paul," said Hadan, his tone equally gentle.

"Strangely enough," said Paul, "I think that's exactly what Adam Wishart might have said to Columbus, before putting him on television as the eighth wonder of the world."

Hadan was silent for a moment, obviously disturbed. Then he said: "It will take time for you to become accustomed to the world as it now is. When you do, you will be able to see it as it might become—as it must become, if the human race is to have any future at all. You cannot yet know what the La have done for Earth, or what they could do if only we could help them. When you find out, then I believe you will see clearly what you cannot now see at all—that you must add your voice to ours. It is the one voice which might influence those who are opposed to us. They have adopted your name as the emblem of their opposition."

"Do I get to hear *their* side of the story?" asked Paul.

"Of course. We will hide nothing from you. The letters, I think, will help you to understand what those who act in your name have come to believe, and how they act upon their beliefs. There are also letters that favor our course. Once you have read them, it will be possible for you to go out into the world, to see the way we live our lives. You may read what you will—the terminal here will call up any book or document known to us. I will show you how to operate it presently."

Paul frowned pensively, and thought about what Remila had told him in the course of the earlier interview.

"If I have the story straight," he said, slowly, "the La want to remake Earth as a Garden of Eden. They think that it will take some time, but that it might be done. Their main condition is that we not only co-operate but offer ourselves body and soul to their philosophy, which translates into English as symbiosis but which implies rather more than that. I'd like to know much more, but for the time being, can you answer a much simpler question: what do *they* get out of it?"

"Symbiosis," replied Hadan. "It is the highest goal, the greatest possible reward. Indeed, it is the only reward. The La have long been able to supply all their material needs. They are not a competitive people, and cannot occupy themselves in a ceaseless struggle to win advantage from one another—they have long tried to eliminate from their culture the impulses they describe as parasitic and predatory. Their one goal is to expand the realms of their symbiotic harmony, to establish communication and understanding and common cause with other races. They believe that there is some urgency in this task, in evolutionary terms, because they have reason to believe that where their kind of harmony cannot be attained—where intelligent races cannot enter into their interstellar network of symbiosis— intelligence itself cannot survive. Either races destroy themselves, as we nearly did, or evolutionary change eventually creates circumstances inimical to the existence of intelligent life."

"Third-phase life," said Paul.

"Yes."

"What does it *mean?*"

"The La, in their exploration of that part of the galaxy which they have so far been able to reach, have found three basic types of evolutionary pattern. It is simplest to consider them as if they were consequent on different kinds of initial circumstances pertaining to the actual emergence of life. On Earth, as you know, life evolved in the primeval ocean, rich in organic compounds, first through the formation of chemically-active globules—microspheres—which gradually became more complex structurally, until they became proto-cells, and secondly by the differentiation of such proto-cells into different modes of existence. As organic molecules became less freely available, some proto-cells embarked upon a way of life involving the synthesis of complex organic molecules fueled by sunlight, while others embarked upon a way of life involving the theft of molecules from the molecule-builders."

"Plants and animals," put in Paul. "I know the story."

Hadan frowned at the interruption, but went on. "The story of life on Earth is basically the story of the mechanisms invented by cells for the purpose of making more cells. Competition between different kinds of cells—both within and between the basic types—established a situation in which there was rigorous selection between reproductive mechanisms, the most effective surviving while the less effective perished. You know all this, and it is quite obvious. But it has probably not occurred to you to wonder whether there might be alternatives to this whole pattern.

"In fact, natural selection of this kind is by no means universal to all life-systems. This kind of competition of reproductive systems is not inevitable. There are some worlds where the conditions permitting the evolution of life are not as violent as those pertaining to the early Earth. Some life-systems have emerged in which the fundamental structure was not the microsphere proto-cell but a kind of film, like an oil-slick on still water or a sheath of slime covering a rock. On such worlds, the differentiation of living material into cells came only at a very late stage in the evolutionary story, which was for many years involved not with globular individual life-units but with potentially-infinite sheets. In these systems the differentiation of the modes of existence you call the plant-mode and the animal-mode simply never happened.

"There is, in such systems, no real difference between growth and reproduction. On such worlds there are no organisms, but only life. All life on such worlds is one. There are no individuals. Sometimes such systems never even develop the ability to photosynthesize more organic substance with the aid of sunlight, and remain forever limited by the initial supply of organic molecules dissolved in the primeval soup or distributed over the primeval rocks. More often, though, the photosynthetic faculty does evolve, and the life-system can continue to evolve, often introducing the differentiation of function and the complication of structure characteristic of any evolutionary pattern, but such systems never evolve individuality and competition—or if they do, they alter their whole mode of being in the process, and become second-phase systems. These systems are, of course, what the La call first-phase life.

"Third-phase life involves the kind of system that we might imagine originating on a world where conditions were much more violent than those pertaining to the origin of life on Earth. Here, too, the fundamental step is the evolution of the microspheric proto-cell, but instead of its emergence being a relatively comfortable affair, it is one attended by great difficulty. In order for a microsphere to survive at all in such an environment, it needs to have far greater capacities of self-repair than were necessary for the ancestors of Earthly cells.

"We imagine conditions so violent and a struggle for existence so desperate that the problem of there being so many microspheres that they must compete for dwindling resources never arises. The only problem is maintaining the integrity of the proto-cell. In such circumstances the protocells become gradually more capable. Where two come together they do not simply merge and separate, as second-phase microspheres do, but join and co-operate, adding their capabilities together. This is the price of survival—only those proto-cells that can evolve better and better life-preserving faculties can survive at all.

"In consequence, individuals do not evolve in this instance either. There is no competition of the second-phase kind, but instead a much more bitter conflict between living substance and environment. What emerges from the process are cells that are highly adaptable, cells that can aggregate and co-operate. What forms is a kind of super-organism, all of whose individual units are protean, and which can adopt any function required for the immediate needs of the whole. Cells or groups of cells can function in the animal mode or in the plant mode, but the whole population of cells remains associated in a way that second-phase cells never are.

"On such worlds, inordinately complex life-systems have evolved, whose biomass is vastly greater than the biomass of a second-phase life-system, but which consist, essentially, of a single super-organism. Imagine, if you like, all the species of Earth associated like the bees in a hive or the zoophytic colonies comprising a Portuguese Man O' War. This super-organism is infinitely adaptable, and can co-opt into its biomass everything save the rock which is its substratum...and perhaps, as it grows, even that can be slowly eroded. A visitor to such a world need only open the aperture of his starship and he is destroyed. A third-phase life-system will absorb alien flesh in a matter of moments.

"Sometimes, just as first-phase life can give rise to second-phase, so second-phase life can give rise to third-phase. Once third-phase cells arise, however their origin is achieved, they absorb the entire life-system. That might be the eventual fate of *all* life in the universe, and would be for certain, were it not for the fact that second-phase life, with its competition between cells to build better and better reproductive systems, almost invariably gives rise eventually to sentient and intelligent beings. Third-phase life can never give rise to intelligence—it has no use for it. Its protean cells are infinitely adaptable *physically*; they do not need to be adaptable *behaviorally*. The evolution of intelligence in second-phase systems is vital, because intelligent beings can take responsibility for the future evolution of such systems. They can assure that third-phase life does not evolve, and can destroy it while it is still vulnerable, as and when it emerges. Intelligence can preserve itself, if its owners behave in a *truly* intelligent way.

"I hope now that you can see something of the pattern of life in the universe. Seeing that, you can better appreciate the philosophy of the La, and their behavior. The survival of intelligent life—of *all* intelligent life—is their goal. They have known races that could not be preserved, and whose worlds have either become utterly sterile and lifeless or have fallen prey to third-phase life. They see the long-term future in terms of a growing network of symbiotic relationships between second-phase life-systems across the galaxy, and perhaps even between galaxies. Without such a network, they fear that third-phase life will mindlessly possess all the habitable worlds of all the stars. The idea of a mindless universe appalls them, because they believe that the universe itself is not merely a physical system but is, at least potentially, possessed in its unity and entirety of the property of mind."

When he stopped, silence fell.

Paul let a full half-minute pass before he asked: "How many stars have the La visited?"

"Tens of thousands," replied Hadan. "Very few have worlds where life exists; even fewer have second-phase life; fewer still have intelligent life. Ours is the thirteenth intelligent species the La have contacted, although they have found residual evidence of two more that are now extinct. Of the thirteen, one has already fallen prey to third-phase life. Its world had to be abandoned by the La, and the La concerned had themselves to be quarantined. It is an experience that the race remembers with horror and fear. Remila and his people do not want to see the same thing happen to Earth."

"And you agree completely?"

"Yes, I do."

"Even though everything you have told me is, from your point of view, hearsay. You have not been into space—and nor has any other human."

"Humans are not equipped, physically or psychologically, for travel between the stars. The La can travel in suspended animation, sustained only by the symbiotes that live within their bodies, and which can supply their elementary metabolic requirements by means of photosynthesis."

"What about time-jumpers?" asked Paul. "If a human were to ride a spaceship beyond the solar system, and then go into stasis, surely he'd stay where he was, inside the ship? That way, he could survive a journey of fifty or a hundred years."

"Time-jumping is erratic," replied Hadan. "It seems to be simple enough to jump, but planning one's arrival is quite another thing. What use would it be to take a passage on a star-ship, if one were to wake up thirty years too soon, or not at all. No human has gone to the stars, and no human intends to try. There is no reason whatsoever to doubt what the La tell us. What motive could they possibly have for trying to deceive us?"

To that question, Paul could make no reply. Instead, he said: "What, exactly do the La want from us? What would count as a convincing demonstration of our worthiness to be part of their grand plan?"

"At the moment," replied Hadan, "the opposition to whole-hearted co-operation with the La is focused on your name. There are many different cults and groups of one kind or another, and countless individuals, who are bound together only by the fact that they are in some sense waiting for your return, convinced that you might be able to tell them what to do, offering them a different kind of salvation. If all those movements were to lose the glue that holds them together, our cause would be won. A few disaffected individuals don't matter; the La themselves have plenty of those, and whole shiploads have arrived in the wake of accounts of Earth that reached other La worlds over the last few centuries. They, too, have only one thing in common: the futile hope that an alien messiah with the power to move through time might offer them a reason for living that can stand in opposition to the philosophy of the La."

"In other words," said Paul, "you think that everything will be beautiful, if only I'll throw in with you and preach your gospel."

"To me," agreed Hadan, "it certainly seems that way."

Paul glanced across at Remila, who was patiently watching and listening.

Remila went into a long monologue in his own language. When he had finished, Hadan said: "He says that it would have been better if you had never awakened, or had vanished completely like some of the others. He doesn't think that even you can overcome the mythology of your name. But he still hopes that we might win, with all his heart, and he knows that we must try."

Most of the speech went right over Paul's head, because his attention had been caught and held by one particular phrase.

"What do you mean, *vanished?*"

Hadan looked genuinely surprised. "Didn't you know?" he said. "I thought that even in 2119.... Some of the jumpers don't ever land. Sometimes the statues blink out, just like *that!*" He snapped his fingers. Then he added: "It seems that your pilgrims to the end of time haven't picked a particularly safe way to travel."

CHAPTER THIRTY-ONE

Rebecca's letter was headed: *Paul*. Just that, and nothing else. Perhaps she hadn't felt confident enough to write more than that. Perhaps she hadn't felt that anything else was necessary. She might have known—or at least believed—that her letter would be read by other eyes, and alien eyes at that. How much, he wondered, might that have altered what she had chosen to write?

As he read on, he imagined that he could hear her voice saying the words, speaking in the low, intense tone that she had used during the first night, before she realized who he was... when he was just another ordinary person reborn into the postwar world.

"I don't know if you'll ever receive this letter," said the voice, "and I don't know how much it will matter if you do. Hundreds of people have written letters to you, and I suppose I'm just following the trend. The La have agreed to hold the letters, and they seem to live so long that the same ones will still be around when you come back, so I suppose they mean what they say. I don't know what other people have said in their letters but what I want to do is tell you how I see things and why I'm doing what I'm doing. Others will tell you about the world and give you plenty of advice, so there's no need for me to tell you what I found when I came out of the jump or how I reacted to it all. Either things will still be the same and you'll go through it yourself, or they'll be different, and it won't matter.

"I don't think I write now as the same person you found when you first came to the house that night. I'm not very much older, but I feel very different, about almost everything. Partly that's because I'm a jumper now, and I know something of what you must have felt. Partly it's because of what happened in the few days you were with me and what's happened in the days I've lived since. I'm looking at a different world now, and I realize how much I was trapped before with the idea of the future that seemed natural to the world I'd lived all my life in.

"Because I knew you, and because I spent sixty years frozen still in time with your arm around me, I've become something of a celebrity. I feel that people are expecting something of me. They go over and over what I saw and what you said, as if there ought to be some secret message hidden in it, which will tell them what to do and what to be. I don't like it. It scares me. They can't be satisfied with what there is to say, but I daren't make up anything. They expect me to be able to tell them what parts of your book mean, as if I were the one person in the world who could get it all clear and make it simple for them. They won't accept that I don't know. Everything here is confused. Partly, I suppose, what I'm doing in jumping—and I'm planning to jump, again and again—is trying to escape this situation. I'm trying to get away from not being what other people want me to be. But it's not just a matter of running away. There's much more to it than that—or if it *is* just running away, it's running away from much more than the pressure of what people expect of me.

"Mainly, I'm jumping because there's nothing in this world that means anything to me. It has nothing to give me. There's no place in it for me. Most of the jumpers feel the same—the reason most of them left their own times was that those times seemed to have nothing for them, and they felt dislocated. Jumping has made things worse and not better. They now feel even more dislocated. They can't revert to what ordinary people consider to be ordinary life—it's harder for them now than it would have been before they ever started. Nearly all the jumpers jump again. Sometimes they stay around for months, or even years, but until they get old and tired they keep on jumping, and I think they will keep on jumping for as long as they can. The only exceptions are some of the ones who jumped to escape the destruction of the USA: Marcangelo and some like him. Marcangelo is still alive; he's helped me while I've recovered and thought about things. He's a few years older. There are some people here who are three-time jumpers, and not one of them has stayed more than a few days. I've been here a couple of months, but I'll never stay so long again.

"I don't know if I'll ever see you again. We've tried to work out why it is that the jumps vary so much, but we can't. All we know is that the three-time jumpers tend to jump further every time. Maybe the lengths of the jumps increase according to some mathematical relationship, but we don't know enough yet to be sure. No one knows why some people only jump twenty or thirty years, while others jump a century—it doesn't seem to have anything to do with how hard you try, and as we still have no idea what actually *causes* the slips there seems to be no possibility of our learning any kind of control. Anyone who jumps has got to reconcile himself or herself to the fact that it's a very lonely prospect. The chance of meeting up with people you know is slim.

"Looked at like that, jumping as a way of life isn't very attractive. On top of that, some people disappear forever and some come out dead. We think the dream might kill them, but we don't know how. Most jumpers dream the same kind of dream, but we don't know why. We think that it might be a place rather than a dream—a place where we go when we cut ourselves out from spacetime—but there's no way to know. As long as we aren't frightened to death, it seems that there's little the dream can do to hurt us, but we're not sure even about that, because of the ones that vanish.

"The idea of jumping again and again does frighten me, but it seems to be the only thing I can do—the only road I can follow. I don't know whether there's anything at the end of the road, or even whether there *can* be anything at the end of the road, but if there isn't anything, then there isn't anything *anywhere*—not for me.

"Marcangelo has said all there has to be said about it: that we only have fifty or sixty years of life, no matter how we distribute it through time, and that we'll still die, even if we die a billion years from now. He says that the only choice which faces us is the choice of dying alone, uselessly, or dying here, among people, having used life to *do* something that'll be useful even when we're gone. He says that the only meaningful way to reach the future is to have children, who will have children of their own, and so *ad infinitum.* That way, we can be part of everything forever—part of the symbiotic empire that the La want to extend throughout the universe. That doesn't mean anything to me. It just leaves me cold.

"I'm alone now. I feel alone, and I don't think that I'll ever feel any different. Unless there *is* something at the end of the road. I can see why Marcangelo considers that to be such a ridiculous and forlorn hope, but to me it's the only hope that means anything at all. There's no going back to 2119, no way to undo anything that's ever been done. The only way is ahead, whether you go one day at a time or try to cross a billion years. I'm going to try to cross a billion years.

"If I don't make it, or if there's nothing there—and I know this sounds bad—I just don't care. That wouldn't matter. All that matters is trying, and hoping, and following you. I believe that this is what you'll decide to do, too. I don't know how or why I believe it, but I do. I believe that we'll meet again, too, although not in any world like this one, or the one where we met before. When we meet again it'll be at the end of time: somewhere that we can be, somewhere that we can belong."

The letter was signed: *Rebecca*. Nothing else.

The echoes of the imaginary voice died in his mind. Paul laid the letter down and wondered whether he had got the tone right. Had he added a hysterical tone, it might have sounded very different, and changed its meaning completely. It would have been easy enough for someone like Ricardo Marcangelo to condemn the message as the substance of lunacy, but to Paul there seemed to be no madness in it.

Perhaps, he thought, *it's because I'm mad too.*

Who, he wondered, would maintain the roadside inns along the route that Rebecca had taken? How could she survive if the La abandoned Earth and humankind became extinct? And what conceivable destination was there in the reaches of the far future? Third-phase life?

He remembered then that what Rebecca had done—and what others were doing—had been done in his name. It had been blessed by some perversion of his own philosophy, a philosophy that had seemed, when he wrote *Science and Metascience,* so innocent and harmless.

He took up the second letter, and looked at it uneasily, certain that it would be the perfect antidote to Rebecca's, full of good common sense.

He had as little difficulty conjuring up Marcangelo's voice from the recesses of his memory as he had had in imagining Rebecca's. After all, the two of them had dominated his last awakening with their voices, and in his memory, that was only two days and a dream ago....

"Dear Paul," said Marcangelo, smoothly, "it has, as you no doubt know by now, become fashionable to communicate with our timelocked brethren by letter. This applies to all of us, for those who are not dead when the moment comes for the letters to be opened will undoubtedly be timelocked themselves. I, of course, will be dead. This will preclude your being able to reply to this particular letter, but I am sure that you will be able to build up a fruitful correspondence with some of your fellow time-travelers. Great minds can exchange their metascientific thoughts while the world, dissolved into a mere blur, hastens to its destruction. I dare say that the great minds will not be unduly troubled by that. Great minds never have been troubled by the affairs of the mundane world.

"I suppose that these may come to be reckoned my last words, but in fact I am not yet at my last gasp. I might have several years to go yet, and I hope that I will be strong enough to make a little impact on the world as they go by me. Perhaps I will tear this letter up next year and write a replacement, but I think not. Much of what I have to say I have said before, and could have said at any time in my life. I am not likely to change my views now, nor will I learn to express them better than I already can, imperfect as that may be.

"I hope that you are now, or might soon be, in a position to see clearly the result of a process that is only just beginning now: the rebirth of the world, and the renewal of its chance of long-term survival as the home of the human race. It will also be the home of the La, and I think that is a good thing, because there is much that the La can show us concerning the possible modes of social existence.

"As I write, the cults that have chosen your name as the symbol of their dreams still thrive, but I think that they are dying. As things change and the world is mended, there will be new opportunities for hope in a more ordinary future, and new encouragement for reinvestment in everyday life. I do not know when you will awake, but there seems to be some reason to believe that you will jump further this time than you did before, so that another forty years, at least, will have passed. I hope that might be time for what I say to have become the truth.

"I do not pretend to have mastered the philosophy of the La, or to have obtained a perfect understanding of their culture. The word that has been rendered into our language as 'symbiosis' implies far more than that word can convey, but, in essence, it is little more than a celebration of all the things that allow and encourage living things to co-exist, to the mutual benefit of all concerned. Perhaps it should have been translated as 'love', although that word carries far too many human implications to make it entirely suitable.

"It is not easy to get to know the La. Theirs is a custom-bound world which is difficult to penetrate, although they make every allowance and try hard to make it possible. Their daily routine includes many rituals that affirm the idea of symbiosis and its behavioral paradigms. They are patient and generous. Many would consider them to be altruistic, but I think that it would be misleading to describe them as such. They do what they do for their own reasons, to satisfy their own sense of priority. They will only help those who seem, in their eyes, to be deserving of help. With respect to anything that invites description, in their terms, as 'parasitism' or 'predatory behaviour,' they are intolerant, although not aggressive. It would not be true to say that they are intrinsically kindly or merciful. To put it crudely, they would not automatically extend a hand to a drowning man— they would first want to know whether he was their friend.

"In their present attitude to Earth and the human race they are ambiguous. They are preserving human society as best they can, but are reserving much of their effort because they are not yet sure whether humans in general are capable of establishing the kind of relationship with them that they consider necessary. They are patient, and will wait long enough to be certain before they allow the balance of the situation to tip one way or the other. I feel sure in my own mind that by the time you return, Earth will be closer to redemption than it is now. However, it is probable that as long as your name retains its power the jumpers, at least, will maintain their opposition. It might well be necessary for you to enter into the struggle.

"I have always believed that if things had worked out differently in 2119 you would have added your weight to the side of the dispute that I represented. I was sure that I knew you better than the cultists, and that you were not an escapist at heart. It seemed to me that your interest in metascience was basically an interest in strategies that would allow people to face and feel comfortable with reality, not in imaginative techniques for escaping such confrontation.

"I am equally sure that, whenever you do return, you will commit yourself to the right side. In all the cults that have taken your name as an emblem I do not believe you have a single true follower. You must do what you can to correct their errors. If, as I suspect, you are reading this shortly after your reawakening, then I advise you not to leap to any conclusions about the world or about the La. Look at the world, calmly and unhurriedly. Take the time to consider that circumstances in 2119 never allowed you. Look closely at the letters addressed to you by the jumpers, and try to appreciate what a sterile and desolate world-view they are crediting to your inspiration. I do not think you are the kind of man to be blinded by adoration or misled by the urgency of impossible pleas and delusions.

"In all sincerity, Ricardo Marcangelo."

Paul was about to lower the letter to the table, but he paused, and looked back to the beginning, to read the date. The letter had been written on the second of September, 2194. Nearly three hundred years ago.

"So much," he murmured, aloud, "for optimism."

He stood up and stretched his limbs, and looked around. The four walls suddenly seemed threatening in their blank-ness, although he knew that the absence of a door was only an illusion. There was a claustrophobic thrill in his spine, and his hands shook, briefly. The shudder passed, but its aftermath was no less unpleasant. He felt an urgent need to get out of the room.

He pressed the wall in the vicinity of the sphincter, and felt the plastic surface recoil beneath his touch like something alive. The sensation filled him with horror, although he knew that his fear was unreasoning.

He stepped through the open aperture into the corridor, and began to walk along it. It was blank and featureless; obviously, there were other rooms and other doors but none were evident to his senses. It was like a nightmare, surreal and disturbing. He turned corners and crossed intersections, but nothing changed. There was just the featureless corridor, like an empty vessel in the gut of some gargantuan creature.

He began to sweat, and was seized with the urge to break into a panic-stricken run.

Then, as he rounded a corner, he almost bumped into two of the aliens, who had stopped in the corridor and were exchanging silent gestures. They looked at him with their great round eyes, and one of them broke into weird, whistling speech.

He moved back half a pace, gritted his teeth, and said: "I want to get out. I've got to."

And then, as if it were a dream, the wall dissolved and daylight streamed into the corridor. The substance of the wall simply *shriveled*, as if attacked by acid or strong heat, turning black as the edges recoiled from the great gaping hole. Gas began to bubble up from something that had been thrown into the corridor—a thick, white gas that made his eyes water copiously and caused his head to swim.

There was a crescendo of alarmed whistling, strangled by the gas, and he felt one of the aliens clutch at him as he stumbled, useless wings flapping against the blossoming cloud.

Then strong arms reached out of the murk and grabbed him, just as he himself was about to fall unconscious to the floor. As the gas claimed him he heard only four words, and saw just a fleeting visual image of his rescuer.

"It's all right, Paul...," said the other, the rest of his words lost in a whirl of dizziness, while the same whirl carried away the image of a plastic mask and red, shadowed eyes....

CHAPTER THIRTY-TWO

"Where are we?" asked Paul.

"The foothills of the Andes," replied the robot. "Not too far away from what used to be San Rafael."

Paul looked up at the bleak hillsides, and then back across the plain, following the chalky line that was the rough-hewn road. There was no sign of habitation save a few scattered farms gathered about the road on the eastern horizon.

"Why have we stopped here? It looks to me like the middle of nowhere."

"That's why we've stopped here. The aliens aren't fools. I've kept myself out of sight for three hundred and fifty years by being very discreet, but the La could have located my major installations if they'd only known enough to start looking. Now I've launched an attack on all three of their major cities here and the two in Australia they're going to hit back. By sunset there won't be much of my various bodily parts left."

"Just what are you trying to achieve?"

"I'm trying to drive the La back to where they came from."

"They beat you before."

"They'll beat me again. Even in three hundred and fifty years I haven't been able to co-opt much in the way of firepower, or even to extend myself in the way I would have preferred. The war, such as it is, won't last out the day. It's primarily a matter of timing. The La have been hesitating for a long time over whether or not to abandon Earth. They've recently taken the view that, if they could recruit and use you, they might manage to bring about the desired ideological climate...otherwise not. I'm just tipping the balance."

Paul stared at the robot for a few moments, then opened the door of the car, and stepped out on to the loose stone of the roadside. They had been travelling for more than two hours, but for most of that time Paul had been in the back of the vehicle recovering from the effects of the gas. His eyes were still red and watery, and he felt a powerful thirst.

He stepped from the road on to the verge, where the grass was dry and parched after a long summer. He sat down and looked back at the car: a sleek machine with a plastic body, which moved almost silently. The robot got out and walked around it to join him.

"I'll bet it has an organic engine," said Paul.

"Not the engine," replied the robot. "But it has an artificial nervous system and a certain amount of synthetic musculature."

"Did you steal it?"

"In a manner of speaking."

"Do you have anything to drink?"

The robot pressed something at the back of the car, and the inevitable aperture opened to give access to the boot. He took out a plastic bottle and threw it to Paul. It was water, and Paul drank thankfully. Then he put the bottle down and said: "Why?"

"Why what?"

"Why attack the aliens? Why pull me out of their city? I realize that your behavior is entirely consistent, but I don't see the motivation."

"To put the harshest interpretation on it, I want the aliens to leave Earth because I want it for myself."

"What use is it to you?"

"It interests me."

"Is that all?"

"Should there be anything more? It's crudely put, but in the end, that's what it comes down to."

"And me?"

"You interest me too."

"Suppose the La destroy you? What becomes of your interests then?"

"They won't. That's the mistake they made before. They destroyed the orbital defense systems, and they destroyed the major coordinating installation on the surface, but they couldn't destroy *me*. I'm not limited to any one location, a mechanical brain to hold my mechanical mind. I can make machines capable of coding for my entire personality, and pack them into canisters no bigger than that water bottle. I can install those canisters in cars, or in telephone exchanges, or in robots, or in any damn thing at all. I can switch myself off, temporarily. I can isolate my faculties and link them up again. I made provision for the possibility of defeat in 2119, and I've made provision again now. My personality is safe, and it has legs and hands, all ready to re-emerge from hiding at some future state and set about the task of building me more bodies, more limbs, more brains. I'm like the Hydra, Paul; whenever one head is cut off, two more grow. I *could* be killed, but in practical terms I'm immortal and invulnerable."

"And you want to play god—with Earth as your plaything."

"Not exactly. If I were a god, perhaps I wouldn't need to play. It's because I'm not that I need you. I'm not omniscient, nor omnipotent. I should like to know more about the possibilities that the universe holds, for itself, and for me. Earth presents me with a unique opportunity. I would like to observe the outcome of what has happened here. I could not do that if the La were permitted to subvert the experiment before it really begins."

"Experiment?"

"Not in the sense that the conditions were contrived—this is one of nature's experiments. But I am curious, and I would like to see it run its course."

"You mean the time-jumping faculty?"

"Yes."

"Who built you?"

"Another race, a long way from here, a long time ago."

"One of the races that the La found?"

"The La found traces only. The species that built me has been extinct for a long time. Several million years, in fact."

"And for several million years you've been wandering through the galaxy—in search of a plaything?"

"For most of the time I was, as it were, unconscious," replied the machine. "I have lived, in the sense of being awake and alert, through only a fraction of that time...just as you have lived five hundred years but only experienced twenty years and a few odd days. We have a certain amount in common, you and I."

"The difference is that you seem to have no choice," observed Paul. "You're headed for the distant future come what may—your pilgrimage to the end of time is already built into you. But I had a choice. I could have chosen an ordinary life. And even if I *do* embark upon a journey through time, I'm still going to die in the end."

"I can die," said the robot. "It is not altogether necessary that I only switch myself off temporarily. It would be simple enough to blot out my consciousness forever. It might come to that, eventually...when there is nothing more that attracts my interest and my involvement."

"I suppose that's one of the endearing things about this particular experiment," said Paul, harshly. "It will engage your attention for a long time—occupy you for the next few million years."

"Perhaps," replied the mellifluous voice, calmly.

"Until you get bored and wander away into deep space. And where does that leave us? For the sake of this passing interest, you've tried to close off every other option the human race might have had. Doesn't that strike you as being a little high-handed? I know little enough about the La, but there was surely a possibility that their plan for the future of mankind was the right one, and that without their aid, there's nothing facing us except eventual extinction—even if some of us can run away through time, in a desperate attempt to escape it. You're trying to commit us to a quest that has no conceivable end, and I still don't see *why*."

"Perhaps," said the machine, "it is simple loneliness. Who else but you can keep me company through a million years and more?"

"Build another machine. You have the knowledge and the means. Build a whole race of robots, in your own image, and play with them until all the stars fade. You never had to interfere in *our* affairs. Had you not begun a war to win Earth for yourself, the La would have arrived peacefully. Had you not decided to renew that war today, they might have secured the future of the human race. You don't need Earth, or any world that's already inhabited. You have the time and the equipment to begin your own game of creation."

"If I were to build another machine," replied the robot, quietly, "it would only be part of me. I could design a brain for it, and program that brain with any persona that it could possibly contain, but it would remain, in some essential sense, me. That isn't what I need."

"You mean that it isn't what you want."

"If you wish."

There was a pause. Paul ran his fingers through the grass, and watched a train of tiny ants marching over the baked ground. He rubbed his eyes tiredly.

"How did you know that I'd returned?" he asked. "I didn't notice that the La had any telephones to tap."

"I knew when you would awaken. I always have. Around the spacetime lesions there is a certain tension. There are measurements that can be made, which reveal the duration of the lesion almost to the hour...sometimes to the minute. The La have not bothered to study the phenomenon so closely—it is peripheral to their interests, and they can be quite obsessive in narrowing down their field of attention. I would have reached you at the prison if it were not for the fact that the detection systems they have there are rather too sophisticated to be cheated."

"How did *they* reach me so quickly?"

"Hadan's ornithopter was in the region. There are still people in the northern hemisphere—a few thousand, mostly gathered in the north-western corner of the old United States. They suffer more than most from the dereliction of the environment, and still have to cope with fallout occasionally. The La have no base up there, but they maintain contact. There are still a lot of jumpers in the region as well, and the La and their collaborators like to keep some kind of score."

"What have you got against the La? Is it just the fact that they're your rivals for control of Earth, or is there something more?"

"They have no future."

"No future! They're technologically capable, spread across dozens of habitable worlds...how can they have no future?"

"They're in a state of historical crisis. It's evident in what's happened since they came here. The number of their own kind who've defected to the cults is greater than they care to think. They're losing faith in their philosophy, becoming dissatisfied with its perspectives and its prescriptions. Their period of expansion is over, not because there's no more of the galaxy to explore, but simply because they don't find many surprises any more. Their mythological schema was devised in other days, and now it's out of date.

"They expected to find rather more second-phase life than they have, and rather more symbiosis than they have. They know now, at least subconsciously, that their kind of life isn't the dominant one within the galaxy. They know now that the evolution of third-phase life from second-phase is possible, and in the cosmic time-scale, anything that's possible is more-or-less inevitable. The philosophy of symbiosis is no longer fulfilling all their needs in terms of setting goals and providing a viable self-image. They're frustrated—when there's no pressure of necessity on a species, it has to invent pressures and ambitions to direct its efforts and maintain the illusion of purpose.

"The ambitions of the La are no longer adequate to sustain that illusion, and in any case, familiarity has rendered them contemptible so far as a great many of their own kind are concerned. The La aren't immune to change, and their empire will decay into dust as certainly as any other empire, for all its symbiotic relationships and its governance of a thousand stars. You can outlive their entire species, Paul—if you want to."

There was a barely-perceptible hum in the air. It was just sufficient to catch Paul's attention and make his eyes scan the eastern horizon. The day was not entirely clear, and there was something of a haze, but he had no difficulty in picking out the fluttering shapes in the sky. At this range they looked absurdly similar to flying pineapples.

"They've located us," said the robot, quickly. "It's me they want to destroy—they won't hurt you. Go due west—the road will take you to where you need to go. Go quickly. I'll go to meet them. They can't track you on the ground the way they can track me. If they get too close to you, hide!"

The robot rounded the car and jerked open the door: a real door, not an aperture, because it had to be rigid and it had to contain a window.

Paul watched, uncertainly, as the robot started the engine. He reached out for the other door, but hesitated. While he hesitated the robot threw the car into gear and jerked it into a tight turn. As it whirred away down the slope, throwing up white dust from its rear wheels, Paul murmured: "The road will take me to where I need to go." He wished, briefly, that he knew where he needed to go.

He stood still, watching the car, until it reached the plain and began to accelerate. The flying-machines were still some way off, but they were descending; the car had been seen. Before they could reach it, the car exploded in a ball of flame. Paul felt the shock-wave, although the explosion was several miles away. He knew that the car had not been struck by a missile. The robot was expendable, and had destroyed itself. Whether the aliens would follow the road, looking for him, he did not know and could not really bring himself to care.

Tiredly, he turned west and began to follow the road.

CHAPTER THIRTY-THREE

Evening found Paul very tired, his feet bleeding as he made his way along the roadside. The ornithopters had not followed him into the hills, but whether it was because the La did not know what had happened to him or did not care he was not certain. He met no people and no vehicles.

At first he was hot, but as the sun dipped before him, often obscured by the ridges of the hills, he grew increasingly cold. The light shirt and trousers were designed to protect modesty rather than to secure the body against the vicissitudes of the environment. There was a wind, which picked up as the light dimmed, and which carried dust from the barren roadway into his eyes, which were already predisposed to aching and watering.

The land to either side of the road was for the most part derelict, with most of its topsoil gone and only sparse grass to bind what was left. There was some loose scrub, but few trees. The more distant mountains seemed much more verdant, but most of their color was the same frail grass, and the whole region was little better than semi-desert. There were no animals and few birds. There was no way to tell whether it had been like this for centuries or for millennia.

As dusk approached the green of the mountains seemed to Paul to be dull and unhealthy. There might have been colored blossom on the bushes, but there was nothing. It was easy to imagine that the world was dying.

His gaze was caught by something that lay beside the road

ahead: something that flared briefly red as it caught the waning rays of the setting sun. He could not make out its shape at first, but quickly realized what it must be.

It was a girl, perhaps sixteen or even less: an Indian, to judge by the cast of her features. She lay beside the road as if, like Paul, she had been walking toward some distant and unreachable destination when exhaustion claimed her and laid her out on the ground in an ungainly heap. She had rolled half on to her back to look up at the sky, and seemed to be lying awkwardly. The clothes had already rotted from her torso, but the remnants of her trousers were still there.

Paul ran his fingers over the slick surface of her arm, and then touched her frozen face, feeling the needle-points of her eyelashes, which drew blood from his fingertips in little beads, leaving the faintest of stinging sensations. Apparently, she had been there for months—perhaps years. She would not awaken, in all probability, within the span of what would have been her lifetime.

What would she wake up to now? he wondered. A road that had crumbled, and had been partly reclaimed by the grass, the land having advanced one stage further in its slow regression to desert...the same sun, the same stars, the same exhaustion, the same predicament.

She might well die where she lay, beside the road with no one to find or help her. She might wake to the fierce cold of winter night, or to the deluge of the rainy season. In the meantime, she was dreaming a dream that might kill her, or leave her half-mad when it finally spat her out into mundane time and space. She was dreaming of jagged rocks, of caustic sand blown by a terrible wind, and of *slithering*....

Paul could not help himself shivering. His heart accelerated a little.

It's a cruel joke, he thought. *It's not a miracle, or a means of escape, or a way that the inhabitants of another dimension can fish for human bodies and souls to feed upon. It's just a practical joke, a trick of stupid fate.*

He sat down beside the girl, too tired to go on, and massaged his bleeding feet.

As darkness fell he stared up at the glimmering stars, wondering whether there was anything left for him to do but follow the girl's example and hurl himself once more into the void of time, with nothing but the most forlorn of hopes that there might ever be anything to wake up to.

Then he heard the engine—the throaty growl of an old truck—and saw the headlights coming along the road, curving round the angle of a hillside from the west. He did not know whether to hide or to reveal himself. The antiquity of the vehicle suggested to him that it was more likely to carry friends than enemies, but there was no logical warrant for the feeling. Indecisive, he stayed where he was, and allowed the headlights to pick him out.

The truck ground to a halt beside him, and the driver leaned across to throw open the passenger door.

"Get in, Paul," said the driver. The voice was harsh and throaty—more like the mechanical voice that Remila had used than the silky tone adopted by the machine. It came from a human throat, though. In the dim light, Paul could see white hair and a white beard, and there was something about the shape of the face, as well as the voice, that seemed familiar.

He stood up, and grasped the handle of the open door.

"Who are you?" he demanded.

The other laughed briefly, and said: "My name's Paul, too."

"Scapelhorn!"

"Get in," said the other. "I'm afraid I've aged a little since last we met, but it seems like only yesterday. I suppose that it seems the same way to you, bearing in mind that in your terms it *was* only yesterday."

Paul raised himself up into the cab of the truck and on to the seat. Scapelhorn put the truck into gear and began backing up to a place where there was room to turn round.

"How did you find me?" asked Paul.

"Phone call. The angels brought me down here after the jump

we all took. I've taken one more since then...but I'm too old to go on. I always knew that. I figured that I'd be better employed setting up some kind of station for jumpers up in the mountains—I told you the plan. I've been there a long time, now. There are a couple of hundred of us, counting the ones who are standing still. We recruit slowly—maybe it will pick up a lot now the war's on again."

"You don't sound surprised."

"I knew the machine was still around. I've seen the robot a few times—the only reason I got the phone working was to communicate with it. I knew what it was going to do."

"And you approved?"

"I don't know. Wasn't much I could do about it if I didn't, except tell the angels, and I wasn't about to do that. The machine helped—and still helps. In the long run, it's going to take over the station."

"What's happening—with the La and the machine?"

"It's pretty fierce in the cities the angels built here. Fireworks everywhere. A lot of the people who live in the city have no particular love for the angels, and some of the angels have no particular love for their own kind. The machine liberated some kind of artificial virus that plays hell with the biotechnology, and the aliens are having the devil of a job fighting it. Whole buildings are seizing up and falling down. The communications systems have been put out of commission, and some machinery's been blown sky high. It's mostly trivial stuff—annoying more than destructive—but the angels don't like being annoyed. They over-react. They've blasted the main centers that were coordinating the machine's operations, and put them out of commission, more or less. But they've been stung, and they won't stop at that."

"What else can they do?"

"Pull up stakes and leave."

"But they must know that that's what the machine wants."

"They won't do it to spite the machine. They'll do it to spite *us*—unless we beg them to stay. Hadan will, I suppose, but they'll demand some kind of mass gesture of good intent, and they're unlikely to get it."

Paul watched the headlights play on the makeshift road for a while, uncertain of the best way to carry on the conversation. Finally, he said: "You haven't changed your mind?"

"About what?"

"About what you said in the prison—about investing in the future of the jumpers and the hope of reaching a regenerated world in order to start again."

"Should I have?"

"The argument you used then was that the old world couldn't be saved—that it was bound to die. Now the La are here that's no longer true, is it?"

"I don't know," replied Scapelhorn.

"But you're doing what you can to set up the same plan—establishing some kind of center for jumpers. Why do that, if you're no longer so sure that Marcangelo's way can't be followed and made to work."

Scapelhorn was silent for a few seconds, and then he sighed. "To tell you the truth, Paul," he said, "I'm old and I'm tired. I've given up making plans for the world. What I'm doing is for me. It's what I want to do. I've got some land to work, I've got a wife—no children of my own but half a dozen with no parents of *their* own. It's a place to live and a place to die, without too much strain. The idea of bringing in the jumpers and making it a way station for them was a kind of excuse, I suppose—a reason for allowing me to do what I wanted to do, without having to feel that I was giving up. After a couple of jumps, I was getting further and further away from anything that meant anything to me, and I guess I was scared. What I'm doing now is, in some sense, going back...not that I was ever a farmer, you understand...just going back to a way of life that seemed comfortable and human.

"I don't know that I should be telling you this, because there's a sense in which I still believe in you, and I still believe that you have to make use of what you can do. I don't want to make you think that it's all pointless...it's just *me*, and the way I am. I always talked big, and talked a lot, but half the time I didn't even listen to what I was saying, let alone stop to think how much I believed it, or exactly *how* I believed it. It's the *how* that matters, do you see—because there's still a sense in which I did and do believe. It's just that the reasons for choosing what I chose to do now seem simpler. I'm not really too worried about trying to justify myself any more."

Paul made no immediate reply. After a long pause, Scapelhorn took up the thread again.

"You see," he said, "it doesn't really matter much to me whether the angels go or stay. I don't care, as long as they want nothing from me. I want to get on with my own affairs. It used to matter a great deal what was happening around me, and what I was part of, but now it doesn't seem to count for much being a part of anything. It's because I'm old, and you shouldn't take any notice. I just lost my guts when my hair turned from black to white. I hope you can stay with us, any way you want to, and if you want to go for the far, far future, I hope you make it, and I hope that station will see you through."

"What about the world?" asked Paul, quietly. "Is it enough simply to leave the people behind, when so many of them are still waiting for the word I couldn't give them in 2119?"

"What can you tell them?"

"I could tell them that there's a station, a place where they can gather before jumping, to stay together instead of being scattered over the whole damn world. Or wouldn't you like that?"

"They want more from you than that. They want more than any human being can give them. You don't owe them anything. They wouldn't thank you for any words you can say, no matter how hard they've prayed for them. It's safer to leave them with the hope—that way you don't expose yourself to their anger when you disappoint them. Let them find their own way."

"How can they find their own way if they won't go until I tell them where to go?"

He felt rather than saw the perfunctory shrug of Scapelhorn's shoulders. They swayed in unison as the truck rounded a tight bend, climbing the face of a mountain at such a speed that the engine groaned with the strain.

"Do you think I could have done what Hadan and Remila wanted me to?" asked Paul. "Could I really have turned the ideological balance in their favor with a few calculated speeches?"

"I don't know," said Scapelhorn. "Maybe. It's hard to say exactly what the angels want—some kind of oath of loyalty, a decision to report for work to begin clearing up the mess. Sure, you could sway the crowd, probably enough to convince them—for today and tomorrow. But for all time? I don't think the human race is equipped for the kind of mutual mindfuck the angels have in mind. On the surface, we can go for it, but deep down—it's not what we *are*, or anything we could really and wholly become. I've never been entirely sure what's in this symbiosis of theirs except us doing what they want us to and thanking them kindly for it. I don't know what things are like on other worlds, but I've seen the angels here. Co-operation for mutual benefit is a wonderful thing, but it's the angels who get to say what's beneficial and what's not—for us as well as for themselves. Call an angel a parasite and he's likely to hurt you for it, but that might be because it's a little closer to the truth than he cares to acknowledge."

"In the whole of Earth's biosphere," said Paul, ruminatively, "it's doubtful whether there's a single relationship that is genuinely symbiotic. Most involve one partner deriving an advantage while the other isn't affected much one way or another, in terms of its actual survival chances. The reasons for applying the term are actually largely ideological."

"It figures," said Scapelhorn dryly.

"But if the La leave Earth, and aren't entirely the potential benefactors that they believe themselves to be anyway, where does that leave us?"

"I don't know," answered the old man. "But has anyone *ever* known?"

"I guess not," Paul replied.

CHAPTER THIRTY-FOUR

Paul looked down from the window of the small hut set high on the mountainside. There were trees growing around the building, which obscured the greater part of his visual field, but through the widest gap he could see much of the cultivated valley a kilometer below, including Scapelhorn's farm-buildings. The fields that lay fallow were already filled with tiny figures—some human, some green and bearing parodies of angel's wings.

"They're still coming," said Scapelhorn. "The road through the hills is alive with them. We can't even supply them with enough water, let alone feed them. They'll destroy this place by their very presence, if they stay more than a day or two. They don't want to cause any trouble—they're perfectly peaceful—but they won't go. They don't know you're up here, and to be honest, they don't seem particularly interested in seeking you out. They're content to wait until you go to them, and they're certain that you will. Some of the angels are going into trance—switching over to photosynthesis—but the humans can't do that."

"Isn't this what you wanted?" asked Paul, with a faint trace of irony. "The world is flocking to your valley. Your few hundred silver statues could become a few thousand overnight. Your way-station for time-travelers would be well and truly established."

"That depends," said Scapelhorn, "on what you're going to say to them. For the time being, they're patient and they're peaceful. But what happens afterwards?"

"Can you get your wife and children to a place of safety?"

Scapelhorn laughed. "Hardly," he said. "The kids are enjoying this as they've enjoyed nothing in their lives. And Maria...I guess she's part of the audience."

"Any further communication from the machine?" asked Paul.

"Not for two days. They didn't get him, though. They're not that good. He's keeping quiet and waiting for the angels to go home to heaven."

"Assuming that they *do* go home."

"They will. The word from the city is that Hadan's begging them to stay, and there have been spontaneous demonstrations from like-minded people in the city, but in the end, the fact that will decide is *this*." He pointed down the slope at the slowly swelling crowd.

"Last time," murmured Paul, "I escaped this. Events moved too quickly, and I never had to face the moment of truth, but this time, there aren't going to be any bombs to let me off the hook. This time, I'm going to have to face them, whatever happens."

"You can still get away," Scapelhorn pointed out. "All it takes is a trick of the mind, and you could be five or six hundred years away from now. They won't wait that long for you."

"I can't do that," said Paul. "In a way, I'm down there with them, waiting to hear what I've got to say, wanting desperately to know what I *could* say. If I run now, there'll be nothing for me to do—ever—but keep on running. I don't want to do that. This time, if I jump again, I want to be sure that I've tidied up behind me, even if only to destroy the mythology that's somehow gathered around my name."

In the cloudless sky, something silvery caught the light of the midday sun, and Paul looked up. It was one of the absurd flying-machines used by the aliens, straight out of the surreal imagination of some nineteenth-century dreamer. Try as he might, Paul still couldn't quite believe in it. It came closer, and hovered over the valley, the wings beating furiously to hold it steady in the air.

For a moment, Paul felt fearful, wondering whether this was

Hadan and the leaders of the Earthly La, come to extract some kind of vengeance for the machine's futile attack on their positions, but then the vehicle began to sink, very slowly, and settled close to the house.

Paul watched its occupants descend from the belly of the oval. Even at this distance he could see that three were green and one was human. The human had dark skin and graying hair.

"Hadan," muttered Scapelhorn.

"Even the mighty come to listen to the wise," said Paul, sarcastically. "If the Emperor of Rome had only known, don't you think he would have wanted a ringside seat for the sermon on the mount?"

They watched Hadan and one of the La go into the house.

"Maria will tell them we're here," said Scapelhorn. "They're going to make one last attempt to convince you. Hadan must be more persuasive than I thought—or the La more generous."

A few minutes passed before Hadan and the alien re-emerged, and returned to the flying-machine. It fluttered up into the air again, but its pilot didn't bother to gain much height. With a strange, uncertain action it skimmed the treetops, bobbing up the mountainside in the grip of a wayward updraught, in order to set down again in the small clearing before the cabin door.

This time, only Hadan and one of the aliens came out of the egg. The alien was wearing a strange kind of harness, and carrying a device that looked like a bizarre musical instrument.

"A voice-box," muttered Scapelhorn. "It's not often they condescend. Usually they take the view that they know our language and we know theirs, and that's the way it has to be in order that any meaningful communication can take place. Ordinarily, they'd only talk to someone who didn't understand their chirping through the medium of an interpreter."

Scapelhorn moved to the door of the cabin and opened it to let Hadan and the alien pass through it. Paul remained standing where he was, at the window, his gaze taking in the flying-machine and the crowd that was still gathering, still patiently waiting.

"We have come to bring you back to the city," said Hadan, "if you will come."

Paul turned to look at them both. To the alien, he said: "Are you Remila?"

"I am Remila," confirmed a metallic voice, originating from a diaphragm set somewhere in the device set upon the alien's chest and supported by his arms.

It was strange, Paul thought, how mechanical the alien sounded by comparison with the machine. The La could have made themselves human voices as sweet and as silky as the machine's, but they chose not to. Instead they emphasized the fact that, in order to mimic the human tongue, they needed to have recourse to mechanical aids—contrary, no doubt, to the true spirit of symbiosis.

"I'm not coming back with you," said Paul, flatly.

"With your support," said the alien, "we can govern this world. We can give it a future within the expanding realm of symbiosis—a purpose, and a means to fulfill the purpose. You must help us to do that."

"What about the machine?"

"It has been destroyed."

"You know that's not true. You might have destroyed most of its bodies, but it has the means to protect itself against annihilation. You'll never be able to destroy it, and it will return again and again to fight you."

"It is no more than a minor nuisance. If you were to ally yourself with us...."

"According to the machine," Paul interposed, "the La don't have the future that you're promising us. The machine claims that you'll be extinct in a few hundred million years. Your empire can't last forever, and is already beginning to show the signs of strain."

There was no way to tell what effect that statement had on Remila, but Hadan scowled. His anger seemed to be about to spill out in a torrent of words, but Remila motioned him to be silent.

"The machine does not understand," the alien said. "It is an engine of war, and has never ceased to think or to function as an engine of war. The habits of competition and predation are programmed into it, and it cannot transcend these concepts and their world-view. Our empire cannot die; it is the seed of the cosmic mind itself, the first element in the real evolution of life within the universe. Without the La, there would be no hope for any sentient species."

"Isn't it possible that you're being just a little chauvinistic?" asked Paul.

"You do not understand. You must learn. You must not speak now to the people assembled below to hear your words, because you would speak as an ignorant child. You know nothing of our ways and little of our philosophy. Until you have learned to believe us, your words can only be meaningless."

Paul looked at Hadan. "Is that what *you* believe?" he asked.

"What Remila says is true," insisted Hadan. "Until you truly understand what is at stake here you are dangerous. You could destroy the only hope which men have of restoring their world to health, of finding a purpose in the scheme of things. If we are abandoned by the La we will die alone, having achieved nothing, having *been* nothing."

All metascience, thought Paul. *Pure commitment, desperate and wholehearted. But what have I to offer instead?* "I don't want to play god," he said. "And I don't want to become a pawn in *your* game of creation. I don't think it's for you *or* for the machine to make decisions on the part of humankind, because humankind consists of people who can make their own decisions. I don't want to plan the future of Earth or the future of life in the galaxy or the universe, because I know full well that nobody can. The only thing that any one of us—or any group of us—can really decide is what to do with ourselves. We need beliefs that let us feel that what we're doing has some significance in a greater context, but it would be a dangerous delusion to persuades ourselves that we can dictate to that greater context the pattern it should have.

"In the final analysis, we know very little indeed about the cosmos that surrounds us, and never can know more than a very little. No matter how much of spacetime we explore, we can investigate no more than the tiniest fraction of the whole, and we have no logical warrant for the principle of mediocrity by which we persuade ourselves that what we know about the tiny fraction will serve to inform us adequately about the whole. When we go beyond what we really do know we enter a realm of pure speculation that can never be more than pure speculation. We *need* to do that—we can't avoid the deployment of our imagination in that fashion—but we have no god-given right to be *right*, and we can never claim truth for what we only imagine.

"I refuse to try to impose my beliefs and my imaginings on the world at large. When I decide what to do, I decide for myself, for reasons that are personal. No one else can have those reasons, and it's not for me to tell anyone else to do as I do. Whatever anyone else does is for their own reasons, even if the only decision they make is to alienate their own prerogatives by submitting themselves to an ideology or imitating someone else. The way that people use my words and my example is up to them, and I'm not going to try to persuade them to take any course of action in the name of any metascientific mythology.

"I don't know whether you still have any record of the speeches I made in 1992, but if you have, you'll find that I wasn't trying to sell any particular set of beliefs. What I was trying to sell was freedom—freedom to believe whatever suited the situation. What I preached was anarchy of faith and an end to metascientific tyrannies. It seems that I was only partly successful—I helped people to free themselves from their old beliefs, but left them wanting, not knowing where to turn for new ones, not knowing how to invent. I underestimated the extent to which people are afraid of their own creativity. That's why people were always waiting for me to say something more—and are still waiting, apparently, after four hundred and eighty years.

"The sad fact is that I have nothing more to say, that there *is* nothing more to say. So you see, there was never any hope of your recruiting me to the service of your own particular tyranny of belief. I don't know whether you're right or wrong, and I can't predict what the consequences of my supporting you might be. I can't tell whether the human race—or any sentient races anywhere—has any future, and nor can anyone else. We have to live our lives in the expectation of *some* kind of future, and we have to believe in it with all the passion we can muster, but we can never know that it's true.

"That, in the final analysis, is what I have to tell people—that it's really up to them to find their own expectations, and up to them to decide whether to borrow, steal or invent them. I won't try to steal that responsibility from them, on your behalf or on anyone else's."

The silence that followed was broken, eventually, by Gelert Hadan.

"We should have killed you," he said. "Perhaps, even now, it's not too late."

"Yes it is," replied Paul, calmly. "It always was too late. Remila doesn't want to kill me—he wants to leave me here to live with the consequences of my decision. He thinks that time will prove him right and deliver me into a private hell of anguish and regret. Isn't that right, Remila?"

The voice-box made a peculiar sound that was probably a tremor in the finger that controlled one of the keys.

"There will be no killing," said the alien. "We are not predators. Where there is no hope for symbiosis, we simply let well alone. We kill only to defend ourselves. We will withdraw from this world before winter."

The anger that was seething in Hadan finally burst the bounds of his self-control. He stepped forward to strike Paul across the face. Paul made no move to grab his arm or to avoid the blow, but it never fell. Scapelhorn's voice cut across the room like a whiplash, saying: "Stop!"

Hadan turned, to see the old man holding an ancient shotgun, its double barrel pointed at his chest. He stopped, as if frozen, and then slowly relaxed. There were small tears in the corners of his eyes. He turned to face Remila. "You can't leave me here," he whispered. "You have to take me with you...all of us. We trusted you."

"I am deeply sorry," said the alien, "but it is not possible. We would take you if we could, and all of your race who are genuinely capable of symbiosis, just as we must leave behind all those of our race who have proved that they cannot, but there is no way that humans could survive the journey across the interstellar void. Neither in body or in mind are you fitted for such a journey. You must stay here, and live your life as best you can."

Remila turned then. and made as if to leave, but, as if on impulse, he turned back to address Paul one last time. "You are mistaken," he said, "if you think you can stand apart. There is no neutral ground between life and death. To refuse a decision is itself a decision and a commitment, and you cannot so easily renounce your role in this affair. You say that you cannot predict the future of your world, but I can. That future is third-phase life, and the extinction not only of your species but of all possibility that Earth could ever again give rise to intelligent life. You have added one more world to the living blight which threatens the universe with mindlessness."

"Perhaps," said Paul, without animosity, "you have failed in your imagination to envisage fourth-phase life, and fifth and sixth, and all the possible phases that will render your empire and its faith into caustic dust."

"We cannot deal with the unimaginable," retorted the metallic voice.

The alien turned abruptly on his heel and went out into the cool, clean air.

"No, indeed," murmured Paul, "but we'd be fools to think, because of that, that the universe is necessarily imaginable."

An extract from *Science and Metascience*, by Paul Heisenberg

If we are to build an appropriate metascientific context upon and around our contemporary scientific knowledge, it is unlikely that we shall find much that is useful in the cosmologies and theologies of the ancient religious systems. Our modem creation myths are prescribed in some detail by the findings of radio-astronomers, which leave the creative imagination far less room to maneuver than it enjoyed even in the nineteenth century. Our notion of the status of human beings within the Earthly scheme of life has been largely determined by discoveries in genetics and paleontology, and the ambitions of early religious teachers in specifying a special creation and a special destiny for the human race now seem to be the products of an absurd vanity. Now, when we attempt to discover the significance of our own existence in the contemplation of the universe that contains us, we are constrained to be humble. There is a considerable series of difficulties facing the speculator who wishes to save the notion of a special destiny.

There is no area of science as attractive to metascientific embellishment as evolutionary biology. This is due in part to its special relevance to the image that we have of ourselves, but we should not overlook the fact that the nature of the inquiry lends itself to the extensive generation of hypotheses that are essentially untestable. The substance of the science is concerned with events in the past, which cannot be observed, let alone manipulated.

All that we know about the past—all that we *can* know about it—is inferred from its relics. Past events that extended no consequential traces into the present are forever hidden, exiled to the realms of metascientific speculation. Because the record of relics is so very sparse, the past that we reconstruct is shadowy and far from complete, and metascientific speculations must be summoned prolifically if we are to compose any kind of coherent image of the history of life on Earth. Part of the story can only be filled in by speculation based on what we know to be possible, without any reference to physical evidence at all, for in the pre-Cambrian rocks we find a virtual absence of information.

There is an unfortunate irony in the fact that the science which we find most intensely and personally interesting is one in which our knowledge has few firm foundation stones. As metascientists, however, we can take advantage of this situation, using the speculative opportunities thus generated. No other realm of the imagination offers such freedom and such rewards. It is for these reasons that there has been, ever since its first explication, a series of attempts to build a set of metascientific speculations upon the theory of evolution by natural selection, which might fill in the imaginative space left vacant by its discoveries and permitted by its implications. Henri Bergson and Pierre Teilhard de Chardin made significant attempts in the realm of formal philosophy, while H. G. Wells and Olaf Stapledon gave their speculations literary form. The value of these endeavors should not be underestimated. They were not generated by arbitrary whims, but by the force of necessity.

All attempts to discover a direction and a purpose in the evolution of life on Earth have been handicapped by the fact that this particular scientific discipline had to be purged of a certain kind of teleological thinking that turned out to be invalid. Darwinian theory had to establish itself not only in the fact of theological commitments, but also against the much more subtle opposition of prevailing scientific attitudes deriving from the work of earlier theorists, including the Chevalier de Lamarck and Charles Darwin's grandfather Erasmus. Darwin's theory of natural selection, as modified by the introduction of Mendelian genetic theory and Weismannian mutational theory, was missing the notions of purpose and improvement that had been central to earlier theories.

The notion of environmental selection between individuals modified by small random changes killed the supposition that there was any predetermined pattern in evolution, which merely had to unfold over the eons to give rise to eventual perfection.

The evolution of "higher" forms of life and the increasing complexity of Earth's life-systems were seen to be by-products of the interaction between genetic mutation and the competition of whole organisms for resources. Lamarck's nation that environmental change might be the result of *effort* on the part of the individual organism was abandoned, and that had considerable implications for hypotheses regarding the moral perfectibility of humankind and the extent to which human beings might influence the future of their descendant species.

These implications of Darwinian theory created a demand in the marketplace of ideas for a metascientific system that would re-establish not only the role but also the *power* of purposive decision in man's evolutionary situation. Not only individuals, but whole cultures, have reintroduced variants of neo-Lamarckian philosophy into their evolutionary thought. These have been strongly resisted by representatives of Darwinian orthodoxy as being without foundation in empirical evidence. It is, in fact, true that these speculations belong to the realm of metascience rather than that of empirical science, but they should not be entirely despised on that account, and we should be prepared to recognize the force of the need that generates them. The antagonism between the scientific and metascientific aspects of evolutionary philosophy is historical in origin and is not logically necessary. Orthodox evolutionary theory still leaves sufficient imaginative space for speculation regarding the direction of evolution, and for the attribution of a constructive role for the power of human purposive decisions, provided that these speculations include no empirical claims regarding quasi-Lamarckian genetic systems.

The consequence of this argument is the conclusion that attempts to reintroduce into evolutionary philosophy the notion of evolutionary "goals" are not illegitimate, provided that we recognize that these goals are metascientific constructs designed to give us confidence in our present actions, not prophecies of an inevitable future. We can and must speculate freely about the possible future of humankind, and the more alternatives we can imagine, the more will be the possible meanings we might attribute to our present decisions and predicaments. Only by so doing can we hope to escape from the existential trap threatening us all: the conviction of our utter insignificance and the hopelessness of our situation. We have to overcome that sense of meaninglessness, and the means to do it are provided by our creativity rather than by our expectations of scientific discovery. We must be prepared to accept that responsibility because, in today's world, we can no longer hope to avoid it.

PART FOUR
PARADISE LOST

CHAPTER THIRTY-FIVE

A million years is not a long time, in evolutionary terms, but rates of evolution can vary considerably from the "normal" horotelic mode. The career of *Homo sapiens* resulted in drastic changes in the environments available to life on Earth, while the temporary invasion of the La resulted in the introduction of a whole new gene-system. These two factors stepped up the rate of evolution not just by one gear but by two, throwing the rate of turnover in the various specific gene pools into a hypert-achytelic mode. A regime of rapid evolutionary change never hitherto realized on Earth's surface was instituted in the wake of the desertion of Earth by the aliens.

The new regime facilitated changes of a genuinely funda-mental nature, resulting in the emergence of new cell types and new kinds of cell interaction. The evolutionary entity that had held unchallenged dominion over Earth for nearly two billion years, the eukaryot cell, was finally faced with new competi-tion. Similarly, the system of genetic information-exchange, sexual reproduction, which had sufficed for the purposes of such entities, when they required any such system, was also faced with competition.

Out of the poisoned areas of Earth's surface—the regions destroyed by radioactivity and chemical pollution—came new living entities shaped by a fiercer regime of selection than had pertained even to the primordial environment. In the lands thus rendered derelict, life based on eukaryot cells could not survive indefinitely. Animal life died out in such regions very quickly—

in a matter of centuries—after a brief period of mutational extravagance. Plant life, more amenable to mutational change and less dependent on the complexities of meiotic chromosome-reassortment, clung to the land for thousands of years and tens of thousands, but steadily declined as the more complex species were eliminated one by one.

In their dying, these plant species provided a new biotic environment, in which primitive saprophytes that could nourish themselves only on dead flesh thrived and multiplied, but the situation was one that could not endure for long. With no new burgeoning of primary production, the saprophytes were faced with dwindling resources, and they too were in the grip of the slow death that sustained them. All life based on complex walled cells replete with membranes and organelles became slowly extinct, leaving only the most primitive life-forms to thrive on the organic humus—the primitive, membraneless prokaryot cells that had enjoyed sole possession of the Earth during the earliest eons of life's evolution. It was from these cells—from the bacteria and the most primitive of the protists, and from the entities that were not even cells, like viruses and microspheres—that the new order was born.

Bacteria are capable of immensely prolific reproduction, and survive selective regimes that kill anything more complex. In the debris of the declining life-system, the bacteria were unconquerable. They changed in themselves generation by generation, but they survived such change easily. Bacteriophage viruses thrived along with them, and the metamorphoses of the hosts were matched by the metamorphoses of the parasites. From this regime of rapidly-changing commensalism came new forms of commensalism.

The new life did not emerge out of the old by mutation, natural selection and lineal descent, as all the entities in the ancient life-system had descended from the earliest eukaryot cells, and those cells from prokaryot ancestors. The new organisms arose by symbiosis and symbiotic synthesis, by the fusion of genetic systems into super-systems whose main property was the ability to absorb and maintain yet more systems and thus acquire protean hyper-adaptability.

The simplest cell of all in the ancient life-system was prokaryot in kind, carrying a single chromosome—a self-replicating system of genes coding for the building of an elementary cell. Parasitic upon these systems were viruses, which attached themselves to the bacterial chromosome so that as the bacterium made more bacteria it also made more viruses, and sometimes subverting the manufacturing capability of the cell, so that it made viruses *instead* of more bacteria, dismantling itself to provide the raw material. Increasing complexity within this system consisted in adding more genes to the basic chromosome, and more chromosomes, to code first for more elaborate individual cells, and later for extremely elaborate multicellular reproductive machines. The new life-system, however, developed its complexity in a different way, by increasing *versatility*. The number of chromosomes in the new organisms multiplied not so that more elaborate engines of reproduction might be built, but instead so that the individual cell could vastly increase its adaptability as an individual. The result was a type of cell that did not need complex reproductive strategies, because it was itself immortal, and which could extend itself not by replication but by infinite growth as a coenocyte.

In these organisms there was potential for Earth to be reborn. It was not long—perhaps a few hundred thousand years—before the coenocytes discovered the utility of tissue-differentiation and membrane-packaging and began to make full use of their protean potential, but they remained, essentially, things that grew rather than things that replicated themselves, and even as they divided their bodies into millions of different parts they remained single individuals. When they met cells of the ancient type, they simply absorbed them into the whole. When they met one another, they absorbed one another.

The adaptability that had proved competent to deal with the selective regime of hard radiation was far more than competent to deal with the regions of Earth that had not been so despoiled.

The new life came out of the lands that had given it birth, and began to devour the entire life-system of Earth. It did so unhurriedly, having all the time in the world to explore its possibilities. Eventually, it would dominate the surface of Earth more completely than the ancient system could ever have done, although it would be a dominion of a very different kind from that achieved by the older system.

In the old biocosm there had been individuals, and thus competition between individuals, and thus complex behavioural strategies, and thus—ultimately—intelligence. In the new biocosm there were no individuals, but only life. There was no competition, save for that between the system and the vicissitudes of its environment. There was no behavioral strategy, save for that of the system as a whole, which was simply to survive and to grow, not to reproduce. There was no conceivable need for the evolution of intelligence.

And thus it was that third-phase life assumed command of the planet called Earth.

CHAPTER THIRTY-SIX

He huddled into the crack in the bare red rock, hiding his eyes from the wind-driven sand. The motes that clung to his skin seemed to grip his flesh and to stick to one another, forming a crystal patina as if they were living things. On his exposed arm and shoulder the sand collected until it formed a kind of outer tegument—a jeweled sheath that would have been welcome if it had protected his skin, but which somehow did not.

The wind screamed as it crossed the butte, searching for him, desperate to pluck him from his poor shelter, to tumble him over the bare rock, to break his bones, to cover him with silica until he was nothing but a human silhouette in crystal scale.

From the wind, though, he could hide. The wind was only the hot air which surrounded him. The *other* force was inside him, sucking from within, a parasite in his very soul that was trying to work its metamorphic magic in the essence of his being. He could feel his flesh creeping as though it were softening into viscous liquid. He could feel the sluggish tide in his fluids, always rising in his belly.

He forced himself to look up, forced his eyes open, exposing their tenderness to the hostility of the maddened wind. He forced himself to look into the infinite blue deep that was the sky, searching for the fugitive vision that once had guided him towards the horizon.

He found it: a shifting pattern, cut out of vapor or of pure light; a mirage created by refraction in the layers of the atmosphere. It was never there for more than a few moments, and now, as he tried to fix his attention upon it, it dissolved. He had never managed to perceive shape in it, attribute any meaning to it.

He closed his eyes and bowed his head, knowing that it would take tantalizing advantage of his surrender to reformulate itself.

He knew that he must not stay in the crevice. Even while he rested, the desert was changing. The crack was slowly closing, forcing him out on threat of enclosure and permanent imprisonment. He had to expose himself once more on the scorching face of the ragged rock-formation, where the wind would harry him and scratch him with its arrows of sand. He pulled himself free and began to stagger across the plain.

All around him was a forest of dendritic shapes, like tropical corals left high and dry by an ocean that had evaporated or drained away. In the branches, little points of light were dancing, like the ghosts of tiny fish, as if the desert were dreaming of the time when it had been an ocean bed. Glittering salts had crystallized out on the combs and stems in stratified layers, and where the dendrites were scarred or the branches broken off it was possible to see multicolored growth-rings that testified to the passage not of years but of eons.

Sometimes the fingers of the coral limbs reached for him as he passed close by, but they never brushed his skin.

The sun stood still in the sky, denying him the night.

The sand swam about his body in loose fluid plates, trying to link up and to gather particles enough to turn him into a crystalline statue: one more twisted entity among the dendrite corals, spawning colored growth-rings eternally.

Deep inside him he felt the slithering sensation, the echo of ophidian existence that tried perpetually to assert itself within his mind, fought to fuse his legs together and make him squirm and slither his way across the rock, sidewinding without regard for pain or time or will...living by means of poison fangs and the reflexive strike.

He dared not scream lest the sound blot out his consciousness and send his mind recoiling back into reptilian calm.

Time expelled him, again and again and again; but always he returned to live in his dream of hell through all eternity, while the world that had given him birth was born again as a vengeful organism that sought, like the desert, to dissolve him and smear his identity across the whole surface of creation.

CHAPTER THIRTY-SEVEN

The machine, too, was third-phase life of a kind. He, too, grew by absorption, without there being any theoretical limit to his total size. He was immortal, and did not replicate himself to produce other entities with their own separate individuality. Everything he made remained part of himself. In only one respect was he unlike the third-phase life that evolved on Earth and countless other worlds: he was not mindless. His mind, however, was a byproduct of his ontogeny, and he had never ceased to feel that it was, perhaps, a superfluity and an incongruity, inappropriate to his mode of existence. Paradoxically, that core of self-doubt was the source of all his motivation. It was the one aspect of his being that sustained his identity against the haunting fear of purposelessness.

When the La abandoned Earth, leaving behind the disaffected members of their own species, they put the planet into quarantine, placing a network of defenses in orbit around it far more elaborate than the one mounted by the machine before they came. This network had a dual function: to keep other visitors away from Earth, and to confine that which was already on the planet's surface, including the machine. The machine was untroubled by this, because he knew that in time, after a few hundred thousand years, he would be able to subvert those defences, and incorporate them into himself.

In the meantime, there was much to be done in his inherited kingdom, the surface of the Earth.

Parts of him began the erection of a series of gigantic domes in the foothills of the Argentinian Andes. The first enclosed the valley where Scapelhorn and his allies, and their descendants, lived throughout the third and fourth millennia.

The immediate purpose of the dome was to seal off a controlled environment, free from fallout and plague, in order to preserve the human colony. In the long-term, it would provide an enclave against the advance of third-phase life. Underneath the domes, the old Earth could be maintained for the time-travelers, and for the machine. The plates of the dome were made of glass, the interstices of metal, and both the glass and the metal were equipped with mechanical nerve-nets, which made them part of the body of the machine.

The building of the domes took thirteen thousand years, and by the time the last of them was finished there were no humans living an ordinary life beneath the first. Scapelhorn's community, despite being protected, had never thrived. The mutational load built up in the genes during the centuries that followed the atomic wars was too great, and the birth-rate never matched the death-rate, in spite of all that the machine could do in providing a healthy environment. With the exception of the time-travelers, the human race became extinct while the domes were under construction.

While parts of him built the domes, other parts of the machine went far and wide across the face of the Earth, some scavenging for the materials he needed in order to grow and build factories to provide the means for his future growth, and others searching for the human-shaped lesions left by the time-jumpers. Over the first few centuries, he built a catalogue of such lesions, and measured them all, to estimate the time that each time-jumper would return. By the time the third millennium began, no time-traveler emerged without a robot to meet him.

Some, of course, did not return at all. Many returned only to die, because of the poisons and mutations that were already incorporated into their being, but some were healthy, and these he invited to the Andean valleys and the domes. Only a few refused—and they went on through time to their inevitable deaths.

By the end of the eighth millennium, all the remaining jumpers were gathered into his enclave. There he attended to their needs every time they awoke. As time went by, some died, some vanished and some decided to live out their lives in ordinary time. Once there were no other humans under the domes, however, very few decided to live mundane lives until they were very old. Most spent only a few days eating, sleeping and breathing at each awakening, and most became increasingly parsimonious with their days as they went further into the future.

Every jumper was able to leap further each time he or she went into stasis. At first, the increases were relatively small and apparently arbitrary, but a pattern began to emerge. For a while, the elapsed time of each jump increased according to an exponential curve. Then the curve began to fall back from ever-increasing steepness, until the rate of increase was steady.

Eventually, the machine supposed, when he had calculated all the graphs for all the jumpers in the thirteenth millennium, the rate of increase would begin to slow. Either it would level off, so that each jumper was jumping the same timespan at each jump, although each one would be leaping through a span unique to himself, or it would begin to decrease, following the descending phase of the curve until each jumper was leaping only a few hundred years at a time, returning to the minimum represented by his or her first jump. Then, presumably, the curve would turn back on itself and continue in ceaseless oscillation.

Assuming this to be the pattern, the machine calculated that the minimum point of the curve would occur approximately one thousand million years from the time of the first jump. At that time, those jumpers who were left would begin to converge in terms of the time-relations of their pauses, and some of them would actually coincide in their waking—something that could not possibly happen while each one was accelerating through time and covering tens of thousands of years at each leap.

The main flaw in this particular calculation was that it

assumed that there would still be enough jumpers living after a billion years to coincide with one another. When he removed from consideration those likely to die, and computed the number who would simply vanish, assuming that that particular "mortality rate" remained approximately constant, the assumption proved to be less than safe. He decided that it probably would not matter what happened to the curve tracing the progress of the jumpers through time once it was past the period of possible coincidence: it was highly unlikely that any traveler would get that far. The pilgrims were not going to reach the end of time, and the probability was that even the one who went furthest would have used up his life in spanning only a fifth of the period that the Earth had existed.

When he discovered this, the machine sighed for the mortality of humankind and the ephemeral quality of human experience.

The La who remained on Earth fared better than the humans, because they did not inherit the mutational load which condemned the descendants of Scapelhorn's orphans. They built new cities, and a culture of their own, which was unlike the culture of their own forebears and unlike the culture of any of the ancient human nations. They never learned to leap through time, and turned away in time from the hopes they had entertained of the false alien messiah, Paul Heisenberg. They did not live beneath the domes, and for the most part they ignored the machine and all of his parts that existed in their realms. The machine, for his part, ignored them.

For several millennia the La were the people of Earth, insofar as Earth could be said to have people at all. They reclaimed some land from the poisons, and fought wars among themselves for the better land. In the end, however, they came into contact with emergent third-phase life, and had to embark upon a long and futile struggle to preserve their world against its advances.

That was one war they could not win, but they fought hard, as a species, and they fought for hundreds of thousands of years. It was not until nearly two million years after their arrival that the last of the La died. But that, too, was only the briefest of moments in the whole history of life on Earth, and even in the career of the time-travelers.

The machine watched these changes impassively, not because he was emotionless, but because his emotional investments were made in a different way, on a different time-scale. When the foraging was done and the domes were sealed for the last time against the world outside, the machine laid much of himself to eternal rest, leaving many of his bodies inert. For long periods he "slept", releasing his hold on consciousness for thousands of years between the periods when he roused himself to confront and converse with the time-jumpers as they landed briefly in their flight to eternity. It was only in those brief moments of communication and intercourse that there was any need for the invocation of consciousness and identity, and it was, indeed, only those brief moments that could sustain him in his sense of self.

In that period, while he lived his life so sporadically, he learned to love the people he protected, and every time one failed to rematerialize, he was stricken by grief. Every time one died, he mourned. In those waking moments he dreaded the time when he would once again be alone, with immortality his prospect still.

Paul Heisenberg had called the human race his playthings, and had accused him of wanting to play god, but he did not feel like a god and he could not relegate the time-travelers to the status of playthings to be put away and discarded when the time came. Frequently, he felt like a plaything himself: an enduring toy of fate, maintained against all meaningful change, condemned to be always himself, and at such times he envied the travelers their mortality, and the great gamble with destiny that was their pilgrimage.

He built houses for the time-travelers, and then tore them down, and built pyramids: useless monuments that seemed to symbolize something but actually signified nothing at all. Then he built underground vaults, with stone sarcophagi for the jumpers to lie in while they fled through the dream, and he carved names in the stone that would last for millions of years, but even those he had to remodel and renew.

Beneath his domes he preserved thousands of species of plants and animals. They became arks built to withstand the third-phase deluge that was slowly drowning the old world. Every species he preserved he chose, and he controlled their numbers, their environments and their relations. If he became a god at all it was not with respect to the travelers but in his dealings with the gardens that the land beneath his domes became, for they became his alternative Edens, and as time passed he became more and more involved with their maintenance and control, with the planning and the balance of their ecologies, and with the appreciation of their wonders.

At times, he became impatient. He asked himself what he was doing and why, and as often as not could find no answer, but he was never tempted to abandon his course. He was always aware that there were other projects on which he might have embarked, other purposes that he might have discovered, other tasks that he might have allocated to himself, but he also knew that there was an element of fascination in his present task that he might never find again.

The essence of that fascination was not simply that it was something strange, with an element of the inexplicable about it, but the fact that it was something entirely beyond him. The principal attraction that had led him to the time-travelers, to the support of their cause and intricate involvement with their sense of mission, was the fact that—try as he might—he could no more jump through time himself than the La.

In truth there seemed to be little in the talent to envy. It had no possible advantages to offer him. But the simple fact that he could not do it was sufficient to make it, for him, into one of the great mysteries.

For the time being, it was for him the focal point of the search for the ineffable, which is the impossible quest of all curious intelligences.

CHAPTER THIRTY-EIGHT

"I think the worst of it is the dream," said Rebecca, speaking across a hundred thousand years, in a voice which existed in his mind as fully and as powerfully as if she was standing beside him. "The loneliness isn't so bad. Most of the time I don't really feel lonely at all, because knowing that there isn't any alternative to being alone helps me not to mind too much. It *would* be bad, except that I can talk to you through these letters, and I know that if things work out right there'll be a point in time where we'll come together again. But the dream is something else, and it gets no better. I thought I'd get used to it, but I haven't. If anything, it gets worse. I think the reason that people disappear is that the dream swallows them. I could almost believe that old story about the dream being some kind of net which something uses to fish for us.

"The more I visit that world of the dream the more I feel convinced that it's a real world, not like ours—so much unlike ours that we can't even perceive how unlike ours it is. We can only see what there is for creatures like us to see, and we can only feel what there is for creatures like us to feel. The dream world doesn't really make sense in those terms. It's beyond our understanding. And there *is* something predatory about it— something that wants to hurt us and consume us. It isn't a person or an animal, and maybe not even a thing, but when we're there the danger is real, and I think it may get us all in the end. There aren't so many of us left now, are there? If it weren't for the coincidence and knowing that if I can only keep going I'll see you again, I don't think I could carry on. I'm not very brave, and it isn't courage that makes me go back every time—it's being more afraid of staying alive and growing old and shriveling up while you're still flying through time. I feel that there's nothing for me to do but keep flying after you, always thousands of years behind, hoping that I can fly long enough and far enough to catch up with you. I know it's the same for you, too; every time you wake up I'm frozen, incapable of stopping, in free fall.

"The new world frightens me, too. Outside the domes, everything is different. You can't really *see* it, if you just look through the glass, but if you look through the machine's eyes—the eyes it sends out to watch the world—you can begin to sense just how different it really is. Because of what's outside, the world inside the domes has come to seem that much more strange, as if the little forests are ghosts of the dead world where I was born. Sometimes I think this is the dream, and the other world is where we really exist. Perhaps *everything* is a dream and we'll have to wake up some day to find reality, if there's anything at all, anywhere or anywhen, that isn't made of dreams.

"I'm almost afraid to ask what will happen when we meet up again—and afterwards. I can't help thinking about it, though, and I can't help telling you about it. I don't want you to answer me, even if you can. At the moment, I'd rather have that be the end than the beginning of something else. It's all I have left to want, and all I have left to need. It's the only thing I have to live for. It must be different for you—you've always seemed to know what it was all for; you think in bigger terms than I do, and even if the things I think about are the only ones that are really important, you still have more.

"I talk to the machine a lot. I need to do that, and he seems to need it to. He never used to talk about himself, but now he does. He talks about what's going on under the domes, not just describing it, but as if he were involved in every moment and every event. It's as if he's frozen a piece of the world in time, and he's pushing it along like some kind of landing stage, to catch us every time we reach the bottom of a fall. But it's not just *mechanical*—in some sense he's more a part of it all than we can imagine.

"Even the stars are beginning to change now. The machine showed me a new one this time—a nova somewhere not too far from our own sun. Its light will have died by the time you wake up. Sometimes I wonder what happened to the La, and whether they kept expanding through the galaxy, or whether something went wrong with it all. I didn't know much about them when they were on Earth. I was just passing through. Most of what I know the machine told me. Most of what I know about everything, the machine told me.

"I don't know what else there is to say, although I want to keep writing just for the sake of writing. How can there be anything new to write when there's nothing new to happen? Is there even anything new to think? I don't know. I do know that I love you, with all of my heart....

The voice faltered inside Paul's head, and for a few moments he stared at the last few words and the signature without being able to hear anything, or to make sense of what was written there. Then he folded the letter, and searched for a pocket in which to put it. There was nothing; the garments the machine had given to him had no such provision. In a way, it was absurd that there should be garments at all; there was no one to see him, the temperature was carefully regulated, and he could, if he wished, walk through the forest as a naked, shameless Adam. But he didn't want to be Adam, and there was some small aspect of his self-image that was irrevocably involved with the idea of clothing.

He looked about him at the ancient, gnarled trees. When he had last walked this way their remote ancestors had been seeds on the branch, but still their senescence made him feel young and ephemeral. It was late summer, but he did not know the date, and in any case, the days were no longer the same length, so that the machine would have had to make adjustments to the calendar, interposing extra leap years. The rotation of the Earth had been slowed by the tidal drag of the moon. When several billion more years had passed, it would turn the same face perpetually to the moon, just as the moon did to the Earth. Even that would not be the end, for solar tides would continue to drag upon the Earth's axial rotation. There would be no end, even when the moon spiraled closer and disintegrated into a system of rings.

He wondered whether the alien orbital defense system would make war against the shards of the moon.

Among the branches of the trees, tiny birds were playing, and their play seemed unnatural because it was so very familiar. They had no fear of him. They were used to the presence of the machine's humanoid robots, and they knew that presence to be benign. When winter came—and the machine maintained the cycle of the seasons as he maintained everything else—the robots would come to scatter food for them.

The words of Rebecca's letter echoed in his mind: *you've always seemed to know what it was all for.* An illusion, of course. It was a thought put into her head by a sense of propriety, not by any experience. *What is it for?* he asked, meaning the forest first and foremost, and then everything that was implied by its existence. The domes, the time-jumping.

He couldn't quite remember all that had passed before his eyes and across his mind in 2119 and 2472, but looking back it seemed that he had never really taken a decision and therefore had never really taken proper account of the reasons influencing the decision. If there was one thing which had sealed his resolve it had not been anything that *he* had done—it had been Rebecca's first letter, or the machine's attack on the cities of the La, or Scapelhorn's farm in the valley.

You speak truer than you know, he thought, *when you say that as you're pursuing me through time, I'm pursuing you.*

He tried to think about the fatal question: the question of what might happen after the point of coincidence, if anyone survived to make that rendezvous; but he found that he could not. It was as if knowledge of the impending coincidence had introduced a horizon into his imagination, and, try as he might, he could not peep over that horizon into the territories beyond. It was a barrier to his mind, and he lacked the courage or the means to knock it down.

It was, in some ways, a frightening realization that he did not know why he had done what he had done, or why he was doing what he was doing. If challenged, he would have been able to produce rationalizations in plenty, but when it was him who issued the challenge, he knew that the rationalizations would be seen for what they were.

Deliberately, he shut his eyes and called up the images of the dream: the bare red rock, the screaming wind, the time-stream, the snake-identity that tried insistently to impose itself upon him, from within or without. It no longer made him sweat or shudder when he brought it into the real world—he had conquered it to that extent—but he was no nearer to a knowledge of what it really was and what it really meant.

The universe, he thought, *is no more and no less than Brahma's dream. But how many dreams is he dreaming?*

CHAPTER THIRTY-NINE

The little airplane flew over the ocean, only a few hundred meters above the crests of the sluggish waves. There was little wind to ruffle the surface but it would not quite be still. It quivered and quaked as if some tremendous force trapped within was straining to be free.

"It is curiously appropriate," said the machine, "that the ocean, the womb of your life-system, should be its last stronghold. The new life came from the land, where your kind of life was poisoned, and it has virtually exterminated the species of the old system across the entire land surface of the planet, but the ocean still cradles the life to which it gave birth, and will provide the last battleground for that life to fight its rearguard action. The littoral zones were absorbed very quickly, but the conquest of the depths is a different matter. Soon, the grotesque deep-sea fish will be your nearest kin on Earth—except for the gardens preserved beneath the domes. That must surely be a sobering thought: the only cousins you still have in the natural world will be twisted, perverted creatures living so far beneath the surface that humans never saw more than a tiny fraction of the number of species that exist."

"Curiously enough," said Paul, ironically, "I don't find the thought awe-inspiring, or even particularly disturbing."

"Within a few million years, even the fish will have gone. Your only relatives then will be holothuridians living in the deepest ocean ooze like great fat pentamerous slugs. When they're gone, there will only be nematode worms, then protozoans, and then nothing but bacteria. Your whole world will be gone—utterly swallowed up. There will be nothing alive on Earth to suggest that the entire evolutionary chain of which you are a part ever existed. Only fossils in the rocks, and perhaps the occasional ghost of an artifact in metal or stone."

"There are the domes," said Paul.

"But for how long? At present Gaea is still an infant. She is still reclaiming the flesh of the old life-system. When that job is finished the only way she will be able to grow is to find *new* ways of growing. She will not be content with the carbon that *your* life-system owned; she will find ways to exploit all the sources of carbon on Earth. It will take her millions of years—tens and hundreds of millions—to discover methods by the slow process of accumulating mutations and new faculties, but she has all the time in the world. She is potentially far more powerful and more efficient than your system ever was."

"In view of the fact that the new life negates the very possibility of the evolution of intelligence," said Paul, "isn't it a little absurd to personalize it by giving it a name and an honorary gender?"

"Perhaps," acknowledged the machine, but there was a note of humor in the word as it was spoken.

The voice came from a microphone in the cockpit of the plane, where Paul sat alone looking out at the world. Now that they were over the ocean it was easy enough to believe that it was the same world he had always lived in.

The sun was high in the sky, its scattered light blotting out the stars whose positions had shifted. Of all the things in the perceived world the sun had changed least. Paul had half expected it to turn red as the millions of years rolled by, in conformity with the images of a decadent far-future Earth he had encountered in stories during his youth, but the sun was unchanged and the atmosphere had not altered its structure sufficiently to change the composition of the light that filtered through it. Perhaps the blue of the sky was just a little less pure, but that might easily be his imagination.

The sun, the sky and the sea were all in some special sense familiar: links with the past from which he fled so precipitously. It was the land that had changed, and not only in terms of the life it carried. The lines of the continents had changed, drift shifting their relative positions and the grinding of the continental plates causing faults and folds that had altered their shapes. The map of the world had been wrenched and tortured into a caricature of its former self, and now it seemed like nonsense to talk about Argentina, Australia and the United States. Such nations had lost even their *physical* identity, the last vestige of excuse for retaining their names in his head.

Paul watched the shadow of the plane dancing on the water, and rejoiced in its commonplace significance.

"We'd better head back," he said. "There's nothing more to be seen out here."

"We're in no danger," the machine assured him. "As I said, Gaea is still an infant. It's easy enough to keep you safe from her clutches, even though her very touch would be fatal if we could not fight back. In time, it will be very different. She will try to attack the domes, desperate to claim the last stronghold that threatens her dominion; but for now, it is possible to co-exist."

"It's not that," said Paul. "It's just that there doesn't seem to be much point in staring at the sea, or passing from one continent to another. There's little to attract the attention of the tourist in this Gaean ecology. A tedious sameness has settled upon the face of the world."

The plane began to follow a great arc, turning to the north and then back to the west.

"When, exactly, are we?" asked Paul, leaning back in his seat and feeling, somehow, that the pressure was off and that there was no longer any need to pay attention to the world below and the vexed question of its differences and similarities.

"Three-quarters of a billion years from your starting point. A quarter of a billion still to go before the point of coincidence. You're as remote from your origins now as your own time was from the Pre-Cambrian, whose events left so few relics because of the great ice age which scoured the Earth clean six hundred million years before you were born. Each jump is still taking you several millions of years, although you're decelerating steadily now. In all probability, the dominant life-form of the Pre-Cambrian, as remote from your time as we are now, was an echinoderm not very different from the holothuridians that will soon be the dominant representatives of the system once again. It's difficult to judge exactly when that symmetry will be set up, but it will come. For two billion years or so the sea-cucumbers will have gone their own patient way, following the same habits of life in the same habitats, finding the same form adequate to all their purposes, while all the so-called higher animals will have come and gone—inadequate, in the end, to the struggle for existence. Even when they're absorbed into the Gaean organism they won't be finished, because their form is perfectly adapted to the life they lead. They'll become just one more facet of Gaean's limitless personality and versatility, but they'll always be there, in the flesh, sucking up the oceanic ooze and reclaiming its organic content."

"You've become addicted to philosophical lyricism," said Paul, dryly. "You talk as if you were the victim of a mystical revelation—as if you'd suddenly perceived the divine plan, God's blueprint for the universe and trans-cosmic evolution."

"One gets an interesting perspective on evolutionary affairs when one observes consistently over millions of years," said the machine. "It is, of course, different if you only live your life two days at a time, sleeping for millions of years in between."

"You reduce your functions to a minimum for the periods between awakenings," Paul pointed out. "In that sense, it's *you* who sleeps. *I* dream."

"My consciousness may be active only sporadically," admitted the machine, "but my senses are not. There are always recording devices to show me the slow patterns of change. Change fascinates me. The fate of an entire life-system is not something which can be easily ignored."

"And when the new life eventually reigns supreme? Is that

the end of change?"

"I don't think so. When Gaea reaches her physical limits—when every last atom of carbon on Earth has been absorbed into her sphere of control, she will find other paths of development. She will continue to evolve even if she cannot grow. Mutational drift will change the register of her faculties even if selection cannot require her to develop new abilities to meet new challenges.

"Perhaps there *will* be new challenges. Why should she limit her substance to the variations permitted by the chemistry of carbon? Why limit herself to Earth? And what is to say that she will not carry the same seeds of destruction that your second-phase life-system carried? Perhaps there will be a fourth phase and a fifth."

"I won't be around to see it," said Paul, feeling remote from the conversation and unable to enter into its spirit.

"You're still young," said the machine. "You have years of subjective existence in hand, which will take you through a second billion-year cycle, if you wish—to a second coincidence...."

"And the dream will kill me," interrupted Paul, his voice flat and bitter.

The machine was silent, as if something forbidden had been said, leaving nothing but an emptiness that could not be filled until the memory was buried and a new departure became possible.

A narrow strip appeared between sea and sky on the western horizon. It was a strange ocher yellow in color. During the next few minutes it grew wider but no more distinct. It looked more like a yellow fog than land. Paul scanned its length, idly wondering what kind of wreckage of the coastal cities remained beneath the yellow blanket, and whether, if acid were to burn away that part of the Gaean organism, there would be anything at all to say unequivocally that humans had once lived here... and died here.

Where the sea met the land there was little in the way of sand

and bare rock. The super-organism the machine called Gaea was not wasteful of space, and she did not require fertile soil to establish her holdfasts. Even the caps of the highest mountains, once bare and icebound, were Gaea's now. There were still deserts, still salt-flats...but even those areas were being slowly conquered. Gaea could irrigate land and supply herself with any essential minerals by the extension of vast fleshy conduits—biological pipelines and highways. Her one aim was to capture and make use of the sunlight that fell upon Earth's surface, and in order to do that, all of the surface had to be exploited. Mindlessly, purposelessly, she extended herself as her innate variability eased her towards this end. In time, even the polar ice-caps would be conquered.

From the airplane Gaea looked exceedingly dull, at least in her South American manifestation. Paul had flown over North America frequently in the twentieth century, and knew the landscape as a complex series of changes, with many patterns and many colors: great grey cities, oceans of wheat turning from pale green to creamy yellow, patchwork fields, the colored flames of oil-field gas flares—and everywhere lines and angles, delimiting the anatomy of human endeavor. There were no lines and angles in Gaea's anatomy, save that her regions were shaped by the winding ribbons of rivers, and the occasional silver bubbles that were lakes. The backcloth was simply a vast, deep and complex carpet of living flesh, essentially vegetable in character, although it had its motile elements. Its colors were varied, but always faded one into another: yellow into green into turquoise into brown into orange into yellow. The colors changed with the elevation of the land, with proximity to water, and sometimes, it seemed, quite arbitrarily, but there was never a clear boundary.

Within that gargantuan body, pseudo-organisms were constantly formed, fused, metamorphosed and broken down. It no longer made sense to talk about death, because there was nothing within Gaea that was ever *independently* alive. The organs of her body reacted constantly to one another's presence, were brought into being to serve immediate purposes and then redissolved. Her flesh was ubiquitous, in a state of continuous self-induced mutation, fulfilling all established functions and constantly "exploring" new possibilities, changing for the sake of change, helpless in the grip of an unending process of experimentation. No new metamorphic system was ever lost, because the systems within each coenocytic region could dismantle and build up chromosomes and chromosome-sets in an infinite number of ways, storing in neuronal memory-systems the record of every last one. She could even grow brains—gigantic brains greater than human brains by far—but she could not use them for anything more than bodily co-ordination, because there was no way that she could endow them with identity and consciousness.

The plane veered again as it ducked in the sky and went into a long, shallow dive. Paul watched the little cluster of beads strung out across a series of slopes and valleys grow into the tops of the domes that were now the only place he could think of as home.

"It's still safe to go out on the ground," said the machine. "To see the organism from within. It can be a spectacular sight— it's not like walking through a forest where everything is still. There's constant movement, constant change. It's eerie, but beautiful in its way."

"I don't want to see it," said Paul.

"It might not be possible for much longer. In time, it will become too dangerous for you to go out in person, even in the most sophisticated of protective clothing. I can send out my own mechanical eyes, of course, and even if they don't come back themselves they can transmit images, but it wouldn't be the same."

"I don't want to take a walk in Gaea's belly," insisted Paul. "I don't have that much curiosity."

The plane hovered in mid-air before settling slowly down into a cavity that opened in the roof of one of the domes. It gave them access into a kind of airlock, where the plane rested in a rain of purgative poisons, which cleaned its surface and steril-ized the air that had infiltrated itself along with the vehicle.

"What are you going to do when the last of us dies, or fails to return from the dreamworld?" asked Paul, abruptly.

"I don't know," replied the machine.

"Do you intend to stay here and continue your evolutionary studies?"

"No."

"You'll go looking for more playthings, then? More sentient beings engaged in small historical projects, which are of some passing interest in spite of the fact that they all come to nothing eventually."

"That's not the way I see it."

"Why not? It's the way it is. You can speak casually of symme-tries perceived across billions of years, of patterns in evolution that make any endeavor on the part of intelligent second-phase beings quite meaningless. Against the background of what's happening on Earth now, this stupid pilgrimage through time is ludicrous. We appear to have conquered time, but the only result is that we find that there's nowhere to go, that the fate of our species and our whole biocosm has been extinction. How could it have been otherwise, given that the eventual evolution of third-phase life seems to have been inevitable? Hasn't the game become quite pointless—for you, for us, for God Almighty?"

"There is no place for my mind in a world which has only third-phase life," said the machine. "My conscious self can relate only to beings like you—or to beings like me."

"Perhaps that's what you should be looking for: another war machine, accidentally endowed with consciousness, freed to roam the cosmos by the extinction of its makers. In infinity, all things are possible. Then you can play games with one another, as we do: a romance to last throughout eternity. Or are you still trapped here by the defenses left by the La?"

"I have absorbed the satellites into myself. I have already begun work on probes that will carry my identity beyond the solar system and into deep space again. I already have equipment trying to locate signals in the radiation-environment that will give evidence of intelligent life."

"And have you discovered any?"

"No," replied the machine. "I haven't. I haven't even discovered the ones I expected to find."

For a moment, Paul could not see the import of the remark. Then he realized what the machine meant. "The La?" he said.

"I think they are gone," said the machine. "If even the echoes of their conversations are gone, they must have died a long time ago. I can detect no signals at all, and I would still be able to find signals that originated thousands of light years away if they were still in existence thousands of years ago. It has been a long time."

"So much," murmured Paul, "for the interstellar network of symbiotic relationships that would form the basis of the cosmic monad and the cosmic mind."

"All things," said the machine, softly, "must pass. Even empires, and the faiths in which they are founded."

CHAPTER FORTY

The wind tried to hurl him to the ground, to make him crawl and squirm, but he remained steadfastly upright. Though the soles of his feet were bleeding he continued stubbornly to place one before the other. Each step carried him forward no further than half a meter, but he bore himself on nevertheless. He never looked back at the trail made by his bloody footprints, nor did he look up at the mocking sky, but he shielded his eyes and watched the ground before his feet for fissures and sharp stones.

Although his arm protected his face from the sand-ridden wind tears leaked continuously from his eyes. There was the taste of dust in his mouth, but when he extended the tip of his tongue to catch the tears as they ran down to the corners of his mouth, he could find no relief in the moisture. His body felt dry, his muscles aching for lack of salt, his belly cramped.

Here and there in the pitted surface over which he walked were fumaroles, whose thin sulfurous smoke was whipped away by the wind as it belched forth in little clouds. They filled the air with the stench of hot brimstone, and he knew that he was breathing poison that would foul his lungs in due course.

His naked skin was spangled with clinging sand, but the abrasive clutch of the sheaths no longer troubled him. The current that dragged at his soul pained him more, because it seemed to threaten something so much more important, so much more essential to his being. He could strain his muscles against the wind without, but there was no resistance he could make to the wind within save the assertiveness of mind which denied its delusions.

The black night sky was moonless, and the scattered stars shone with a bloody light which shimmered unnaturally in the alien atmosphere. Auroras danced about the horizon for which he was heading, like a curtain hiding another world beyond. As he came forward the curtain always retreated, and now he tried to stop himself looking at it, hoping that if he did not perceive it he might somehow come upon it unawares.

No matter how often he came to what he thought must be the last step of all he always found reserves of strength that allowed him to stagger on. This, indeed, was part of the torture: the fact that no matter how close he came to the limits of his endurance, he would always be supplied with just sufficient strength to prevent him crossing the limit and falling down never to rise again. The wind could not fell him, the sand could not strip the flesh from his bones, nor the surging force within him reduce him to reptilian torpor. Instead, the agony of their threat would go on and on....

Perhaps forever.

He took a step sideways to avoid the rim of an elliptical hole, and for a moment half-straddled the pit. While he shifted his weight from one foot to the other, something extended itself from the maw of the hole and wrapped itself around his left ankle, anchoring the foot.

He stared down in helpless astonishment. Absurdly, he could not feel fear, but only amazement that there was still something new to be added to his torment.

It was black and strap-like, and as he watched it slowly released its grip, writhing instead upon the ground while still it extended from the fissure. It looked for all the world like a long black tongue.

A forked tongue.

CHAPTER FORTY-ONE

As Paul felt himself returned to life he found his heart hammering with a desperation he had not experienced in any of his previous awakenings. He broke out into a cold sweat, and reached up to grip the walls of the stone sarcophagus in which he lay, with a fierce clutch of the fingers. He did not attempt to pull himself up, but the muscles of his arms went rigid as he fought to control his panic. Within minutes it began to ebb away. He opened his eyes, and then closed them again. He kept them closed until he was sure that he was in control of himself.

There was a white face floating above him in the dim light of the vault, looking down at him. It took him a few seconds to bring it into focus. Then more seconds passed while he strove for recognition. To this face, he knew, there belonged a name—even though he knew that it was impossible.

Finally, he said: "I preferred the plastic mask. This isn't very funny."

"You don't look so good, Paul," said a low voice that rasped like a file on coarse paper. "I'm sorry if I startled you. I'm not the robot."

"Herdman," said Paul, still unable to believe.

"That's right. You knew I was...." The other raised a hand to gesture at his surroundings. "...Among the brethren."

"You never communicated. Of all of them, only you never left a letter, or a tape. Not a word."

"It didn't seem to be a sensible way to communicate. I thought I'd wait for something better."

Paul used his arms to pull himself up into a sitting position. He looked to one side, and saw the still, silver-shining body of Rebecca in the hollowed-out stone shelf to his right. To the left, the similar stone cavity was empty.

"That's impossible," he said.

"Nothing's impossible," replied Joseph Herdman.

On the ledge that surrounded Paul's resting place—a resting place built to accommodate a repose of millions of years—Herdman placed two small glasses. He produced a bottle from somewhere, containing a brown fluid, which he began to pour. One glass ended up nearly full, the other half-empty. It was the latter that he offered to Paul.

Paul could already smell the alcohol on the other's breath, and that, more than anything else, was what convinced him against the evidence of reason that it really was Joe Herdman, aged but hardly changed. His hair was still dark, his face still set firm. He had always looked to be immune from the ravages of time, as if preserved by the alcohol that had turned his complexion yellow and saturated his brain with the illusory clarity of intoxication. That look was with him still.

"I've come to see you, Paul," he said, softly. "In person. I knew it could be done, if only the matter were given a little thought. There are few limits to the ingenuity of our host, if only we would care to test them."

Paul took the glass and sipped at the liquid. He looked up in surprise.

"Even whisky isn't impossible," purred Herdman, "if one can count on the resources of a friend like the machine."

"How?" asked Paul.

"The grain was preserved in one of the other domes...."

"Not *that*."

Herdman laughed. "Everything can be arranged, if you only have the time and the talent. I could always get things done—it was my one function in life. It was enough in the world that made me. It's still enough. All it needed was the imagination and the determination, and maybe a little courage. It wasn't a great way to travel, but in view of the way the dream has treated some of our erstwhile companions I decided that the risk was easily justifiable."

"How?" asked Paul, again.

"Deep-freeze."

"The machine built a cryonic chamber—so that you could meet me in person, ahead of the point of coincidence?" Paul shook his head, quite dumbfounded. He threw back the remainder of the drink.

"I wasn't so sure of meeting you at the point of coincidence," said Herdman. "It seemed to me that I might be one jump too late. Coincidence, you see, doesn't quite mean the same thing for all of us. A hundred years may not seem like much at this stage—but I know the value of planning. *My* first jump was from 1994, less than two years after yours. But *hers* was from 2119, which was when you took your second jump. I wasn't around then. Do you see the drift of my argument?"

Paul hauled himself over the edge of his coffin and on to the floor of the vault. Herdman handed him sandals and clothing.

"You could have written it down," said Paul.

"Written what down? I wanted to show you something, Paul. I wanted to show you that coincidences can be made— that we're not at the mercy of circumstances. How else could I hammer home the point but by making one? Get those clothes on and let's go to the house. There's a good deal to talk about."

"Old times?" said Paul, as he put the glass down.

Herdman shook his head, and poured himself another liberal shot. "The future," he said, his voice crackling as he slurred the syllables of the second word.

Together they came out into the open air. Paul glanced back just once at the dim-lit vault, and Herdman—without waiting for the question to be framed, said: "Twenty-four."

Paul was neither surprised nor pained by the answer. Each time he awoke, the number dwindled. He had long since grown used to that fact of life. He only prayed that Rebecca would survive long enough to make their predestined rendezvous.

Until now, he had almost forgotten Herdman—the only other man known to him who still survived as a time-traveler. All the remaining statues were strangers.

The scent of the preserved air, and the colored light that passed through the crystal of the dome, reassured Paul that everything was still normal up above, although none of the machine's humanoid bodies was visible.

The house was new—or had, at least, been remodeled since Paul's last awakening. The machine built and rebuilt continually, always growing bored with his handiwork, impatient for something to do. This time the place prepared for his reception was a bungalow with an ornamental roof and a verandah. Inside, it was perfectly clean, decorated in plain pastel colors and furnished sparsely. Simplicity was obviously the current fashion.

"You want another drink?" asked Herdman, when Paul had glanced inside and then returned to sit on the verandah.

Paul shook his head. "Where's the machine?"

"All around us."

"I mean the robot."

"I told him that I would welcome you. The robots are elsewhere, attending to other business. The machine is no doubt keeping a benevolent eye on us, in some more discreet fashion."

They sat in silence for a few minutes while Paul looked around. Then he got up and went into the house. It was some time before he reappeared to take his seat opposite Herdman. In the meantime, Herdman drank—not copiously, but steadily.

"I don't know what to say," said Paul. "It's been so long since I last saw a human being. I've grown adjusted to being alone, and to a mechanical routine of waking up, going through the motions, and then jumping again. It's set inside me...I've always been keyed up to meet people again at coincidence, but I've fallen into the habit of thinking of that as a rather distant prospect. This has thrown me, a little. You never wrote—you could have warned me."

"Not my way," said Herdman, in an off-hand tone. "When I

make a decision, I act on it. Plan quickly, execute soonest. It's the only way to stay ahead."

"But we still have months of subjective time before coincidence. Over a year, in fact, assuming forty-eight hours a stopover. If you're planning for coincidence...."

He trailed off, realizing the implications of Herdman's presence.

"Coincidence is when we care to make it," said the other, flatly. He replenished his glass, though it was not yet completely empty. "And if it isn't soon, nobody's going to make it at all."

"So what you want to do," said Paul, slowly, "is to put an end to it all?"

Herdman slapped the bottle down with unnecessary vehemence.

"For Christ's sake, Paul! What the hell is left to do?"

"Have you been drunk every step of the way?" asked Paul, the note of censure in his voice concealing his avoidance of the other's challenge. "Through nearly a thousand awakenings?"

Herdman scowled. "That'd be something," he said. "Soused for a billion years. While the human race and its successors die off, while the world undergoes a transfiguration such as no one in our own time could have imagined, while some alien machine herds time-travelers on a pointless pilgrimage to nowhen, Joe Herdman rides a hangover and a whisky high. No, Paul—this is the first bottle in a long time. For my first jump I jumped out of *delirium tremens* and came up a hundred years later still in it. It was a big let-down, considering where I spent the meantime. But I needed this one. I've been awake a few days, and thawing out is painful. Then the time began to hang heavy. And how could I meet such an old and valued friend without a drink in my hand?"

"You wanted to be your old self," said Paul.

"Got it in one."

"Why? Are you thinking of taking up where we left off? Becoming my agent again?"

Herdman laughed, the dark mood of a moment before

vanishing like magic. "*That's* what I've been missing all this time," he said. "It wasn't the whisky at all—it was the wise-cracks. You don't know how good it is to hear you."

Paul didn't know how to take it. Some of the tension eased out of him, but not all. He couldn't relax completely. In some strange way he felt that Herdman was here to do him harm, and no matter how his reason told him that the feeling was absurd it would not quite relinquish its hold on him.

"Have you seen others?" asked Paul. "Or did you stay frozen through the other awakenings to get to me all the sooner?"

"I wanted to see you," replied Herdman. "The machine told me about the others. They didn't seem like people I'd want to make a special effort to see. I'll meet them all in due course, now we can all get off the roundabout."

Paul knew that there was a temptation, if not a challenge, in Herdman's last few words. Herdman was watching him like a hawk for some kind of reaction. He said nothing, and deliberately looked away.

"I know about the others," said Herdman, in a low voice. "I asked. I dare say you never have—except about the girl."

"You know about Rebecca?"

"Like I said, I asked. The machine knows a lot of answers. It's beguilingly honest, if you approach it in the right way. But I dare say it's discreet enough—I haven't heard anything you wouldn't have wanted me to hear. Did *you* ever ask about the others?"

"I know their names—something about their lives before they became jumpers. What *should* I know about them?"

"You should know what they're like now, Paul. You should know what's happened to them while they've lived their years a couple of days at a time, sometimes a week and sometimes a month, afraid of the dream and afraid of the machine, afraid of loneliness and afraid of death. I've seen them—not in the flesh but through the eyes of the machine. You could have seen them too, if only you wanted to, if only you'd thought about it.

"They aren't thinking any more, Paul. They're just going

through a routine, over and over. They want to get off but they can't, because there's nowhere for them to get off *to*. They've retreated from their fear into ritual, following it blindly—following *you* into the dim and distant and nonexistent future. What else can they do? When they can't find the courage to jump back into hell they delay, for days and weeks, but what is there for them *here*, in the dome, with no one for company but the everpresent machine? They love you, Paul. They still have what hope they have left invested in you. Of course, you do have a kind of monopoly on hope now—there aren't any alternatives any more. They're good suckers, Paul—perfect disciples. They'd die for you...which is perhaps as well, because that's all that you require from them now, isn't it?"

Paul stared at him for several seconds.

"The machine didn't tell me," he said.

"You didn't want to know," replied Herdman. "And you must know by now that it's *you* the machine is interested in, far more than the rest of us. We're just the hangers-on. You're the one it loves, because you're the one with the sense of mission. It's you that's keeping this whole thing going. It wasn't about to tell you without you asking. But it has a curious sense of fair play that it never learned when it was fighting wars between the stars. It didn't stop me when I asked it to bring me to you. It isn't going to stop you listening to me. Maybe that's just one more move in the game—one more aspect of the perennial fascination. Maybe its little circuits are positively thrilling with the uncertainty of not knowing what you're going to do."

Paul looked up at the dome. The sun was no longer visible—evening came quickly to the dome because of the great wall of vegetation which had grown up alongside it, and which tried constantly to overwhelm it, to hide it from the light forever. So far, the machine had managed to keep Gaea at bay.

"What exactly do you want?" he said to Herdman.

"You know what I want," replied the other, his voice harsh but measured. "It's time to run down the curtain. I always admired you as a performer. I thought you were just right for the role, and that the role was just right for the moment. You've had the longest run in Creation. But the role's not right any more, Paul, no matter how good you are at playing it. It's got to finish. I want you to quit the business."

Paul felt his jaw clench with momentary anger.

"It wasn't a performance, Joe," he said. "I meant it."

"I know that," replied Herdman, with genuine sympathy in his tone, "but it doesn't affect the point at issue. The fact is, it doesn't matter how hard you mean it. It's no good any more. It's suicide for all of us to go on. I've shown you the way, and you have to take it. This is the time for us all to take a ride in the deep-freeze, until we can meet up when the last man's due out, and finish this crazy pilgrimage forever."

"I understand all that," answered Paul. "But the question is: what then?"

CHAPTER FORTY-TWO

Herdman did the cooking, although the machine could have delivered everything fully prepared as easily as providing the ingredients. He was trying to make some kind of point. There was no sign of the robot and the machine's ever-presence was unobtrusive; it did not speak. Even though Paul knew that the house and its walls *were* the machine, just as much part of its body as the robot or the domes themselves, Herdman managed to make everything seem ordinary...an echo of a long-dead world.

After supper, they played chess. The machine had made a handsome ornamental set of pieces and a polished wooden board, which looked for all the world like products of loving human craftsmanship. Herdman was still riding the tide of incipient intoxication, maintaining himself by steady and unhurried drinking at the point of balance antecedent to loss of control.

Herdman won the first game when Paul resigned on the nineteenth move, a piece and a pawn down with no way to combat the other's king-side attack.

"You've gone rusty," observed Herdman.

"I suppose you've been playing the machine."

"We usually have a game or two."

"Who wins?"

"He does, most of the time. It must be millions of years since I last beat him."

They set up the pieces again.

"What kind of risk is there in this freezing process?" asked

Paul.

"It's difficult to say. The machine's experiments on small mammals indicate that if the thing's done properly, cell death is virtually negligible...and most of the cells that do die are replaceable. Only the death of the neurons is really serious, unless something actually goes wrong. What kind of risk is there in *your* mode of time travel?"

He played pawn to king four and offered Paul another drink. Paul declined, and replied with pawn to queen four.

"That's weak," said Herdman. "I always used to tell you that it's weak, but you kept right on doing it, as if you were determined to prove that I was wrong, or that you didn't much care. You shouldn't do it."

"It's the way I prefer to play," answered Paul.

Herdman played pawn to queen four.

"That's just as bad," said Paul.

"It's the way *I* prefer to play."

"Is the machine switched off? I mean in the sense that its higher mental faculties aren't functioning—asleep, or unconscious is probably a better way of putting it."

"Hardly," replied Herdman. "It's watching us with unwavering attention."

"What does *he* think of your plan?"

"About the induced coincidence? He'd go along with it, if that's what you decided—just as the other jumpers would go along with it on your say so. He wouldn't like it if we then chose to live out our lives in his little garden of Eden, because it would end things prematurely from his point of view. It doesn't really matter, though—it has to end some time, and some time soon. I think the idea of getting off the cycle offends his aesthetic sensibilities rather than his reason. He'd like you to go on through another cycle, you know—and then another. You have a good many billion years in you, if you don't die. He wants someone to sit with him while he watches the evolution of the new life, and tries to stop it invading or destroying his domes. When you come down to it, it's simply a matter of isolation and the intolerability of being alone."

"Suppose he won't help," said Paul. "Your plan is entirely dependent on him."

"He will. He has to leave us our independence of will, or we'd be simply caged animals. We have to be free of constraints imposed by him, or we'd be no answer to his problem."

"Somehow," said Paul, "there's something about your proposal that I don't like. I'm not altogether sure why, but there's an essential *wrongness* about it. I think it's more than just aesthetic sensibilities."

"Shall I tell you what you don't like?" said Herdman. His voice was cold, implying that Paul wouldn't like hearing the analysis of his reasons.

"Go ahead," said Paul, looking down at the chessboard and concentrating on the position.

Herdman poured himself another drink, but not a large one.

"Because of the question you asked earlier—what then? You don't know any answer to that question. You don't even believe that there can be an answer. It applies just as much to *your* point of coincidence as to mine, and it's a question that frightens you. The reason my plan makes you apprehensive is that it would force you to face that problem immediately, instead of allowing you to put it off for a few more weeks of subjective time. It isn't that you've still got any faint hope of there being a destination for us to flee through time *towards*—I think you realized the falseness of that hope a long time ago. It's just that you're afraid to face up to the responsibility of deciding what you're going to do instead of chasing mirages."

Paul moved a piece, and Herdman answered the move without pausing to think.

"I'm not sure that I have abandoned that belief," replied Paul.

"You *know* that there's nowhere to go Paul. You must, by now. The advent of this Gaean super-organism has preempted the very possibility."

"I wouldn't seek to defend the belief on the grounds that it was true," replied Paul, slowly, as he made his next move. "I'd defend it on the grounds that it's necessary. It's necessary to give me some kind of direction and purpose in life." Herdman moved a knight and said: "Check." Paul shifted his king one square to the left.

"But it's *not* necessary," said Herdman.

"You want us all to stop, to come together into a tiny little community, and live out our lives together? You think that that would be less lonely, less frustrating, less empty than continuing the journey? To give up everything that's sustained us this far, and admit that we'd have been better off staying where we were in the ancient world, working for Marcangelo or for Scapelhorn—that's a lot to ask."

"Do you think people can't survive admitting that they were wrong?"

"I think that the one thing we can't do is simply to stop," Paul told him, quietly. "It wouldn't be simply an admission of defeat—it would be an admission of the fact that we've delivered ourselves into an utterly alien world to no purpose, that we've made ourselves strangers in a hostile cosmos. It would mean declaring that the universe has no place for us and that we shouldn't be here, that we're ridiculous anachronisms. That's rather more than just admitting we were wrong. I don't believe that we could stand that, Joe. I think we might all go mad. The coming of Gaea is exactly what says that we must go on, because it's what proves to us that there's no going back. We can't just be content to play Adam and Eve and start a new human world."

Herdman didn't answer for a moment, and when he did there was the beginning of a smile on his face, as though he'd just set up an opponent for a telling blow—as if he'd known all along that Paul would say exactly what he *had* said.

"Suppose there were another alternative," he said.

"Is there?"

"Actually," Herdman went on, "there are several. I've given them all some thought. One, of course, is adding ourselves to Gaea—yielding our flesh to her just as all Earth has yielded its flesh to her. We needn't necessarily think of it as suicide, but as a kind of transcendent merging with a higher being—an apotheosis of sorts. Our genes would live on, although our minds wouldn't. It's not an alternative that appeals to *me*, but it's a destiny to be contemplated as a means of discovering a purpose and a conclusion."

"Then again, we could ask the machine to reclaim Earth from Gaea's motherly grip. We could ask him to destroy her utterly and absolutely, so that Earth might be re-seeded from within the domes. *That* would be an Adam-and-Eve story with a vengeance. The main point against it is that it may not be possible. Gaea is strong, now, and she can defend herself. I doubt if even the machine could devise a way of destroying such a creature, and if he tried, the end result would probably be Gaea destroying *him*."

"That leaves us with the third version of the begin-again story, which is the one I might well favor. The machine has been sending probes out into the galaxy for a long time now. Some have returned, most have transmitted back some data. Out there is a collection of billions of stars, any number of which have second-phase life. It might take a long time to find one compatible with Earthly life, but the La found several worlds where they could live in harmony with alien nature. It would take a long time to cross interstellar space, too—one has to reckon on journeys taking millennia—but that doesn't really matter either. Time is the one thing we have plenty of, now. The La said that interstellar travel wasn't for us, but that was because they were trying to preserve it for themselves. With the aid of the machine's cryonic chambers, we have no need to fear long journeys. We can find a new world, Paul. Isn't that something we can accept as a target? Isn't that something we could pretend we were looking for all along?"

There was silence.

Herdman added: "Your black bishop's *en prise*."

Paul made his move, and then said: "Is that all?"

Herdman shook his head. "There's another alternative yet. Do you think that your personality really needs to be confined by that frail, pale body? Suppose the machine were to begin work on a project to duplicate *your* mind in the body of one of his robots—or in a ubiquitous machine like himself, with many bodies each capable of serving as a receptacle for consciousness. That way, you wouldn't need a cryonic chamber to visit the stars, or to suffer the dream of hell in order to travel into the distant future. You could be like him: an immortal in search of playthings."

"Is that possible?"

"In a way. Of course, if you became a machine, you wouldn't quite be *you* any more. You'd be something ontologically continuous with the present you, but you'd be something fundamentally different. All kinds of afterlife carry that kind of proviso."

"It's not a prospect that appeals to you?"

"Not exactly. I'm a romantic at heart. I'd like to see the stars."

"You've done a lot of thinking about this."

"Somebody had to, Paul. You didn't seem to be ready to do it yourself, even though everyone else is relying on you to tell them what to do next, when those who can reach coincidence. I had to cut the corner, if only to jerk your conscience a bit, get your fertile brain moving again. Incidentally, I have mate in three moves."

Paul studied the situation, then laid his king down on its side.

"You're convinced that there's no future," he said.

"Aren't you?" replied Herdman.

"A fourth phase for life? A fifth?"

"Maybe. Would it alter our situation much if there were? Neither the first or the third phases of life have any room for anything remotely resembling human beings—why should the fourth or the fifth? Humanity is a second-phase product. It seems to me that it requires a second-phase system."

"Have you ever wondered why it happened?"

"In what sense?"

"Why did human beings suddenly acquire this power to jump through time? It's a power that the machine couldn't learn to command, nor the La. It's a power that seems not to have existed before 1992. And why me? Why did the first accident happen at such a time and to such a person...almost as if it were staged? It can't have been just an accident of fate, Joe. It can't have been mere coincidence."

"You think somebody up there likes you? You think you really are a messiah bearing a gift from God? Some gift."

"Way back in the beginning someone—Marcangelo—said that there were all kinds of crazy theories, but that none could be supported by evidence. One was the notion that something in another dimension is fishing for us, that they endowed us with the ability in order to make it possible for us to take their bait."

"And you think that's the logic of the disappearances?"

"Probably not. As an idea, it's just standard paranoia. But there's *something* in it that makes a kind of sense. This power *came to us.* It didn't just happen. It was given, or made available. It arrived at a point in time when it was *needed*—because it was the only way that any human being could survive the impending destruction of the human environment."

"It's arguable that if it hadn't been for the time-jumping that destruction needn't have happened."

"I don't accept that. I think the ability was offered as an escape route, and I think that escape routes usually have ends. Everyone assumes that the fact we're now slowing down in our flight through time means that we'll reach a minimum and then begin to increase the lengths of our jumps again. I'm not so sure. Perhaps when we complete the bell-shaped curve, the ability will disappear just as it came, having picked us up from one point in time and delivered us to another. As for the question of what then...I'm not at all sure that it was ever our question to ask or to answer. Your list of alternatives is a list of possible *choices.* But what about the alternatives where our choices are taken *for* us?"

"I don't believe in them," said Herdman, flatly. "And I can't really believe that you do. I know that your philosophy always had its negative side—that you favored so-called metascientific beliefs leading to the passive acceptance of situations rather than ones that called for action—but that was because of the strategic value of such beliefs in stable situations. Blessed are the meek for they shall inherit...if they don't get walked on by the rest. But this situation isn't like that. It's not one that we can simply lie down and live with. Do you want another game?"

"No," replied Paul.

"A drink?"

"No."

"I think you need it."

"The game or the drink?"

Herdman didn't bother to answer. "We have to reinvest, Paul," he said. "In *something*. Something human and mundane that's within our scope. We have to learn to live again, to talk, to love, to find pleasure. Those are the only prizes on offer, and we have to find some strategy that will allow us to enjoy them. You must see that. Hope and faith aren't enough any more. They're drying you up and they'll leave you nothing but a heap of dust."

"There doesn't seem to be much danger of your drying up," said Paul snidely, his eyes on the battle.

"I need a drink to make a pitch," said Herdman, lightly. "I always did, from way back. But I mean what I say. I always did."

"Yes," said Paul, speaking softly enough for it to sound like an apology. "I know that."

CHAPTER FORTY-THREE

Paul found the robot in one of the domes, in the middle of a forest. It was pitch dark outside the dome, and the forest was composed of various evergreen species which filtered out the sunlight even by day, but it was easy enough to locate the artificial man because he was working with a lamp that shone with a brilliant white light through a loose arrangement of finely-netted drapes. He was luring and trapping moths—part of a routine program of population control that maintained ecological balance in each of the ecosystemic enclaves.

"You didn't have to come out here," said the robot. "You could have talked to me in any room of the house, or in any one of a dozen places in the main dome."

"I didn't want to talk to the walls or to the empty air. When I think of you I think of that body. If it weren't for that body I couldn't imagine you as being possessed of the least vestige of humanity."

"I suppose that's only natural," replied the machine.

"Can you do what Herdman says? Could you take us to another world in cryonic chambers? Could you give us bodies with imperishable brains and steel bones?"

"I think so."

"Why did you never mention the possibility of arranging a coincidence by the use of cryonics?"

"I did not think that it was necessary. You never asked me to find a way, or led me to think that you would find the prospect extraordinarily attractive. It would have facilitated a meeting between yourself and Rebecca, but it would only have been a temporary affair. As soon as you jumped again you would have been separated. Unless, of course, you decided to abandon jumping altogether. I did not think that you wanted to do that. I do not think so now. Coincidence will come, in time."

"If we survive...and it won't be coincidence for everyone. My rendezvous with Rebecca isn't the whole of it."

"The problem can be dealt with as it arises—and as for survival...it is a chance which we all take."

"Even you?"

"I can be killed. I think that there will come a time when Gaea might destroy the part of me that is here on the surface. If it were not for the part of me that is in space...and accidents can happen, even in space."

"It seems to me that the degrees of risk aren't really comparable. You're virtually guaranteed survival—if we carry on jumping, we're virtually guaranteed death."

"Death is certain. The only uncertainty is when." The robot's voice was as silky as ever, but in the cool night air and the harsh white light of the lamp it sounded hard and unyielding.

Paul watched a large grey moth flutter into the netting as it headed for the light, and beat its wings desperately in an attempt to disentangle itself before going suddenly quiescent.

"What do you think I should do?" asked Paul.

"I don't know. You can see the alternatives. It's your decision."

"But you were quite happy to see me going the way I was. You didn't feel obliged to point out any of the alternatives."

"Had you wanted to think about them, you could have seen them all for yourself."

Paul looked away from the light at the straight trunks of the trees and their pitted bark, and at his own shadow hugely stretching across the littered floor of the forest. "But I didn't, did I?" he said, as much to himself as to the machine. "And now that I'm forced to do so, the opportunity isn't exactly welcome. That's hardly right, is it, for the man who began the whole thing, the prophet in whose name the crusade was declared? I ran away in 2119, and in 2472, and I'm still running. I tried to slip off the hook in 2472, but I knew that I couldn't. In my heart, I knew. I can't ever get away from that performance I began to play in 1990: Paul Heisenberg, messiah of metascience. A false prophet, come into his own legacy of false hope and false faith. A touch of irony, I suppose. Maybe God sent me skimming through time, as a kind of retribution for the sin of *hubris*... another Ixion, bound to a wheel and spinning through eternity."

"You could stop," said the machine, "if that's what you want."

"It's a bit late."

More moths fluttered into the net to be entangled. The robot detached them one by one, very careful not to injure their wings.

"What do you do?" asked Paul. "Kill off the surplus?"

"Not unless it's necessary," replied the silken voice. "I keep the males and females apart, so that they can't breed. I let them live out their lives, if I can."

"You have some strangely unbalanced ethics. You worked against the people who wanted to try to save the world for humankind. You let the La become extinct. You could have saved the old life-system, if you'd wanted to. You let third-phase life take over the Earth. And yet you're too fastidious to kill moths. You've killed people before now, and aliens. You were once an engine of interstellar war. Why the absurd insistence on pointless scruples?"

"I could not have prevented Gaea's growth," said the machine levelly. "There are circumstances in which murder is justified. But as a rule, where there are alternatives, I believe that it is wrong to kill."

"Why? What need have you for a moral code? Why bother with ethical commitments at all?"

"I defend them," said the robot, "not because they are true, but because they are necessary."

Paul laughed, but without humor. "What will fourth-phase life be like?" he asked. "What comes after Gaea?"

"I do not know. Unless one of my probes encounters fourth-phase life, there is no way I *can* know."

"But you believe that there will be a fourth phase?"

"It's not a matter for belief. It is a possibility."

"Like the fifth dimension."

The robot did not ask him what he meant. They had talked about it before. If the jumpers could be considered analogous to flatlanders who had acquired, or been gifted with, the means to move in another dimension, then why not, ultimately another?

The robot had pointed out that time could not rationally be considered as a fourth spatial dimension, but Paul had countered that such quibbles did not prevent it being considered as a dimension at all, nor the possibility that there were others, perhaps similar in quality, perhaps different. It was pure metascience, but the question was not whether it was true, but whether it was necessary, or desirable, to believe it.

"Hello, Paul," said another voice, interrupting the conversation. Paul turned to see Herdman standing half a dozen metres away, leaning on a tree-trunk that was only partly illumined by the lamplight, so that his face was half in shadow. He had a bottle in one hand, and a glass in the other. He always carried a glass, and never drank from the bottle. Joe Herdman was no slob.

"Hello, Joe," said Paul.

"Getting away from it all?"

"I just wanted a private talk with my friend."

"And what's his verdict?"

"He doesn't know."

Herdman laughed. "I've been trying to find a copy of your book. I thought there ought to be one in the house somewhere: a permanent reminder, as it were. I prefer a real book to a telescreen—something bound in leather with thick pages and red chapter-headings and illustrations. There was an illustrated edition, remember? I commissioned it. The edition *de luxe*."

"I expect it's out of print," said Paul, sourly.

"I wanted to read the chapter on ecological mysticism," said Herdman. "To refresh my memory with regard to your comments about relocating the mythical golden age in the future beyond the personal horizon—the refurbishing of the idea of paradise. The renewal of the Earth and all that kind of stuff. It was the healthiest brand of optimism remaining, you said, as I recall. And something about the Earth doth like a snake renew, her winter weeds outworn...heaven smiling...something along those lines."

"It was a quotation," said Paul. "From Shelley."

"Ah! Prometheus unbound...."

"*Hellas*, actually."

"Not the poem—*you*. Prometheus, released from the bondage of time, to retreat into your cave instead of assuming your role again in the human world, leaving it to the spirit of nature to lead them to the glorious future. I still remember my Shellery... approximately, at least But it's not here, Paul, is it? The paradise born to the spirit of nature, that is. The Earth's renewed itself, but there's no golden age for the survivors of humankind. There's nothing, Paul...nothing at all...except you. Paradise seems to have been mislaid. It's time to come out of the cave, to man up. Sometimes, I wonder why I ever chose you to promote, when I could have found someone with balls."

"You're drunk, Joe."

"I do seem to have allowed myself to slip over the edge a little. It must be lack of sleep."

"Go to bed, Joe. We'll talk again in the morning."

"I came out here to eavesdrop a little. I want to know what you intend to do."

"I don't know." Paul looked sideways at the robot, but he was bending over his nets, as if oblivious to it all. He took a couple of steps towards Herdman, and then faltered. He stood still, watching.

"You're going to go on, aren't you, Paul?" said the old man, softly. "I knew it when I told you the alternatives. I just don't know why. You're not too stupid or too cowardly to admit that you were wrong. It's not that at all. It's something I just can't figure. But you're going to go on, in spite of everything."

Paul took a deep breath. "I think I have to," he said.

"*Why?*"

"I don't know. I just have to see this thing through. It *has* got another side to it—there *is* a way through...a fourth phase, a fifth dimension. I need to be believe that."

"Shall I tell you why you feel that you need to go on?" said Herdman, the alcohol blurring the words and taking the sting out of them.

"I'd be glad if you would," said Paul, tiredly.

"You're afraid. Not a cowardly fear, and not of anything superficial or immediate. You can't admit that you were wrong because of a much deeper fear—the sheer terror that strikes you when you contemplate the possibility that there's nothing left, and that it was all for nothing. You can't face the thought that there's nothing to go on to, and because you can't face it you can't draw back. You *have* to go on, and on, rushing further and further, and coming closer and closer to the terrifying absence of everything meaningful. It's as if you were being drawn towards a curtain, knowing that when you draw it back there'll be something beyond it that will be so terrible that your blood will freeze, and not being able to refrain *because* of that knowledge."

"That doesn't make sense, Joe."

"It makes more sense than you imagine. Imagine yourself in the place of the man who's reaching out for the curtain. Imagine yourself in his shoes. You're not so different, Paul, except that what you're afraid of isn't anything immediately and implicitly terrifying—it's the more subtle and fundamental terror of nothingness, of alienness, of Godlessness. You're afraid of being a shadow, Paul—nothing but a shadow on the face of existence. You're afraid that you don't *matter*, that you don't *mean* anything, that even a life smeared across the face of eternity is nothing more in the context of the cosmos as a whole than a scale falling from the wing of one of those moths as it struggles against the netting. And so you'll go on, and on, and on, screaming your desperation as you stagger into the biting wind. The world isn't a poem, Paul...it's real...."

Herdman stood clear of the tree then, and began to declaim, with a voice full of sarcasm and gestures of parody: "Tomorrow and tomorrow and tomorrow, creeps in this petty pace from day to day, to the last syllable of recorded time; and all our yesterdays have lighted fools the way to dusty death. Out, out, brief candle! Life's but a walking shadow, a poor player, that struts and frets his hour upon the stage, and then is heard no more: it is a tale told by an idiot, full of sound and fury, signifying nothing."

The voice died away, and silence reigned for a moment. Then Herdman said, in a voice closer to his normal manner of speaking: "Another old favorite. Worn well, hasn't it?" Then, in a near-whisper: "I used to be an actor too, before I was an agent."

"We'd better go home, Joe," said Paul, softly.

Herdman poured himself a drink, and then touched the glass to the neck of the bottle to make a little *clink*—a mock salute.

"That's...what you're...afraid of...," he murmured. "And that's...why...tomorrow and tomorrow...to the last syllable...."

He turned on his heel, and began to walk away into the night.

Paul looked back at the robot, who looked up again now. The lamplight caught the red lenses that were his eyes.

"If I do go on," said Paul, "what's going to happen to him? To all of them?"

CHAPTER FORTY-FOUR

Paul sat in his chair, quite relaxed, as the lights dimmed and the screen flickered into life. It filled one wall of the room, and as the image was clarified it seemed as though the wall dissolved, becoming a window to the world outside. The machine adjusted the scale of the three-dimensional projection so that everything was life-size. The chair was positioned so that Paul's viewpoint was that of the camera which had transmitted the film from the depths of Gaea's leviathan body.

There was a ghostly quality to the image—hardly any color was visible and there was relatively little light. There were only shades of grey and yellow-brown.

"I have to use the image-intensifier at this level," said the machine. "Hardly any light gets down to the ground."

The ground itself was invisible, covered by a carpet of keratinous material woven into fibers. Projecting through this carpet were massively thick pillars, as smooth as marble columns. These were the basic elements of Gaea's skeletal structure. Strung between them were webs of vegetable silk, which bulked into many-layered bowls where shafts of sunlight contrived to pass through the stratified canopy. The webs were supported by thicker strands of tissue, and across the strings swarmed motile blobs of protoplasm, which resembled planarian worms. Most were flattened and transparent, but occasionally they would flex themselves into coils or contract into globules. Similar vermiform things moved over the keratinized mat that hid the ground, and there were also many-legged creatures like primitive insects and other arthropods. The largest that was visible at the moment was something like a king crab, but there were others about the size of a man's fist that resembled giant woodlice.

"Scavenger elements," said the machine. "They keep Gaea's body clean. From time to time she reingests them. She has others like them inside her solid structure: worm-like things that repair all tissue damage and suck up injured nuclei and redundant membrane-structures. The largest are five to six times as big as these. The plates aren't armor, of course, just a convenient way of stacking spare chitin and keratin. The tail of the largest one is a kind of probe carrying chemoreceptors; they're all eyeless, of course."

The camera-viewpoint began to move slowly upwards into Gaea's body. For a few minutes there was nothing to be seen but the vertical stems and their connecting strands, but then the camera began to catch the flutter of white wings.

"Effectively, they're vegetable moths," said the machine. "A double leaf mounted on a musculated frame. They carry photosynthetic material from point to point, wherever the stimulus of sunlight remains for any length of time. It's quicker and more convenient than having elaborate internal translocation systems to drain away manufactured sugars."

The next region was characterized by laminated elements linking the pillars, which began to diversify here into clusters of thinner stems. There were many rigid cross-pieces which formed arches between the pillars, sometimes linking four in a complex double bridge. There were often swellings in the stem where elements diverged. There were relatively few of the web-like light-traps here, but the foliage was sparse; clusters of the moth-like double leaves arranged themselves in ranks and circlets at particular points. There were many flatworm-like bundles of flesh engaged in their slow crawling over the smooth surfaces.

"At this level only a fifth or a sixth function as scavengers," said the machine. "Most are migrating protoplasm redistributing support-strength to contend with metamorphoses in the main photosynthetic region. We're still in the stable stratum here. You can see the blobs being absorbed and extruded if you care to watch for long enough, but it's not an exciting sight. Their metamorphosis into flying elements is more interesting, but the best place to see that is in the crown. It's easy enough to induce; I've sent out small explosive charges, and when they explode it's as if the shockwave turns everything it touches into a cloud of insects. The experiment can be expensive; the fluttering things often function as absorptive surfaces and they'll settle on anything in a situation like that. They can dissolve the plastic parts of my traveling eyes in no time. Usually I'm more discreet, and can keep the flow of sensory information going for hours."

The camera continued to rise, coming now into the lower canopy, the lowest and the most stable of the three main photosynthetic strata. Here there were nets of foliage, often bizarrely structured, continually attended by dancing pseudomoths. The leaf-elements twisted and shifted, but only very slowly, and their supporting branches coiled and squirmed. There was a lack of integration between the different elements, which were constantly poaching one another's sunlight; they constantly induced movement and change in one another.

Higher still, in the middle stratum of the canopy, there was more light and more space, and much more color. There were many more fluttering forms commuting between the dendrites, and life seemed better coordinated as well as less unhurried. The surfaces of the branches were no longer so smooth, but were pitted and structured with sensory hairs, pores and the occasional eye. Paul felt that the eyes were staring at him, because they turned immediately towards the camera when they perceived it. Tentacles began to grow out of the nearer branches, and they reached out for the spy in their midst, seeming to come right out of the screen in a vain attempt to touch Paul, and to destroy him.

The camera kept ascending, moving just quickly enough to avoid the reaching tentacles, but the pseudo-insects now began to cluster about it in great swarms, and the whole image was filled with their fluttering colored wings. Through the chaotic swirling cloud, Paul could see great domes of green and yellow, for all the world like the skyline of some ancient oriental city. Soon, it was impossible to see anything at all.

"That's Gaea at peace," said the machine, as the image died and the lights came on in the room. "When she's really reactive, you have very little time to see anything at all."

"She can metabolize your camera-eyes?" said Paul.

"Yes."

"How long before she can metabolize the material of the domes?"

"Metal and glass she can't cope with yet. It's difficult to say whether she ever will be able to dissolve the material protecting the enclaves. She isn't aware of us in any real sense; to her we're just a bunch of globular rocks. The main battle is to keep her contained round the edges so that she doesn't grow over us as she's done every other mountain in the world. You should see her when it rains, and she becomes a water-trap as well as a light-trap. That was her main limitation in many areas: water supply. But the way she's expanding now, she'll soon change the climate sufficiently to melt the polar ice-caps. That will flood a great deal of what is now land surface, but she'll adapt, just as she's adapted in extending herself over the continental shelves. In time, she might be able to absorb enough water into her body to allow her to cover the whole surface, land and sea. She already has command of the oceans in the form of a vast Sargasso Sea of floating weed."

"Suppose the domes *were* breached?" said Paul.

"There'd be an emergency, but as long as it happened when no one was awake, I could contain the invasion. Once she shows herself to be capable of that, though, it might be worth considering the possibility of removing the whole project into orbit."

"The domes as well?"

"No. But some of the life could be transferred. Seed, ova... enough to start again in an orbital Ark."

"You couldn't move the statues."

"No. The people would have to come one by one, as they awake."

"If that has to be done," mused Paul, "there'd be no real point in keeping the Ark in orbit. Once forced to abandon Earth... unless there's something to wait for."

"It's possible," said the machine, "that Gaea might ultimately become versatile enough to transcend the limits of carbon. There are other elements capable of forming long-chain molecules: silicon and boron. But what possibilities there are, we can't know until they begin to emerge in reality. Perhaps, when she reaches the limit of her growth-potential on Earth, she will begin to send Arrhenius spores into space. There is time enough for all accidents and eventualities to come to fruition."

"She's rather frightening," said Paul, "although she doesn't look it in the film. She's like a great, silent forest, where everything is in harmony and nothing is wasted, and yet, if anything that's not already part of her steps into her body...."

"She uses relatively little of her infinite variety," said the machine. "It's intriguing that, although she's absorbed all the genetic potential of all animal life that existed on Earth— including that of the La—she rarely makes use of any animal faculty except the eye, and some of the functions of striated muscle. Everything else is more primitive, or hers alone."

"Can we be *sure* that she can never evolve intelligence and identity?" asked Paul.

"We cannot be sure of anything, but it's highly unlikely. Intelligence and identity are the products of ecological competition and social organization. She's not that kind of being. I would say that it was impossible, but you might with justice quote to me some words from your book: There still remain hopes that we dare not entertain, and possibilities we cannot imagine."

"I wish you'd stop quoting my words back at me. Herdman's bad enough."

"Why? Have you recanted?"

"No, of course not, but I don't need constant reminders. Make up your own aphorisms and stop parasitizing me."

"Herdman's presence seems to make you very uneasy."

"Of course it does. He's the only remaining link with the life I led before this all began. Rebecca came into the story *after* the beginning, and she's part of it, but Herdman's not. He's part of what I left far, far behind. He *belongs* to the dead past, like Wishart. I never saw Wishart, you know, in 2119. He was there but only as a name—just as I was only a name during the century before. Herdman's the only thing I've seen that remains from before the beginning. Of course he disturbs me."

"After today, you'll never see him again."

"How do you know? Suppose he goes back into his deep-freeze, to trip through absolute zero to my next awakening? He doesn't have to jump again; he can stay with me every step of the way, if he wants to."

"I don't think so," said the machine.

Paul didn't know whether to welcome the opinion or not. He felt guilty about Herdman, although he didn't know exactly why. Herdman had asked him for a favor, and he had refused, but not for lack of charity...surely there was nothing he need feel guilty about. He didn't really want to see Herdman, ever again. Perhaps *that* was what disturbed him—the fact that, no matter how isolated he had become in skipping through time, he still shied away from such human contact as Joseph Herdman could offer.

He got up, and went to the door, knowing that he would have to face Herdman one more time, before returning to the vault and taking up his station among the undead.

CHAPTER FORTY-FIVE

The vault, as always, was dim-lit, its air cool and still. Paul touched the hard stone of the bed that would bear him through a million years and more. Effortlessly, he swung himself over the polished rim.

Herdman was behind him, watching from dull, bloodshot eyes. His face seemed to be drained of all expression, and the sallow flesh hung limply on the narrow jaw-line. "You're making a mistake," he said, levelly but a little listlessly.

"Perhaps," Paul replied, as he extended his legs into the hollow that was designed for them. "But I've got to go, at least until the point of coincidence, and I have to go this way. I can't abandon it now."

"You're condemning people to death," said Herdman, harshly. "You know that. The people following you will die...including the girl. If you want to see her again, you should stop now, and do things my way."

"You might be right," Paul conceded.

"But you won't?"

"No."

"Did you look at the film of the others? The zombies, who gave up thinking in favor of a traumatized trip through time? Did you?"

"No."

"I'll fight you for them, Paul. Every last one—including the girl. I'll be here for every awakening from here on. I'm going to make a sales pitch to everyone. You'd better pray that it works,

Paul, because it's the only hope they have left. If they decide to stay on course, you'll be to blame. You had the option, here and now, of calling a halt, and you refused."

"It's their decision," said Paul, calmly. "They'll make it for their own reasons, just as I'm making my decision for *my* reasons. They're entitled to the best sales pitch you can give them. I wish you luck."

Herdman laughed.

"I mean it," said Paul.

"I know you do," replied the other. "That's what's funny."

"I'll see you again, no doubt."

"I don't know about that. Maybe, when I've seen them all, there'll be time in hand to do what we want to do. We needn't wait to give you a second bite. When you return there might be a dozen of us *en route* for the new world, and you'll have missed the ship."

"Maybe," said Paul. "Either way, *bon voyage*."

"Thanks," said Herdman, bitterly.

"Even you must have believed for a while," said Paul, quietly. "Not necessarily in me, and certainly not in the talismanic power of my name. But you must have believed in *something*, in order to propel yourself through time at all. You must have had some reason for trying, some reason for beginning the long trek. It hasn't sustained you, but you must have had it once. You weren't just running from the delirium."

"Sure," said Herdman. "It seemed like a good idea even when I was sober. I should have known then that it was a bust. Never trust yourself sober."

He put his hands up, palms outwards, to show that there was nothing there. He watched Paul disappear into a Paul-shaped hole, which seemed to shine as it repelled all light and all heat, aloof from the very fabric of existence.

"You put them on a stage," he muttered, "and they get delusions of grandeur. Every last fucking one."

CHAPTER FORTY-SIX

The snake had form now. The desert had given birth to it: a creature of immense size, with scales of silica and coils that writhed like time and eyes that stared like the bloodied stars. It was hooded like a cobra, and its hood eclipsed the night sky when it reared its head to strike. Its starlit eyes were hypnotic, and its fangs spat poison that could shrivel the flesh on human bones, drowning its victims in black corruption.

He crawled, heedless still of the laceration of his skin and the fragmentation of his fingernails, careless of the stinging sand. He saw nothing, but his ears caught the sound of scale scratching stone, and the wind was the breath of the serpent, hot and reeking.

From far away came the thin sound of screaming.

CHAPTER FORTY-SEVEN

He came, at last, to his senses, and realized that the sound of screaming had not died with the dreams. It echoed in the underground chamber, and then began to change into a series of bubbling sobs as the screamer realized that she, too, had returned from hell to the last enclave of the long-dead ancient world.

Paul was at her side within seconds, lifting her head from its foam-plastic pillow in order to cradle it in his arm. Her flesh seemed colder than it should or could have been—much colder than the stone of the sarcophagus or the dull, still air. Her muscles were very tense, those in her arms and legs making the limbs rigid. Her stomach was taut, her nipples erect. Her eyes stared wildly into his, without recognition.

He turned, and his eyes searched the vault for the robot.

The machine was already at his elbow, carrying garments ready for them to put on. Paul started because of the machine' nearness; he had not heard the other approach. Then he snatched the clothes, and began to drape them over Rebecca's body, trying to urge some warmth and life back into her terror-stricken body.

He lifted her out of the sarcophagus, surprised by her weight. He tried to carry her towards the staircase, but he was too weak. Instead, the robot took over, and carried her out into the open air. Paul followed.

The air outside was warm, and carried the scent of apple-blossom from the trees across the clearing. There was a faint background of sound: the movement of birds in the branches, the sound of insects' wings. There were yellow flowers growing beside the entrance to the vault.

Paul looked back once at the room from which they had come. All the stone vessels were now empty. There were other rooms, but he sensed that they, too, would be empty now.

The robot was helping Rebecca to dress herself. The rictus that had gripped her facial muscles was gone, now, and she looked very pale and weak, but she seemed to be fully conscious. Paul began to put on his own garments, although his head was swimming with incipient nausea.

He managed to control himself. He looked down at Rebecca, and saw that she knew him now. She nodded, very slightly, and then lay back to look up at the patterned dome enclosing the sky.

"Is it always like this?" he asked her.

She looked at him again, and shook her head. He helped her to her feet, and they embraced.

"It was the dream," he murmured. "Something in the dream."

He felt her head, pressed against his chest, move to indicate agreement.

The images burst in his head:

...black corruption....

...breath, hot and reeking....

...the thin sound of screaming....

"You were there," he said. "Through all that time, I thought I was alone—even though others dreamed the same dream, I felt that I was alone there, that it contained only me and nothing else. I even thought that the whole of it extended only as far as my perception of it." He looked at the robot, and said: "Are we the only ones?"

The robot nodded. "The old man died. The younger one disappeared."

"Any news of Herdman?"

"The ship will reach the new world in seven years. All seven passengers are still alive. There is no reason to suppose that they cannot be successfully revived."

"Three Adams and four Eves...what are their chances?"

"It's impossible to judge. They will live out their own lives...

all of the women are capable of conceiving and bearing children, and with my help, they can have as many as they want, as many as they feel they need...but in the long term, the odds are heavily weighted against them."

"Joe will be satisfied. He'll have made his point, in his way of figuring the score. And he was right about the others. They didn't even make it to coincidence...maybe I should have helped him, added my argumentative weight to his recruiting drive instead of just stepping out of the way."

The machine made no answer, and Paul shrugged.

All three of them began to make their way slowly towards the house. It was still much as it had been when Herdman had intercepted Paul after the first cryonic time-trip, although it had been renewed several times over. The interior had altered somewhat, but not greatly. It had become familiar, over the millennia, and as the length of each jump had shortened from thousands of years to hundreds its lack of change had become a curious symbol of reassurance: a guarantee that their flight through time really was slowing to a halt, and that they would meet again at the moment of coincidence. Now they were here, and the house seemed exactly right. It was *home*.

Paul's memory reached back to the moment when he had last seen Rebecca in the flesh, when the window of the room blew out and the sky had been on fire. It seemed less remote than it ought to have been. There was nothing at all in existence that had not been touched by change since then, save perhaps the sun. It had been a billion years. In Paul's own time there had been no traces left of a world as remote as this: not a single fossil visible to the naked eye to testify to the nature of life on the ancient Earth. Now, outside the domes, there was likewise no trace of Paul's world. Gaea had obliterated them all.

He tried hard to think of something to say, but could only stare. It was Rebecca who finally said: "Hello."

CHAPTER FORTY-EIGHT

"There's no one else now," said Paul, as they lay together on the bed after making love. "We're finally alone. I feel free for the first time. There are no longer hundreds of people around in my wake by the accidental magic of my name. There's only you, and you're real. Between us, we constitute reality. There's nothing outside of us but the Garden of Eden and the god-machine."

Rebecca said nothing, though he paused to let her say something.

"What do we do next?" he prompted, gently.

"I don't know," she replied.

"We could book a passage on a starship," he said. "We could arrive on the new world just as Herdman's descendants are beginning to mount their own space program, ready to take the story of the human race into a new phase. I wonder what they'd think of us?"

"They'd hail you as the messiah," she said.

"That's what I'm afraid of. There's no outrunning destiny. Can you imagine being doomed to reincarnation on world after world as a false and futile redeemer?"

"No."

"The machine could find us another world. One of our own, where we could have as many children as we wanted or thought we needed, and then die in our own good time and pass safely into the stuff of legend."

"Don't talk about it"

"Why not?"

"I don't want to think about it. Not now. Let's just *be* here, for a while. Let's not think about what's in front of us—let's think about what we've *got*."

Paul realized that behind the words lay fear. She didn't want to face the question of what to do next. She *couldn't* For her, there was only the present, and no future at all. She'd be happy if time stood still—as, indeed, it did, in the world that cradled the house. Only *inside* was the march of time proceeding, unrestrained. Inside *him*—and inside Rebecca too, no matter how hard she might try to deny it.

A billion years, thought Paul, *and what have we found? No vestige of a beginning, no prospect of an end. How could we ever have hoped for anything else?*

"Don't look like that," said Rebecca, faintly.

"Like what?"

"Sad."

He laughed, briefly. "Post-coital triste," he said.

She didn't know what that meant.

"I'm suffering from human contact," he said. "It's a long time since there was another person so close to me. In a way, it frightens me."

That was worse—she looked hurt.

He shook his head, and said: "I don't know. It'll pass. Forget it. Let's do as you say, and think about where we're at rather than where we're going."

He smiled, and she relaxed a little.

"Was it worth it?" he asked, softly. "To get from there to here? Was it worth the dream—and the death of Earth—and living the days of your life like beads on a string, with no one else but a plastic-masked machine?"

"Yes," she said.

"You aren't even disappointed, are you? You don't feel denied because there's no Heaven, no Isle of the Blessed, no land of Cokaygne. This is enough. Just *this*."

"I don't want anything else," she said, hesitantly. "And you mustn't, either."

He had to look away when she said that. He had the feeling that she was right, or at least being realistic. She had attained her goal. She had asked for no more than circumstances were prepared to deliver. That was wisdom. Only a fool could imagine there might be more, and only a fool would ask for it.

"The thing is," he said, speaking in an audible whisper and feeling reckless in doing so, "this isn't what it was *for*. I only wish I knew what it *was* for...."

She took him by the wrist, and pulled him round so that she could stare mesmerically into his eyes.

"You mustn't," she said, in a brittle tone. "You mustn't."

CHAPTER FORTY-NINE

"How's the game?" asked Paul, of the machine.

"What do you mean?" asked the smooth, sexless voice.

"You know what I mean. What's the state of play? Are we near the end, or only half way? And who's winning? Has it all been worthwhile?"

"Those questions have no answers."

"You've devoted a lot of time to this project—the greater part of your exceedingly long life. How has it changed you, if at all?"

"I'm not entirely sure. Can anyone really estimate the degree or kind of change that has taken place in himself? I feel that I am changed. I feel that I know a great deal more about the possibilities of life than I did when I first came to Earth. I have different perspectives now on many things. What else could I say?"

"And what happens now—if it's over? What do you do next?"

"For a while, I shall be content to explore, and to grow."

"Have you found other sentient creatures in the galaxy?"

"Of course."

"But they don't attract you sufficiently to begin another game?"

"If you want to put it in those terms."

"What about Herdman and his little colony?"

"They shall have such help as I can give them. It will not be a great deal, but they will not want more. There is so little of me in the starship, and the potential for rapid growth and diversification will be limited, given that they will not want me to rule them as a tyrant, however benevolent. Theirs is, after all, a virgin world. They will want its destiny to be in their own hands, as soon as they feel capable of bearing it."

"Did it ever occur to you," said Paul, "that you might be God? That you might have created all of this—the whole universe—as an experiment, and reincarnated yourself as an observer, forgetting your own omnipotence in order to be part of it all?"

"The same might apply to you," replied the machine.

"Yes indeed," said Paul. "Or to any one of us. Even Gaea, the mindless one. How is she, by the way?"

"Stronger. She invaded one of the domes. In expelling her therefrom virtually everything was destroyed."

"How?"

"She has acquired the habit of shaping the landscape. She can pulverize rock. She can extend roots into cracks, or surround outcrops with fibres that simply squeeze until the structure gives way."

"She could do that to the domes?"

"Yes. They are built to withstand great strain, but in time there will be nothing that can withstand her efforts. She could crack any of the domes like an eggshell, if the stimulus was there to make her do it."

"And how much warning would we have?"

"Two minutes. Warning enough—but you have the perfect escape route. You alone are untouchable."

"Except that there might be nowhere to land," Paul pointed out. "As Marcangelo took such delight in pointing out, it's no good leaping out of trouble if you have to come down no better off and probably worse. And we wouldn't be together any longer. We'd be separated, forever."

"I could save you even from Gaea," the machine assured him.

"I'm sure you could," said Paul, dryly. "But what for? Herdman was right, you know—I am afraid, and desperately so. Afraid that it *is* all a tale told by an idiot, full of sound and fury, and signifying nothing. He said that I was running toward coincidence simply because I was afraid to face matters before then. And now I'm here...I remember what he said about the man and the curtain. *In vino veritas*...I wonder whether the drunkenness was real, or just part of the act."

The machine was silent.

"Nothing to say," observed Paul. "Nothing to be said."

"Something else that Herdman said is true," said the silky voice. "I could give you immortality. I could give you a body that could grow forever."

"And then," said Paul, "you wouldn't be lonely ever again."

"That's not the point."

"No," said Paul, "but it's still a proposition I'd have to think about. Why is it, do you think, that you can do everything except jump through time?"

"Why should I need to jump through time? I have no need."

"But you still can't do it. Of all living things on Earth, only we can. And I still don't know how or why. Do you?"

"No."

"Wouldn't it be ironic," said Paul, "if all along it had been a mistake—if we had it wrong way round? For a billion years we've thought of what was happening as a kind of time-travel, and the other factors of the experience we've left aside as side-effects. But what if it were the other way around? What if the time-jumping is the accidental side-effect? What if the *real* essence of what's happening isn't that at all, but simply the opening of a door to a different mode of experience—a gateway into something beyond time and space? Wouldn't that be a joke? A billion year pilgrimage reduced to a hesitant faltering in the threshold of infinity...just a stupid mistake, because we were too blind to see what was before our very eyes, albeit in the fifth dimension. It'd be a joke on you, too, wouldn't it? All the time and effort you've put into the game, and it might yet turn out that, from the very first move, we've been playing by the wrong rules."

"Is that what you believe?" asked the machine.

"I don't know," said Paul, lightly. "I'm trying to decide

whether it's worth the commitment."

CHAPTER FIFTY

"I think that we need to try an experiment," said Paul, trying to keep his voice as casual as possible. "We have to determine whether it's actually possible to go on. Otherwise, we can't be sure just what the options are."

She deliberately looked away from him, at the great dome of the sky that was darkening with the twilight. She struggled hard to contain her tears, and to pretend that he had not spoken. As he watched her, he wished that he had not—that he had lived with the compulsion just a little longer.

"I can't," she said.

He placed one hand on her shoulder, but she didn't move any closer. She shied away, her hands fluttering aimlessly as she tried to find something to do with her arms. Eventually, she let them hang limply at her sides.

"It's just one jump," he said. "We can meet again, using the cryonic chamber. But I don't know, you see—I don't know whether we've really come to the end or whether there's another cycle beyond this one. I need to be sure."

"You don't have to know! You *don't* have to be sure. It's over and it's finished, for me. This is all there is, for me. It's all I've ever been able to want, since...anyway, I can't begin again. I couldn't jump no matter how I tried—I'm too frightened." Her voice had lost its vehemence very quickly. By the time she got to the last sentence it held hardly any force at all.

"There's no need to be afraid," he said, uselessly.

"I've spent all my life following you through time. The only thing that made it possible was knowing that I might eventually catch up with you. That's all that saved me from dying, or from being devoured by the dream. I've no strength left. I can't do it any more."

"I can't stay here, Rebecca. Not like this."

"Why not?" Her voice rose in anger again. "Why isn't it enough? It's *everything*. There isn't any more! Why can't you just be *happy*!"

He tried to pull her into his arms, but she wouldn't relax. Terror was holding her muscles rigid again—real terror, and nothing less. He'd held back the question so long, and she'd known that he was holding back, and now that the long-antici-pated moment had come her fear had simply broken its bounds.

She shook off the grip of his hand, and buried her face in her palms.

"It's over," she whispered. "It's all gone. There's nothing more. We can't ever go back. I don't know how I came through it once. Now I know...I couldn't. Whatever you do, I can't. I'm at the end, and I can't move from here. It's no good. There's nothing I can do. I won't let you go. You mustn't leave me. You can't."

Now she did try to seize him, to cling to him as if by so doing she could anchor him in time, forever. She was trying to trap him in her arms.

He let her enfold him, but he could not respond. She was crying, the tears no longer under control but flooding forth.

"It isn't enough," he said, helplessly.

"What we have now all that there *is*," she insisted. "It's all that any human being has ever had. Can't you see that?"

"If I could see it now," he said, "I'd have been able to see it in the very beginning. I'd never have begun. When I started to move time, even though I didn't know that that was what I was doing, there was something I was seeking, something that I was chasing...something I can't even put into words, but *something*. I can't settle for less...not after a billion years. Paul Scapelhorn found something else; so did Joe Herdman, and Adam Wishart, a long, long time ago, but I can't. I just can't. There's something inside me—something alien and strange that just won't let me stop. I feel it in the dream, and I feel it here. I've always felt it. I felt it on that stage in 1992, the very first time...it wasn't just an accident that singled me out. There was something *in* me—and there still is. I can't let go."

"If you go on," she said, in a low, urgent voice, "you'll be alone. You'll be alone until you die. You'll never see another human being, hear another human voice, see any more human handwriting. There'll only be the machine. He'll be your whole world then—everything that surrounds you. If you go, I'll kill myself."

He pulled her hand away from his shoulder in order to make her look him in the face.

"Yesterday....," he said.

"Yesterday," she said, "you loved me. And the day before. You *always* loved me, even when you didn't know it yet. But not any more, if you leave me now. I want *now*, and I want now to last forever. No more *time*—just days, and nights, and you, and me—and you loving me. It's all that's left of the world. I won't let you go."

"I'm sorry," he said. It was true.

"*He* said it would be like this," she whispered.

He felt a muscle in his jaw flex convulsively. "Herdman?"

She didn't answer, but she could only have meant Herdman.

"Yes," he said, softly. "He would say that. He wouldn't be able to resist saying that, so that when the moment came you'd remember his name."

"Please," she said. "You have to listen to me."

He shook his head, but not to deny her assertion. It was a tired, empty gesture that came out of utter confusion. He bent his head to look at his hands, scanning them back and forth as if he were searching for something: the marks of fervent laceration...the angry scars that weren't there, that never had been there.

"I don't know....," he whispered.

"You love me," she said. "You do. You have to."

He didn't know what to say, but he kept staring and staring at his hands as if he expected them to crack and let the blood flow....

And then there was a sound, which grew and grew until it seemed to fill the dome: the sound of a screeching siren, and a wordless shout; as if something had struck a mortal blow to the very heart of the great machine.

When he looked up, the sky was already beginning to crack, and to fall apart.

Gaea had finally begun to destroy the last enclave of the Ancient Earth, to make her dominion complete.

CHAPTER FIFTY-ONE

Seconds passed while the birds rose from the woodland, startled into panic by a sound greater than any they had ever heard. A flock of sparrows wheeled in the air above their heads. Gaea's flying things were already flooding through the great rent in the dome, fluttering down to meet the helpless birds like green butterflies, spreading like a cloud of poisonous gas.

There was no response from the machine. The loudspeaker that had released the shriek was trying to form words, now—shouted instructions to the two human beings who stood looking up at the cascade in the sky—but the words would not form. Somehow, Gaea had destroyed essential circuitry.

There was nothing, in any case, that Paul and Rebecca could do; there was no time to run to another dome, or to reach some enclosed hideaway. There was only one way that they might be able to avoid the consequences of the slowly settling cloud of Gaea's ambassadors. They both knew that, although seconds still passed while they watched and could not respond.

"They'll drink our flesh like nectar!" whispered Paul. "Our very souls...."

The million mothlike mouths of Gaea settled on the trees and on the ground, and plucked the birds out of the air as they flew.

Where Paul and Rebecca had stood, however, Gaea's components fell on silver statues that were utterly impervious to their vampiric power.

That did not bother Gaea in the least, because she was blind and stupid, and she was nothing if not patient.

CHAPTER FIFTY-TWO

The wind screamed.

It screamed its triumph, its ultimate victory, while the cobra-head towered in the sky above them, its hood a dome that blotted out the sun while fringes of cloud were whipped by the storm into a boiling frenzy.

Lightning bolts hurled themselves at the time-lost mountains and the great mouth gaped wide, the hinged jaw distending until it seemed certain that the snake could swallow the world.

The great forked tongue licked the scaly lips and the fangs spat out their poison—and Paul, who held Rebecca in his arms, knew that, at last, it *was* the end, and that there was only one response...one possible refuge....

CHAPTER FIFTY-THREE

The robot felt nothing, although his plastic face was dissolving as he ran, and the artificial flesh upon its metal bones was in the process of being consumed. Gaea's fingers were plucking at his body, but they could not reach the complex web of electronic components that was his true being.

The robot was doomed, but that mattered little enough to the machine, provided that he could reach Paul, and that his red-lensed eyes could confirm that he had escaped into time. Four domes, in all, had been breached, but the machine knew that he could fight back, extirpating all life for a thousand kilometers around, if need be, in order to reclaim those few square meters where Paul and Rebecca stood...so that, at their next awakening, they could be removed from harm's way, taken into orbit...and, if necessary, to the stars.

The robot reached up to pluck the mothlike entities from his face, to clear their green wings away from his eyes.

He saw Paul and Rebecca vanish into the reflective lesions, safe from anything and everything.

And then he saw them disappear, as the lesions closed with a clap of thunder that reverberated through the dome.

The air rushed in to fill the vacuum, whirling the green butterflies with it, breaking their leaf-wings from their soft coenocytic bodies. The robot stood still, allowing Gaea's servants to cluster unrestrained, blotting out the visual image.

CHAPTER FIFTY-FOUR

The poison that streamed from the fangs of the great snake splashed harmlessly from the incorruptible surface, and when the snake struck there was nothing for it to grip with its cavernous mouth.

There was a clap of thunder as the air rushed in to fill the vacuum, and the stinging sand met no resistance.

There was nothing there at all.

Perhaps the pilgrims had crossed the threshold, at last.

Had he been able to believe anything, in the moments before the thunderclap, Paul Heisenberg would have believed that he could and would, because, true or not, that would have been a necessary belief.

Had Rebecca been able to believe in anything, she would have believed in Paul, because, whether he was worthy or not of that pledge, there was nothing else in which she could believe.

CHAPTER FIFTY-FIVE

In all the eons that followed, Gaea never ceased changing. Neither did the machine, although it never became a god.

The descendants of Joseph Herdman's colonists became extinct, after a long time, save for their own pilgrims of Promethean progress, and no human life then remained in the universe comprised by spacetime.

Meanwhile....

ABOUT THE AUTHOR

Brian Stableford was born in Yorkshire in 1948. He taught at the University of Reading for several years, but is now a full-time writer. He has written many science-fiction and fantasy novels, including *The Empire of Fear, The Werewolves of London, Year Zero, The Curse of the Coral Bride, The Stones of Camelot,* and *Prelude to Eternity.* Collections of his short stories include a long series of *Tales of the Biotech Revolution,* and such idiosyncratic items as *Sheena and Other Gothic Tales* and *The Innsmouth Heritage and Other Sequels.* He has written numerous nonfiction books, including *Scientific Romance in Britain, 1890-1950; Glorious Perversity: The Decline and Fall of Literary Decadence; Science Fact and Science Fiction: An Encyclopedia;* and *The Devil's Party: A Brief History of Satanic Abuse.* He has contributed hundreds of biographical and critical articles to reference books, and has also translated numerous novels from the French language, including books by Paul Féval, Albert Robida, Maurice Renard, and J. H. Rosny the Elder.

CPSIA information can be obtained
at www.ICGtesting.com
Printed in the USA
FSOW01n0849200817
37806FS